The Keelman's Fortnight - Volume One

Adrian Lavelle

ISBN: 978-1-3999-2236-4

Cover design by: Adrian Lavelle
Printed in the Ireland.

To Anne and Big Marty

To

SEAN.

I SINCERELY HOPE YOU ENJOY THE NOVEL.

HOPE YOU'RE KEEPING WELL.

ALL THE BEST

CONTENTS

CHAPTER 1 --- THE HOUSE OF NOVALIS

The big house used to be a convent, then it was an elderly care home, now it was a commune full of hippies. The exterior of the house used to be a beautiful shade of stonewashed white; now, the exterior was a dirty coral blue.

The walls were scuffed and not well kept, the salty Achill air constantly eroding the rough paint job. Symbols were painted all over the walls, symbols that rang through the eons of time. There was Egyptian hieroglyphics, Celtic mythology, Christian religious art from the Middle Ages, Rosicrucian and Gnostic symbolism, the hippies liked to display what little use of esoteric knowledge they had on to the walls of their commune, to show the world how clever they were.

The statue of Jesus, which stood on the roof balcony, used to bless the Atlantic Ocean with outstretched arms, now, his arms were removed. He was an armless statue, wearing a purple bandana and red aviator sunglasses.

The original plan by the hippies was to renovate his hands, to make it look like he was making the peace symbol. The hippies removed the arms to swivel them upwards, after sculpting the peace sign into both hands, they couldn't glue his arms back on to her body. They tried on several occasions, but the arms kept falling off, this resulted in Jesus being an armless hippie.

Every so often, somebody would climb onto the roof and stuff a herbal joint into the statue's mouth.

The large oval field in front of the house used to be neatly maintained, lavish and green, aligned with clean pathways, flower beds, and dark, lush hedges. Now, the entire area was overgrown, untidy, and full of weeds and nettles. The grass was waist high. The hippies wanted to bring nature back, so they stopped mowing the lawn. Mountain sheep gathered in the field and danced around in the overgrown grass, shitting everywhere. The hippies called the field 'The Garden of Love' – after a poem by William Blake.

I went to the garden of love, and saw what I never had seen.

A chapel was built in the midst, where I used to play on the green.

And the gates of the chapel were shut and 'Thou Shalt Not Writ' over the door.

So I turned to the garden of love that so many sweet flowers bore.

And I saw it filled with graves and tombstones where flowers should be.

And priests with black gowns were doing the rounds.

And binding with briars my joys and desires.

A small chapel sat adjoined to the house. The building, formally stone washed white, was now a painted mess of psychedelic colours. A large sign hung over the wall on the front door, portraying the words 'Magik Theater' in red paint.

When the weather was good, the hippies liked to sit in the grass and drop acid. They would trip on their psychedelic mess, playing guitar and smoking weed.

They would sit in the long grass for hours; sometimes they would sit there all day, until the effects of the LSD would gradually wear off. They would stumble back into the big house like starving animals, and they would feast on marmite on toast, before collapsing on their creaky old hospital beds. The house, when it was a convent, had a hospital ward where they cared for the sick and elderly, it was now the sleeping quarters for the commune.

They would lay awake exhausted, not being able to sleep, staring at the crumbling walls and cracks in the plaster, lost in their own catatonic thoughts, their dreams, ideals, hopes and visions.

They would lie there, until the break of dawn brought beams of sunlight through the dusty, cob webbed windows, warming their faces. They would jump out of bed, feeling relaxed and at peace, and yawn and stretch their way downstairs to the large kitchen, a kitchen that always had the welcoming smell of warm porridge and roasted coffee. The radio was always turned on; they liked to let it play in the background, abolishing the sound of silence.

When the hippies weren't tripping, they would spend their days reading books. They had amassed a huge library of literature, which they kept in the west wing of the house. They had one rule when it came to adding books to the library, no books on psycho analysis, of any kind. They despised any kind of psycho analysis, Jung in particular. 'The Primal Scream' by Janov was the main advocate towards this belief, this hatred they had for headshrinkers, it was the only rule they enforced when accepting people from all races, cultures and backgrounds into their community.

When they weren't reading books, they were

listening to music, cleaning the big drafty rooms, growing vegetables, feeding the chickens, smoking dope, debating, arguing, drinking whiskey, painting, writing poetry and having sex.

Every morning and evening, they gathered in the main common room, sat on cushions scattered around on the floor, and screamed their heads off. The walls of the common room were covered in art, news clippings and magazine articles. It looked like the green room of an underground punk club. It was the perfect space for Primal Scream Therapy.

They would support each other as they took turns partaking in 'primals,' screaming to the point that they were able to get in touch with their feral new-born emotions. Sometimes they would fight each other physically, they would call each other nasty names and pull each other's hair.

They did this to achieve a well-balanced state, not in a docile sweet way, but like aggressive animals, hunters and warriors, like their ancestors were. The group encouraged you to express your aggression towards one another, rather than having it all pent up and bubbling under the surface. Back when it was first invented by Dr. Art Janov, he claimed primal scream therapy cured homosexuality, drug abuse, suicidal tendencies, bi polar disorder and murderous rage. Novalis had taken these theories and altered them, believing free love conquered all, believing a person should be judged by their character and not their sexuality.

They believed screaming like a new-born tapped into emotional issues, all the way back to the time in the womb. *When you get your head straight, you need to get your baby head straight.* Therefore, you could function better as a human being.

They screamed in turn, or together as a group, for two hours per session. If they felt that somebody was on the verge of breakthrough, therapy could last the entire night. Even though the house sat isolated from the rest of the parish, they screamed so loudly the neighbours could hear them.

The locals, particularly the Keel locals, didn't like the hippies. They didn't like anything about them. It wasn't so much the screaming that bothered them, although that did bother them to a certain degree; it was because the hippies destroyed what used to be a house of worship and turned it into a shithole druggie commune. They also despised the hippies purposeful alienation from the community. They felt that the hippies possessed an 'us vs. them' mentality. They were right about the mentality.

The hippies were arrogant in their beliefs and

in their therapy, they felt they were more 'tuned in' than any of the locals were, not seeing how talented the Achill people were in every kind of art, from singing to painting, to sowing, to knitting, to sculpting, to writing and poetry, to culture and language, they couldn't see the tree from the forest in how much their commune could benefit from an actual island community.

The locals missed the sisters of mercy. They missed the olden times when the big house was a warm, welcoming convent with a pleasant peaceful atmosphere. These ladies in black cloaks, who were married to God, helped out a lot in the parish. Their door was open to anybody seeking spiritual comfort. They were forever organising fund raising events, such as bake sales, raffles and table quizzes, to raise money for the poor and needy. They were loved and cherished by every person they knew.

The hippies were the polar opposite. They had no interest in tangling themselves into anything Achill had to offer. They seldom appeared in public, when they did it was the women in the group, who would go drinking in the local, looking to snare one of the local young men back to their nest.

When they all ventured outside, they travelled together; they would all pile into their battered Volkswagen van to do their grocery shopping. They bought their drugs through an IRA contact. They had all they wanted in the big house.

They knew that nobody had any legal rights to kick them out of the big house. It belonged to them, they owned it, the house was bought for them by the founder of the commune, Polly Applegate. She blessed her commune 'The House of Novalis.'

Whilst 'The House of Novalis' was not the first commune to practice primal scream therapy in Ireland, they were the only one of its kind in the west of Ireland. The other one, the more popular one, 'The Atlantis Commune,' used to be located on another island, off the west coast of Donegal, before moving to Columbia.

'The House of Novalis,' much like their Atlantis counterparts, welcomed all outsiders who wanted to learn and practice their innovative therapy.

The hippies had different nicknames. "Let them call us whatever they want, fuck them!" Polly Applegate was overheard saying at the supermarket. "Let them call us the hippie dippies, or the arty fartys, or the loopie doobies, or 'those stupid fuckin druggies,' or whatever it is they call us! I don't answer to them, in fact, I encourage it, if I had to pick one, I'd go with the loopie doobies. It has a nice fuckin ring to it." Henceforth, they were known as 'The Loopie Doobies.'

Polly Applegate was the stamp of American punk singer Patti Smith. The rest of The Loopie Doobies fondly called her Patti, along with variations of her Christian name. She had a long list of nicknames, such as Polly Pat, or Patti Polly, or Polly Apple Pat, or Pee Pee, Pee Wee, Polly the Patti Apple was her favourite.

For the entire commune, when they looked out any of the nine windows on either floor of 'The House of Novalis' or if they stood outside at any of the vantage points, it didn't matter, they could not escape the absolutely, breath-taking view that bestowed them.

Many wept for joy the first time they looked out upon God's creation. A stark realisation hit them that this view would be around until the end of time, they felt blessed, their pathetic existence was merely a pebble in the vast cosmos.

If you happen to visit the house and stand in the garden looking out towards the main gate, to your left, you will see the highest cliffs in Europe, The Minaun Cliffs.

Central to your view you will find the emerald tablet, sitting only meters offshore from Purteen harbour, Inis Galoon, 'The Island of the Meadow.'

To your right stands Croaghaun Mountain, sheltering the most beautiful bay in the world, Keem, from the public eye.

Three cliffs that roll into one another, The Minaun Cliffs are protectors of the bay Keel Beach, otherwise known as Trámore. As you walk the beach the cliffs tower over you, and if the tide is out, you can stand directly below them and look straight up. Each rolling cliff has a grassy mound on top, they stand together, strong and united, like a family.

Mornings and evenings bring their own visual, unique palette to the view, couple this with the unpredictable weather conditions that can hit any time, day or night, the cliffs look uniquely different each day. It all depends on the kind of weather that hits the island, whether that be the King Lear storms that batter the cliffs jagged, ancient faces, or the Greek style heatwaves that magnify every single cove, cave, branch, blade of grass and stone on the face of each cliff.

There are cold days, with rolling grey clouds, where beams of light break through and hit the face of the cliffs, making them ever more majestic, the beams of light look like portals that can beam you to heaven.

There are days so damp and foggy that you can't even see the cliffs and days so clear and close you can almost reach out and touch them. They lift your soul, or make you dread finding yourself, it depends what mood you are in when you gaze upon them. The thunderous spray of the Atlantic waves forever shape and mold them.

The Island of the Meadow is a treasure. It stands a good fifty feet at its most westerly point, before sliding down to sea level on the east. A mat of green grass sits proudly on top, while a wily gnarly jagged stone surface juts out from underneath. It resembles something like a giant whale.

A narrow cove, only about ten feet wide, zig zags its way down along the rocky walls. It is said the devil was cast out of Inis Galoon by a parish priest in the 18th century. He stood unsteadily in a curragh, in front of the island, shouting prayers in Latin as he waved his cross and rosary beads. Curraghs were dotted around him as backup, full of burly fishermen armed with knives and sagarts. It is said the devil shot out of the island and into the sky, leaving a hole in the surface. The island was henceforth known as 'Devils Rock.'

The Loopie Doobies didn't believe the story, but they loved it all the same. They were happy, screaming made them happy. Tapping into their deepest anxieties and fears and screaming them out of their system made them happy. Polly made sure they were happy in every way, spiritually, mentally, physically and sexually.

The Loopy Doobies, with their somewhat pagan characteristics, would discuss what the first settlers must have felt, some 10,000 years ago, when they arrived in Achill, that there must be some mystical practices at work. They would discuss these mythical matters long into the night. It was mostly mere speculative gossip that they would invent on the spot, to make them sound clever in front of the rest of the group and a blazing turf fire.

One day, in early June, The Loopie Doobies decided to take a hike to the megalithic tomb, which sits on the grassy plains under the shadow of Slievemore, Achill's tallest mountain. The Loopie Doobies fondly nicknamed the mountain 'The Loaf of Bread,' because it looked like a big loaf of brown bread. Polly stayed behind to mind the house.

They blessed the ancient tomb with small materialistic offerings, anything shiny the crows could take, and placed them neatly on the mound. They knelt before the tomb and thanked their ancestors for their existence. After that, they all sat around smoking joints, and hazily admired the big loaf of brown bread. Then…they smoked some more and got stoned off their trees, before they turned 180 degrees and gazed out in wonder at the cliffs, the Island of the Meadow, and the rippling Atlantic Ocean. They liked this view the best.

***

CHAPTER 2 --- THE PURGE

Wesley Harding found himself on a fishing boat heading to Achill Island. Wesley Harding was nauseous. Wesley Harding's nausea was a result of seasickness. Even though Achill Island had a bridge, he had managed to get to Keel by boat.

The anticipation of the journey from his hometown of Galway caused him to think irrationally when he arrived in Westport. He heard of a passenger boat in Westport that would take him to the island. Being ever skeptical, he was worried that his journey was going far too smoothly. He never bothered asking *which* island the boat was going to. He just paid the money for a ticket, apprehensive in getting to the commune, thinking that all routes led to Achill.

He stepped off the boat to find himself at 'The Clare Island Hotel.' Dazed and confused, he stopped the nearest local and asked her was he on Achill. She replied with a big hearty laugh and pointed to the hazy, foggy outline of Slievemore Mountain across the ocean.

To Wesley's relief, the locals were extremely warm and helpful in arranging him passage on a three man fishing trawler to Purteen harbour in Keel. The only stipulation was they were stacking and prepping their vessel and it wouldn't be ready to set sail until the following day. Frustrated, Wesley spent a sleepless night in a hotel. The following day, after a hearty meal of haddock and chips, he endured a long wait watching the fishermen prep for their trip. They didn't set sail to Achill until late afternoon.

Wesley was on the verge of vomiting only halfway into the twenty-minute journey.

His inner child, the child that was so awkward, fidgety, futile, crotchety, and bad tempered, was alive once more. Wesley despised his inner child, he lost count of the number of times that he felt shame and embarrassment whilst reliving his childhood memories.

His frozen, purple hands clung onto the side of the boat. The salty ocean spray stung his eyes and black dots blurred his vision. The swaying of the boat caused him to swim through a nightmare of never-ending vertigo. He fought the fuzzy envelopment of blackness fogging his brain. He felt so ill he wanted to die and curl up into nothingness.

A violent, gagging urge rose from his guts. He almost fell overboard as he leant over and readied himself for the first onslaught of vicious vomit.

He watched his hearty lunch of haddock and chips splatter into the viltronic water. He made a sound he had never made before, like he was purging demons. Heave after heave, his entire stomach contents spewed into the wild Atlantic.

He pressed his left cheek against the icy timber of the bow. He prayed metaphorically that his stomach had finally settled, only to have a final heave, the heave that gets right into the depth of your stomach to knock the life out of you. That final heave, that has you guffawing and wrenching and crying and croaking, as you hawk up dry hunks of spit.

He began to second guess the nature as to why he committed to this journey. He collapsed back onto a pile of wet ropes feeling exhausted. A terrible, heavy melancholy washed over him. All he wanted to do was sleep.

He clawed around in his backpack and hauled out a bottle of water. The metallic, copper mineral washed over his tongue before hitting the back of his throat. The water did nothing more than enhance the smell of vomit that lingered around his teeth and mouth. He was so thirsty; he would have sold his soul for a can of coke.

His teeth began to chatter, and he could feel his face swamped in sweat. He focused on the rocking of the boat as a form of meditation to alleviate his seasickness as the sky grew dark overhead. He hoped his savings would be enough to stash him away when he arrived at his destination.

The fishermen left Wesley alone. Judging by the way he dressed as opposed to his middle-class demeanor, his big blue eyes, and his stylish long black hair, they knew why Wesley wanted to go to Achill. They wanted no part of it, they asked him no questions and told him no lies, they were happy to drop him off at Purteen and think no more about it.

They studied Wesley from the steering cabin as he vomited his haddock and chips. They watched this character, with his ripped jeans, army combat jacket and hiking boots and placed bets on how long he would last as a Loopy Dooby.

The skipper put him down for a year, his son put him down for two, and his nephew threw a tenner down and exclaimed he wouldn't last longer than six months before they would fish him out of the water. There was something, they weren't sure what, but there was something in this healing therapy that caused a few of them to shed off all of their clothing, run down to Purteen harbour in the nip, jump into the ocean and try and swim to Clare Island.

The last time they went fishing for Loopy Doobies was the previous year, on the fifth of September, the skipper remembered that day vividly, because it was the day of his sixty fifth birthday, never had he had a more eventful birthday in his sixty-five years as he did that day.

A young woman from the commune had almost drowned after making a swim to Clare Island. Hyperventilating, nude and soaked to the bone, she begged the fishermen to throw her back in the ocean. She was convinced that she was a mermaid, or a pirate queen, or an amalgamation of both.

When the fishermen asked why, she refused to answer; only that speaking about it would force the issue. They wrapped her in a warm blanket that stank of fish and man-sweat and brought her to Westport, where she was checked by paramedics and rushed to Castlebar Hospital.

The last the fishermen heard of the mysterious, nude, mermaid, pirate queen was that she hitchhiked her way to Belfast and joined the IRA. The cause for her 'spiritual swim' was the fact that she was tripping heavily on LSD. She was the fifth person in the commune in as many years that the fishermen had hauled out of the wild

Atlantic current, burned out on acid. None of the five had ever ventured back to the commune.

The skipper had doubts about the IRA rumour, until his nephew spotted the mermaid, pirate queen, when he was protesting international fishing trawlers at Belfast Docks. He spotted her searching a white van, wearing an Aran jumper and a long skirt, with an AK47 assault rifle strapped to her back. As the skipper would say to his son, on many occasions, "It takes all sorts, I suppose."

For all of the disdain that the fishermen had for the commune, they understood the fact that these hippies were lost souls with nowhere to go. They heard stories of the goings on in the big house on Achill. They heard the stories of the screams that drifted from the house in the middle of the night.

For all of their skepticism towards the commune and their practices, they did not like to see these lost souls suffer. Their opinion was, they must have been suffering if they were capable of screaming in the middle of the night. Surely, they thought, surely there must be a better way of finding yourself.

This empathy didn't prevent the fishermen from cracking jokes about Wesley's appearance in their native Gaelic tongue.

Wesley's legs were soft jelly as he was helped off the boat at Purteen Harbour. He had to sit for a minute on the grassy bank of the harbour, to gather his bearings, before continuing his journey. He could feel the wind turn bitter cold and burn his skin. The skipper pointed out the house to him at the top of the harbour road before slapping him on the back and wishing him the very best of luck.

Wesley's steps were unsure and unsteady as he staggered up the steep harbour road. Halfway up he stopped and looked at the house, it seemed like an oasis to a man dying of thirst in the desert, the sheer size of the house overshadowed the dot of whitewashed cottages to its left. He turned his head west to look over the spectacular view, until his eyes rested on Croaghaun Mountain, the mountain with the mystical lake.

Wesley began to fantasize about a hot bath and a comfortable bed, gawping at The House of Novalis from the front gate with a pained expression plastered on his face.

***

CHAPTER 3 --- DO YOU BELIEVE IN ALIENS?

A grey-haired woman answered the door, dressed in a poncho and white denim jeans. "Can I help you?" She asked quietly.

"I've been standing here for a while; I didn't think there was anybody home."

"They're at the tomb; they probably won't be home until late tonight. How can I help?"

Wesley didn't know what to say, the first thought that struck him was how much the woman standing in front of him looked like Patti Smith. His eyes became as wide as a new-born baby. He cleared his throat, hoping it would make some kind of noise that would be deemed passable as an attempt at communication. When he forced himself to speak, his voice didn't have the timber he was accustomed to hearing. It was too quiet, too soft, and too effeminate for his liking.

“I am here to find myself.”

What kind of bollox was that? Wesley’s cheeks went molten red, he fought an overriding impulse to turn and run. He braced himself to having the door slammed in his face. It never happened.

“You’re freezing my darling, where did you come from?”

“Galway.”

“How did you hear about us?”

“I had an episode, I screamed and I felt better afterwards, so I googled the experience and found Primal Scream Therapy, there’s a…list, on the website, with communes, and contact information. I tried calling but all I got was clicks and buzzes. And Columbia was too far for me to get rejected.”

Polly laughed. “Oh not to worry, I don’t reject anyone. I disconnected the phone, the ringing was like nails scraping down a chalkboard, it annoyed me.”

“Well, that’s why I’m here, standing before you.”

“Come on in and sit by the fire and warm your bones.”

Her gentle demeanour relaxed Wesley. His nausea began to subside and he let out a soft sigh of relief. She grinned a goofy grin, and motioned to Wesley to step inside as a heavy drizzle began to cascade. He gladly complied, and was relieved to get out of the cold. He didn't realize just how cold he was, until his face was blasted with positive heavy heat as soon as he stepped inside.

The woman grabbed him by the arm and led him down the long, wide corridor towards the kitchen. This is a nice kitchen, nice and clean. It's a big kitchen, a really big fuckin kitchen. It had a lovely smell of brown bread and the stove fire emanated beautiful warmth that relaxed Wesley into a wonderful feeling of exhaustion. For the first time, in a very long time, he couldn't feel any tremors of anxious energy rattling his body.

She poured tea from a dented pot on the stove, and stirred in some milk and honey before placing it on the kitchen table in front of Wesley, who drank from the cup gleefully; he let the liquid flow down his throat and warm his hollow stomach. She then cut some soft brown bread, and lathered it in butter. Wesley wolfed it down, he never realized how good and sweet bread tasted until that moment.

The woman sat next to him and placed one of his hands into her own. Wesley was taken aback by how warm and gentle her fingers were, they felt more like the fingers of a young lover than that of a middle-aged leader of a commune.

She had to be the leader, when she passes away they will be a religion and she will be revered like Jesus. She would be a patron saint of something or other, the patron saint of tea and brown bread. Wesley had to shake his head with his eyes squeezed closed to get his stream of consciousness to shut up.

"So tell me why you're here." Her voice was welcoming...and trusting.

"Like I've said, I've come here to find myself. I've come here to find inner peace and I'm hoping that you guys are the people who can help me with that."

"How can I do that?"

"You can make me a better person."

"Did you hear we were a cult?"

"I heard...do you consider yourself to be a cult?"

"There's a difference between community and cultivation. We're a commune, not a cult, when you think of the word 'cult,' you think of brainwashing, you think of a doctrine. When a cult begins, negative energy builds up, like an orb, and rattles its way through the cosmos, leading to horrible, horrible consequences. Normally where you find a cult, you find manipulation, alienation and greed. We are a therapy commune. People don't like it, but I find that people don't like what they don't understand. We have never cultivated people and brought them in line, and never will. We're not like the Catholic Church; you're free to leave whenever you want. What destiny brought you here?"

"Destiny?"

"Yes."

"I don't know. It's quite a long story. I had this friend, this special friend, she's gone now. I feel lost without her. I just wanted to see if you were genuine in your answer, and I am so happy that you are genuine and that you have invited me into your home."

"It's your home now too, if you want it to be."

"I think so, yes."

"And if you're going to live in my house, I'd like to know your name. What is your name?"

"Wesley Harding."

"It's very pretty."

"What's your name?"

"Polly Applegate."

Her name sounded sweet to Wesley's ears. He smiled for the first time in a very long time.

"You must be exhausted."

"I've never been so tired in my life."

"Is it okay, Wesley, if I get to know you a bit better? Then you can have a lovely sleep. I'll make sure when the guys come back that they keep the noise down, so you can sleep as long as you want. I want you to answer some questions. They're questions I ask everybody that want to live in my home. It's a process to open up, and build trust. More importantly it's to get you comfortable with me, that you have nothing to fear, and that you can talk to me about anything."

"Oh yeah, sure, no problem, you let me in. I was terrified you would turn me away. Do I have to scream?"

"No, not yet, that'll happen but it's a long, arduous exhausting process and you need to be 100% fit, mentally and physically before I let you do it. The important thing is you answer me honestly and quickly. Don't think when you answer because if you think, you don't speak the truth. This is very therapeutic, and it will help you greatly when you begin having primals. The more I know, the more I can help. Are you okay with that?"

Wesley nodded. He felt excited, and slightly turned on. Polly dragged her chair in closer to him and sat directly in front of him, her face merely inches from his own. Her breath smelled minty and sweet.

"Keep looking at me; keep looking into my eyes."

Wesley took a minute to catch his breath. There was a definite aura of powerful eroticism generating from Polly and he could feel it. It was quite pleasant. Any nerves he had suddenly vanished. Her warm hands enveloped his and she smiled at him reassuringly. Wesley tried with all of his might to ignore the hot, thumping erection that was growing in his jeans.

"Are you ready?"

"Yes."

"Do you make thoughtless remarks or accusations that you later regret?"

"No."

"When others lose their heads around you, do you remain composed?"

"Yes."

"Do other people interest you?"

"No."

"Are you interested in what other people have to say?"

"No."

"Are you impulsive in your behaviour?"

"Yes."

"Do your past failures worry you?"

"Yes."

"Is it difficult for you to take responsibility?"

"Yes."

"Is your life a constant struggle for survival?"

"No."

"Do you make an effort to make people laugh or smile?"

"No."

"Would the idea of making a fresh start in life appeal to you?"

"Yes."

"Do you find it easy to express your emotions?"

"No."

"Does the idea of talking in front of people make you nervous?"

"No."

"Are you clumsy?"

"No."

"Do you find it easy to be impartial?"

"No."

"Do you enjoy sex?"

"No."

"Do you meditate?"

"No."

"Are you careless?"

"Yes."

"Does life seem real to you?"

"No."

"Does music emotionally affect you?"

"Yes."

"Do you condemn people who disagree with you?"

"Yes."

"Are you a deep sleeper?"

"No."

"Do you contemplate death?"

"Yes."

"Are you a critical thinker?"

"Yes."

"Do you accept criticism from those around you?"

"No."

"Are you a jealous person?"

"No…Yes"

"Are you capable of pointing out a person's flaws?"

"No."

"Do you daydream on a daily basis?"

"Yes."

"Do you appreciate the beauty in life?"

"Not very often."

"Do you greet people effusively?"

"No."

"Are you forceful in your action and opinions?"

"Yes."

"Do you put off trying new things through fear?"

"Yes."

"Are you prejudiced towards your background?"

"No."

"Are you logical in your thinking?"

"Yes."

"Do you suspect the actions of others?"

"Yes."

"Do you tend to exaggerate a justifiable grievance?"

"Yes."

"Do you openly admit the beauty in other people?"

"No."

"Do you sometimes feel that you talk too much?"

"No."

"Do you smile often?"

"No."

"Are you easily pleased?"

"No."

"Do you consider yourself handsome?"

"No."

"Can you have your mind changed?"

"Yes."

"Can you adapt to new surroundings?"

"Yes."

"Do children irritate you?"

"Yes."

"Do you dwell on painful experiences?"

"Yes."

"Do you take drugs?"

"No."

"Do you like to get drunk?"

"No."

"Do you find it easy to relax?"

"No."

"Are you a hard worker?"

"No."

"Do you worry about situations that only exist in your mind?"

"Yes."

"Do you cope with everyday problems?"

"No."

"Are you truthful to others?"

"No."

"Do you love your mother?"

"No."

"Do you let others push you around?"

"Not anymore."

"Were you bullied at school?"

"Yes."

"Do you ever feel scattered in your thought process?"

"Yes."

"Do people turn to you for advice?"

"No."

"Do you believe in aliens?"

"Yes."

"Do you fall in love easily?"

"Yes."

"Has anybody ever made you cry?"

"No."

"Do you hear voices?"

"...No."

Polly opened the door to a spare bedroom on the top floor, in the hospital wing, of The House of Novalis. The room brought back fond memories of Wesley's bedroom in his grandmother's cottage in France. Everything was cliché, rickety, and neat. It was everything that he desired. The bed was dressed in soft blankets. There was large hickory furniture and a 19th century chest of drawers. There was even a sink and a mirror.

The view from the window was like something out of Van Gogh's 'Starry Night.' The pale moon shone brightly down on the Atlantic. The moon was so bright that Wesley could see the ocean shimmering. The sky was dense with stars, it was like the parish of Keel was being sucked directly into the cosmos.

Wesley sat on the edge of the bed, his bones aching to be wrapped in warm blankets.

"You can meet everyone tomorrow, and we can make a start, you can run a bath if you want, you can do anything you want to."

"Thanks, I just want to sleep." It was seven o clock in the evening. All of Wesley's apprehension and worry had exhausted him.

"We'll break you in slowly, you can watch at first, but the sooner you participate the sooner you can make progress." Polly smiled and placed a loving palm on Wesley's forehead.

Sleep washed over Wesley.

***

CHAPTER 4 --- FIRST IMPRESSIONS

Wesley awoke the following morning to the singing of birds perched on the windowsill. He remained laying on the bed, too exhausted to move. His clothes were strewn with the natural perfume of damp and body odour. He lay there for what must have felt like half an hour, although it could have felt like an hour. He was wrapped in a warm glow of comfort.

He listened to the hustle and bustle of the morning routine in The House of Novalis. He listened to a woman outside in the front yard. She was feeding the chickens. Either that or she was completely off her nut, he couldn't relate the sound she was making to any other task, her loud beckoning cry of 'chirp, chirp, chirp, chirp!' caused Wesley to assume that was the sound a person made when they were feeding chickens.

He listened to the muffled conversations

through the walls. He couldn't make out what they were saying, it sounded like a male and female. They laughed a lot, they sounded very boisterous. Then everything went silent. After a couple of minutes Wesley could hear the sound of a bed creaking.

He listened to the distant crashing of waves against the shore. He listened to the seagulls crying. He listened to the thumps, footsteps and creaks in the commune. He could smell the fresh scent of coffee boiling.

Through the wall opposite the creaking bed, he heard a strumming guitar. A girl began to sing. Wesley instantly loved the sweet lament of the girl singing. He thought it was a pretty song, one which he had never heard before.

There was a wonderful gush of air as she hit the high notes. From what Wesley could gather, it was a bittersweet song about losing love and lamenting youthful summers, in the universe of her room. He liked the tempo of the song, quick and catchy.

The bedroom door creaked open. Wesley opened his eyes and saw Polly standing over him, holding a steaming hot cup of coffee.

Wesley accepted the coffee with a weak nod and a smile and drank the warm, nutty, bitterly smooth liquid. It tasted good.

“Are you hungry my darling?”

Wesley shook his head; his aches from the previous evening were now replaced by numbness. His chest felt like a warm soft cushion.

“Anytime you want something to eat, you know where the kitchen is. Help yourself my love. We’re all meeting in the main room at 10 o’ clock, make sure you come down and say hello to everyone.”

“What time is it now?”

“It’s half past eight. You’ve slept for a good 13 hours.”

“Are you doing the therapy now?”

“Yes, my advice is to go with the flow, and don’t take anything personally, and most importantly, don’t get involved. Whatever happens don’t worry, don’t be afraid, just let it happen.”

She turned and left suddenly, closing the door loudly behind her. This caused Wesley to shake off his tiredness and to jump out of bed. He stripped bare, and lathered his body in soap before washing himself down thoroughly in front of the sink. He then changed into a set of clean clothes. He couldn’t remember the last time he felt so relaxed and refreshed, as he threw his scummy, sweat stained fish smelling clothes into his rucksack.

He enjoyed the rest of his coffee. He had come a long way, Christ, had he come a long way. Not so much his journey to Achill from Galway, but in life. Fuck, his life was exhausting; a lesser man would have done himself in by now. There had to be a reason to keep fighting. He thought about his life journey, a life that would have drove a sane man out of his mind. A life, where had he lived a normal life, he wouldn't be here in Achill, at The House of Novalis.

This was going to be like his first day of school all over again.

His most vivid embarrassing memory was of his first day at school. He was sent to the bathroom by his teacher after walking dog muck into the carpet. He'd never forget how his cheeks burned with the embarrassment, how his little heart drummed in his little chest, as all the children in the classroom laughed and pointed at him.

He remembered the sheer panic suffered, panic that no grown up should endure, never mind a five-year-old child, as he was forced to wash his shoes under a tap, but his little hands could only spread the muck around. He was terrified of being kicked out of school.

He checked the soles of his boots to see if there was any dog muck on them before exiting the bedroom and making his way downstairs to the common room.

He followed the sound of voices through the upstairs hallway, onto the landing, down the stairs, and into the common room. He opened the door and was greeted to a loud cheer and a generous round of applause by a group of nine people, a group which included Polly.

"Do you all live here?" Asked Wesley when the clapping subsided. The group nodded in unison. "That's crazy, that's really cool." Wesley was over the moon by the reception he received, for the first time in his life, he genuinely felt elated.

Polly grabbed Wesley's hand, as a sign of reassurance. She could tell that despite his elation he shook like a leaf, probably from the excitement, more than likely from nerves and shyness. "Wesley, let me introduce you to everybody. This is my sister Tara..."

"It's so nice to meet you, Wesley!" Tara exclaimed as she squeezed Wesley with a warm, tight hug. Wesley tried not to wince; she felt like a sack full of bones, it was liked being squeezed by a metal coil.

"It's very nice to meet you," gasped Wesley. His sentiment was genuine, but Jesus wept, he didn't want to be hugged by this woman again in a hurry.

"I can tell you're not much of a hugger," said Tara, as she finally let him go. "but don't worry, we'll soon have that knocked out of you in no time."

"This is my niece, Bonnie." Polly said, continuing the introductions.

Wesley's jaw dropped open as Bonnie, Tara's daughter, stepped forward. She was beautiful, her mother's height, petite, with a cherub face, short dark hair, and deep brown eyes which were the size of saucepans.

She was draped in a figure-hugging belly top, and psychedelic long flowing skirt. Her naval, eyebrows, nose and ears were all pierced. When she hugged Wesley, he felt a completely different sensation than that of her mother. He felt this flood of hot energy pulsating through his body. She smelled like jasmine, hot, sticky jasmine.

"Welcome, Wesley, it's so good to meet you."

"You too." Wesley didn't want her to let go. Her stomach and waist felt so warm and pure. When she stepped back, she flashed a pearly, white smile.

"I look forward to getting to know you."

"You too."

Lulu was introduced next. She had blonde hair and deep green eyes, with high cheek bones, and thin features. She was dressed in colourful, handmade, knitted garments, and Wesley could sense that she had a sweet, innocent, loving nature. Her Scottish accent pleasantly tickled Wesley's ear lobe as she hugged him.

"It's so good to have you here, I think me, and you are going to be great friends."

"I hope so."

Ruby was next to greet Wesley. She had wild dreadlocks growing so much they hung all the way down to her backside. She was slim, and extremely shy. She barely hugged Wesley; she was so fragile Wesley was afraid he'd break her if he hugged her any tighter.

She had bright blue eyes and a long roman nose; her skin was the whitest shade of pale he had ever seen. She smelled of cannabis and mint. She was donned in a guns and roses t shirt and ripped blue bellbottom jeans. She didn't say a word to Wesley.

"Ruby is a wonderful singer," quipped Polly, "and a brilliant guitar player."

"Next are the men!"

"Oh yes," replied Tara, "always good to have another man around the place, there's plenty of firewood to be chopping, isn't that right fellows?"

Wesley shook hands with Oscar, a tall, skinny

man with curly hair and a friendly disposition, Gideon, a sullen, frowning man with a large beard and long hair, who looked like he came straight out of Lynard Skynyrd, and Bertie, overweight, balding, with red cheeks, and round spectacles, donned in a technicolour robe.

It was difficult for Wesley to get a first impression from either of the three men, but Tara was right, Wesley wasn't much of a hugger, he guessed that out of the three, the fat looking monk would have no problem enveloping him in a big hug, his hand was sweaty, while the other two had firm handshakes. They probably weren't the hugging type either.

Wesley hoped he could get along with the men in the group. The women seemed like they were willing to open up to him, and he'd be willing to do the same thing. But with having four Irish men in a room, no matter the therapy, or the situation, it was natural that it was going to take a while for the men to open up to each other, what Wesley wasn't expecting though, was how much they were willing to open up to anybody who was willing to watch.

"Okay, everybody let's get started."

The group dispersed and went about laying down on cushions. Polly brought Wesley over to the far wall, they sat down, as some of the moaning and groaning started, Polly explained the process of what happens in Primal Therapy, and what happens in group therapy.

"You can't grow up feeling somebody else's needs and being yourself. You can't grow up trying to be what they want you to be. You can't walk around doing what they want instead of doing what you want. Do you understand?"

"Yes." Wesley said, as he watched the men and women begin to rock and moan. Nobody was screaming. The girls, Ruby, Bonnie and Lulu, were gently crying. Tara was walking around the room, supervising the session. Bonnie was sitting up, almost the way a toddler might. She looked like she was about to throw a tantrum.

"These are the beginning of primals. The idea of group primal is to get you back to the beginning of when it hurt. Uncover the hurts of childhood. Relive them and free the real you. There is a state of being quite different from the one we are used to, the one we know. A brand new life can arise from yourself! You can become yourself and stay yourself, that is the only cure for neurosis."

Polly had to speak louder now as the residents of The House of Novalis began to rock and moan. Ruby was crying harder now. Bonnie was on the verge of having a fit.

"We can call someone who is well balanced,

someone who can get angry when they feel it. Someone who can cry when they feel it, someone who can show love, if that's the emotion they want to feel. It is the people in the world that are "well balanced." The people who think they are calm and smooth, who go with the flow, they are the ones who are terribly unbalanced, do you see Oscar there? Oscar's primals normally tend to be about his mother, his mother was unloving and unwanting. He was one of the first people to arrive, to me and Tara. After getting to know him a bit better, and letting him watch how we do primals, I asked him to call for his mummy. He refused for the first three weeks, he'd cry and shake and moan, but he wasn't in the depths of a primal, it seemed like it was more for show. So when I asked him again, it was a private session, and he wouldn't do it for about twenty minutes. And then, much to my surprise, he took his clothes off and began crying and screaming and yelling, he was writhing, almost to the point he was having convulsions."

"He's not going to take off his clothes here, is he?"

"I honestly don't know. Anybody is capable of taking their clothes off, it just needs to fit into the primal. Like Lulu there. She stripped topless one day and told her father that he could never have her breasts, these breasts were hers and she was going to show them off. The thing about being here, being here right now, is that it may entail crying, or it may entail laughing. Anything, it's just being here, being real, being in the present and experiencing yourself, every minute."

Wesley sat on the floor, with his knees up to his chin as he studied the different primals happening around the room. He wanted to help Bonnie, she seemed like she was regressing back to an age before she could articulate speech, and Wesley didn't get a good vibe coming from that. She was reliving some shit a lot of people would push down so far into their stomach, kept locked with a chain and key. Bonnie was going for it.

"Primal pain lives in the form of tension. The key to undoing neurotic tension is to get rid of the pain, the pains that come to us very early in childhood. When you're a baby, you're too young to deal with trauma, to deal with this tremendous impact that is bestowed upon you. You can't deal with it, so you find functions and distractions. What is so important as an adult is that we are able to feel the weight of these pains, because they won't overwhelm us now, they won't get on top of us, not like they would as a little baby."

Polly pointed to Ruby, who was half lying on her side, with her legs up in the air and her fingers shoved into her mouth. She was gently crying, with her eyes closed, shaking her head from side to side.

"Sometimes when you have a primal, it can be an ordinary scene that sets you off, like your mother depriving you of her breast, or your father abandoning you in the crib so he can go downstairs and watch the football on the television. Then there's Ruby's primals."

Polly began to get emotional; tears sprang into her eyes, Wesley could hear her voice begin to tremble as she continued on.

"Ruby was abused by her father, and her brother, throughout her adolescence."

Wesley went pale. He watched Ruby as she began to wail, rocking her hips back and forth, tears streaming down her cheeks.

"So when she has her primal, she has to relive that memory to get rid of the pain that is bottled up inside. The point is, whatever happens to us in our childhood, doesn't just disappear in an instant, whether it's something ordinary, or in the case of Ruby, without therapy, God knows what she'd be doing right now. This is her way of dealing with the physical abuse, the resentment, the hatred, why didn't her daddy love her? These experiences, especially the ones that are extremely painful, both physically and emotionally, remain locked in the brain as a memory circuit. It continuously reverberates, hence the name, the reverberating circuit. As the circuit reverberates, it continues to pulsate down into the body. Then, they travel back up into the head and produce all of these kinds of bizarre ideas, putting physical pressure on your body. Your early primals are what shape you in life; they cause you to become the person you are. There is continuous tension in the modulator, in the blood cells; it affects your immune system, even your nervous system. It produces musculature tension, so with the help of Dr Janov, and his writings, what we try to do is take the memory circuits and restore them completely. The reason why it's scream therapy is because when you restore the memory, it hurts. It helps to cry because crying restores the natural function of the body, we need to give everybody back their tears, including you, Wesley.

"I never cry."

"Never? Not once?"

"I didn't cry when I was born."

"But all babies cry when they're born."

"Not me, check the hospital records if you don't believe me. Something to do with the trauma of the birth, the pressure I endured coming out of the womb, it rattled me, I didn't cry, not even when the doctor spanked me. I was put into an incubator for a week."

"That there, that could be the answer to your problems, to everything, you feel disconnected from everything because that's how you were born."

He watched as Bertie stood up and began screaming something at the top of his voice, his hands clutched against his chest. His red cheeks becoming more blood red as he wailed, he began pointing at something imaginary, as if somebody was standing right in front of him.

"What the hell is Bertie doing?"

"Bertie is arguing with his dead parents. Bertie was a very religious man. His mother made him go to church as much as she physically could, even when Bertie was in his twenties. His father was such a devout Christian, that when his sister got cancer, they refused to let the doctors give her treatment. They believed that God would take care of her, that she would be cured and that their prayers would be answered; she was dead six months later. Later on in life, his parents died, and Bertie had nobody. He's having a primal about saying goodbye to religion. Religion was his companion and friend, he had nothing else in his life. Now that he's found himself, he finds that he needs it less. I've found that tends to be the case with religious people. Once they find Primal Scream Therapy, they tend to turn their backs on their religious background. Bertie feels guilt for not having religion in his life anymore. He doesn't believe in God anymore."

“What’s wrong with believing in God?”

“It’s a crutch. Something to lean on, we find crutches in our life whether it is drink, or drugs, or materialistic items, or violence, or sex...or religion. Once he found therapy his neurosis subsided, he stopped being afraid of death. Two things can happen when you lose your fear of death, you become overly religious, or you turn your back on religion completely. I find the latter to be the much healthier option. The scariest thing to do in life is to confront yourself. In manifestation, the only cure against the tyranny of neurosis is revolution. The only way to start a revolution is through force and violence, you see that here. You see how everybody in this room is using tremendous force and extremely violent actions to overcome their neurosis.

The search for the meaning of life, seems not only the pre-occupation for philosophers, but for neurotics as well.”

***

CHAPTER 5 --- VOIR DIRE

Detective Sergeant Jimmy Daniels sat glumly in the dock of the Central Criminal Court, watching the sketch artist squint his eyes and study him closely. It was stuffy in the courthouse, and there didn't seem to be a ten-minute break in sight, instead the courtroom watched footage of Jimmy interrogating a young man by the name of Sebastian Rivers, the prime suspect in a murder case.

The footage was crystal clear, and everybody in the courtroom got a chance to study Jimmy's receding hairline and an ever-growing bald spot which was slowly developing on the top of his head.

The audio, for some reason, wasn't as clear, it came across as distant, crackly, Jimmy would have to get onto the IT department regarding this, the media circus surrounding this case was frenzied enough without the Gardaí having to endure more onslaught by the press over their inability to use microphones. Somebody in the department had to transcribe the whole recording for subtitles so that everybody could make out what was being said.

"We've determined, there's no doubt in my mind whatsoever, that you're responsible in what happened to Ryan. That's not even an issue anymore."

Jimmy didn't like to look at himself on screen, he didn't like anybody taking his photograph, he didn't even like hearing his own voice. He could mime along to what he said on the footage on the wide, smart televisions which were dotted around the large, spacious, modern courtroom. Jimmy was using a form of interrogation known as the REID technique.

"I don't think you're a bad person, I know this is hard to go through. The only thing you can do now, to make this better, to make this right for Ryan, is to stand up and be a man and say "yeah, I made a mistake."

Jimmy looked around from his position in the dock at the top right end of the courtroom. His seat was a large leather chair and was quite comfortable, given the circumstances. He felt like the odd man out in the room, mainly because he sat across from the judge, Her Honourable Elizabeth Lyndon, whilst the public sat facing the judge. Jimmy peered over the people crammed into the courtroom. He felt like the character K in Franz Kafka's novel 'The Trial.'

He saw the sketch artist, who must have had about 200 sketches of Jimmy at this point throughout his professional career. He drew in the same way Christy Moore sang live on stage, all fluster and sweat, his bald head glistening from the light which reflected off the monitors screening the interrogation footage.

He gazed across at the judge, sitting high on her 'throne,' peering at the footage through small spectacles, donned in her elegant black robes. There was a mutual disrespect between detective and judge. Elizabeth Lyndon's face reminded Jimmy of a shriveled chestnut. When the woman was not presiding in court she was sunbathing in France or Barbados, depending on the time of year.

Jimmy never had an easy time in court when Lyndon headed proceedings. The Judge found Jimmy to be arrogant, distant and above the law. Whereas Jimmy found Judge Lyndon to be impatient, too emotional and irrational in her thinking process. In Jimmy's opinion, there were far better judges in the country.

"That's all you gotta do bud, just put your hands up and say, "I fucked up." Because we're going to get you for this either way."

Jimmy gritted his teeth, trying not to flinch at the sound of his own voice. He always had to keep a poker face on him, the defence were doing everything in their power to make him look and sound like some tyrant.

He turned and looked again at the crowd, the first three rows were seats reserved for journalists, both from the mainstream media and the independent networks, who were fresh faced and hungry for success. Jimmy could clearly make out the difference between the mainstream journalists and the new age bloggers, it was their dress sense and mannerisms that gave them away.

The mainstream, old school journalists took notes, barely looking at the screen. Jimmy knew they had an agenda, to spin the trial to the public, regardless of the facts. They wore shirts, suits, blouses, and whispered to each other every so often, comparing notes.

The new age journalists wore casual clothing, full of colour and vibrancy, and kept their eyes on every single detail of the proceeding. They studied the footage, the suspect, the judge, they studied if Jimmy would react in any way. Every nuance, every breath, would be reported correctly to their viewers and listeners.

"We both know this happened, in the spur of the moment, all these frustrations that have been hap-

pening in your life build up to the point that you don't even realise what you're doing until you're actually doing it."

Jimmy hated having to attend court. He hated the convoluted manner of the Irish court system. This court proceeding wasn't even the main trial. It was a trial within a trial, a Voir Dire, to speak the truth.

To Jimmy, it was all just a load of bureaucratic bullshit. This was the second day of Voir Dire, to determine if the recorded confession given by Sebastian Rivers to Detective Sergeant James Daniels, for the murder of his two-year-old stepson, Ryan Adams, was coerced by the detective.

It had taken forever to get to this point in the interrogation. Jimmy had to build rapport with the suspect, and listened to Sebastian wax lyrical about everything related to James Bond. It was when the interrogation became intense, that's when Jimmy heard the entire court room shift forward in their seats, becoming more engrossed.

For the past two days, Sebastian River's defence team, led by Mr. Joe Perry, was convincing Judge Lyndon that the confession was indeed coerced, and should not be submitted into evidence, arguing that not only was the confession forced, it would also easily sway the jury into handing out a guilty verdict.

The Judge had to keep the jury in their hotel, under lock and key, without any access to the outside world, until she could decide on what she considered an 'especially important matter.'

Jimmy had no reservations in his belief that Voir Dire was becoming a bane in the existence of Irish Law. Nothing was ever cut and dry anymore. The courts could spend days arguing over the submission of important pieces of evidence before any trial ever began.

Defence solicitors, especially those based in Dublin, had developed a great knack for doubting and finding obsolete holes in the most concrete of evidence the prosecution could throw at the accused.

This case had become a media circus, most notably since Jimmy was one of the top criminal profilers in the country, and an expert in the art of interrogation.

Because of this, the media were having a field day waiting to find out if Jimmy had inexplicably dropped the ball, cut corners, and lied in pursuing a confession. Any scandal that involved a person of Irish authority was always a top news story. And the confession of Sebastian Rivers was no different.

It was a never-ending merry go round of

media coverage on websites and news streams, opinion pieces, so called experts asked to give their two cents on live studio debates as to whether the accused was innocent or guilty, which lead to media coverage on the so-called experts, and more so-called experts called in to give their opinions on the original so-called experts.

The facts of the case could be hidden from the public eye, and the mainstream media, or 'the black mass media,' as Jimmy liked to call them, could influence public outcry by painting an innocent person as guilty or vice versa. Jimmy liked to call it a hivemind mentality. If he had the same thought process as most of the Irish population, he would never have been good at his job.

"I was just waiting to get down to the pub, and have a few pints. My son was screaming his head off and my wife was still at work. So, he's screaming and screaming, now I can't do anything. I don't know why I did this, all right? But suddenly, I just yelled, "Shut up!!" at the top of my lungs, because I didn't know what else to do anymore. I've been where you've been."

That last statement was a lie, it was common for the investigator to create a scenario to build rapport with the suspect. The truth was, Jimmy was never married, and he had no children. To those who didn't know him, he cut a mysterious figure. He was almost six feet tall, with thin features, and wild curly black hair. He liked to dress in fashionable classic suits and was always clean cut and presentable in his appearance. He preferred dickie bows to ties and carried a watch on a chain which was always clipped to a waistcoat. He was able to function to an extremely high degree on four hours of sleep every night.

Jimmy Daniels was a highly intellectual man, who appeared quite aloof in his demeanor. The truth was, Jimmy Daniels was an introvert who preferred his own company, and because of the nature of his profession, was an expert in keeping his emotions guarded. One of the downsides of being a major case detective, was that he spent more time with criminals than he spent with friends or associates. The friends and colleagues he did acquire found him extremely approachable, warm, easy to talk to, and quite friendly, a trait which resonated through his quiet demeanor.

"The difference between good people, and bad people, is that good people make mistakes, they eventually step up and take responsibility for what they've done, it's as simple as that. Now am I dealing with somebody who's a decent person or am I dealing with somebody who's a cold-hearted prick? What am I dealing with here? This is just you and me now. I want you to show me how hard you shook him that day, and I want you to be honest about it, okay?"

Jimmy looked down at Sebastian Rivers, who was sitting with his team of solicitors. He was probably the only person in the courtroom, bar Jimmy, who wasn't looking at the footage. Instead he fixed his gazed toward the carpeted floor. He was slim, with pale features and brown eyes, his thick black hair was slicked back with gel. He wore a distinguished looking blazer and shirt, but no tie. From this angle he could pass as James Bond. It was easy to see that Sebastian wanted to be like his hero. Jimmy watched him like a hawk, as the courtroom heard Sebastian speak in the footage.

"This is hard for me."

"I know it is."

"I shook him like this."

The courtroom watched as Sebastian made the motion of violently shaking a toddler.

"Maybe a bit harder than that, a bit faster, but I shook him like this."

"Did you say anything to yourself, after you did it?"

"What did I just do?"

"I knew I was right about you. I knew you were the type of person who could step up and take responsibility for their actions. You made an important decision today. You stopped lying. You're going

to remember this day as a big turning point in your life, there's no doubt about that in my mind."

Darkness enveloped the courtroom as the footage finally ended. Jimmy checked the time on his watch...it was only half past eleven.

This was going to be a long day. Jimmy sensed the baby shaker was going to get away with it. There was so much focus and attention being given to the nature of the interrogation, rather than the confession itself. Jimmy knew in his heart of hearts he was going to get a suspension for this. More precisely, by using creative methods and diverting away from entitled speech, he was going to get a suspension for doing his job correctly.

The Gardaí danced to the tune of the government sponsored mainstream media, who were going to punish Jimmy for not doing his job the way they wanted it done, rather than the way it should be done. They were going to paint Jimmy as the criminal, while the criminal, the man who murdered an innocent two-year-old toddler, was going to walk free.

***

CHAPTER 6 --- DESOLATION ROW

The death of Ryan Adams had occurred two years previously, when Gardaí were called to the home of his mother, Casey Adams, girlfriend of Sebastian Rivers, on the evening of March 25th.

Casey had called 999, in a state of pure terror, barely audible through her keeling, begging for help, saying that she got home from work and that her little boy wasn't breathing. When the paramedics arrived at the address, 91 Beaumont Avenue, Knocknacarra, they could not resuscitate the child, who was pronounced dead at the scene.

The officers who first arrived at the address notified the Galway Major Crimes Unit, claiming the death of the toddler had looked suspicious. Jimmy Daniels and his then partner, Detective Sergeant Russel Hobbs, arrived at the scene of the crime soon after.

Beaumont Avenue was a council estate, hastily built ten years previously, which quickly fell into shoddy disrepair. Jimmy had nicknamed the area, 'desolation row,' due to the smashed windows, overgrown gardens, junk, and rubbish that could be seen outside each house on the estate.

Upon entry to the residence, a rotten smell of dirty nappies and sour milk hit the back of Jimmy's nostrils, causing him to breathe through his mouth. The house was cluttered with toys and clothes, but it wasn't the messiest house that Jimmy ever had the pleasure to step foot into, that honour went to the hoarder who lived on St. Vincent's Avenue.

Jimmy found the toddler lying face down on the floor in his bedroom, near his cot. The room was painted blue, dotted with white fluffy clouds. Jimmy, without any hesitation, knelt over the body for closer inspection, while Hobbs pretended to take notes in the hallway, too squeamish to witness the death of a child.

The child's face was blue and swollen, and his angelic green eyes were bloodshot red. He wore a cheap knock off sports jersey, and corduroy shorts. One sock was on his left foot while the matching sock was lying on the floor next to him.

This child did not die of natural causes. He

may have choked on something accidently, but this looked like shaken baby syndrome. Jimmy wanted to cover the child with a blanket, to sit next to Ryan and look after him until the ambulance took him to the morgue, but the forensics team were late getting to the crime scene.

Jimmy couldn't even touch the child, he couldn't close the boy's eyes or place a caring palm on the child's head, in case he tampered with the evidence. Instead, Jimmy knelt over the body and said a prayer for the child, and it was then, in the silence of prayer, he could hear the muffled sounds of sobbing and wailing coming from the adjacent room.

Jimmy remembered, upon entering the master bedroom, the opposites in the emotions of the young couple. Casey Adams was hysterical with grief, whilst her boyfriend, Sebastian Rivers, looked like he wanted to be completely somewhere else. He looked distant, uncomfortable, the only comfort he gave his girlfriend was lazily placing an arm around her waist.

The couple were sitting on the bed facing the window, and as Jimmy approached the window to look out, he could see more and more patrol cars, officers, civilian cars and family members trying to make their way into the house. He could see a news crew buzzing its way around the estate, grabbing as much footage as they could on the tragic, unfolding events.

Jimmy Daniels was an instinctive detective, he always followed his gut instinct, it had gotten him out of many scrapes over the years and had led him to finding and catching major criminals. Jimmy's gut instinct was now telling him that Sebastian River's entire demeanour didn't look right. His dark eyes were as cold as marbles, gazing down on the dirty carpet in front of him. He was white as a sheet.

The young man did not portray an iota of emotion whatsoever. Not on Jimmy's first encounter with him, or the subsequent interview that followed, or when he was arrested, charged and interrogated.

It later came to light that Sebastian Rivers had an IQ of 80 and suffered with autism and learning difficulties. No excuse for killing his little stepson, but Jimmy couldn't arrest people on gut instinct alone, he hoped there would be sufficient evidence to back the claim. Sebastian didn't seem to care that his stepson was lying dead in the adjacent room.

Jimmy remembered Hobbs trying to question Casey, and being greeted by ear screeching wails and sobs, the poor woman was so overcome with grief that she could barely string two syllables together. Before Hobbs could press on any further, Jimmy motioned to him to leave the couple be, and to make their way back downstairs to see if there was anybody else they could question.

The detectives spotted Casey's parents through a sea of strangers, sitting at the kitchen table, with tears in their eyes, their faces red with grief and despair. Jimmy made his way through the crowd without much curtesy, he didn't suffer fools gladly and didn't think so many people were needed at the crime scene.

"Mr and Mrs Adams, my name is Detective Sergeant Daniels, this is Detective Sergeant Hobbs, I'm so sorry for your loss, is it okay, would it be all right, to talk to you? I want to help."

For as long as Jimmy would live, he would never forget the mountain of grief that was etched on the Adam's faces. Their grief would haunt him for months afterwards, giving him many a sleepless night.

Jimmy quietly sat down next to them at the round kitchen table and let the father shout at him until he was so upset that all he could do was cry. Once the emotions died down, they began to open up about Sebastian Rivers.

"We never liked him. There is something wrong with him. And people turn their nose up at us because we treat a person with disabilities with such disdain. He gets everything given to him. Money, training, he has his own flat but he never stays there. And look where tolerance got us. It wasn't because Casey was going out with him when she was six months pregnant, that happens, that didn't bother anyone, but for him to practically move in with her after a matter of weeks, that felt wrong to us."

"Where is the father in all this?"

"Prison...we think, we never met him."

"What is it about Sebastian that you don't like?"

"His personality, he's very cold. At first we thought that was just his way, not to make too much out of it. Casey liked him, he seemed to make her happy, so we stayed out of it. Then he moved in here. We thought that was odd. He does not say hello, he doesn't smile, he just spends all his time playing them video games in the sitting room, that feckin 'Goldeneye' or whatever it's called, the one with the shooting. And Casey is a good girl, she has a good heart, and anybody who thinks she has something to do with this should go and fuck themselves."

"Did he look after the boy?"

"Not the way we wanted him to, there were plenty of evenings we'd come around, when Casey was at work, she works hard, and we'd come in and the house dirty, and clothes everywhere, and the baby crying, and him playing them fuckin video games. Completely tuned out. He didn't care about the child. He just wanted someone to look after him. So, we'd feed the baby and change him and play with him, and Casey would come home, tired, and we would always stay late. There was one day when Sebastian was in his own flat, and we begged Casey to stop the relationship. The argument became so heated she threatened to disown us and said if we didn't start being nice to Sebastian, that she wouldn't let us see our grandchild. She was in love with him, and it's not his fault he has autism, Casey's heart has always been so pure. So, after a few weeks, we wanted to see our grandchild, so we apologised. Now…he is dead."

***

CHAPTER 7 --- CROSS EXAMINATION

"Detective, can you be so kind as to go through the nine phases of the REID Technique, and what they involve?"

Mr Perry stood in front of the dock; his thumbs hooked into his robes. This was the part of the process Jimmy dreaded the most, the cross examination.

The prosecution was very straight forward in their line of questioning, very matter of fact in the way Jimmy conducted the investigation. He only needed a couple of hours briefing from the prosecution, and they gave him a rehearsal on how the cross examination would go, Jimmy had an idea what kind of trap Perry was leading him into. He slowly cleared his throat;

"Would I be correct in presuming there's more than just deceptive indicators when reading a suspects behaviour?" Perry's accent had gotten posher over the years, to the point one would mistake him for being British.

"Well, I generally rely on my gut instinct."

"How so?"

"Intuition occurs when your brain sends out information and matches what is happening in that precise moment to experiences that you have had in your past, the cognitive recognition doesn't reach your conscious awareness, for scientific reasons I can't tell you the precise chemical process on how this takes place, you'd need to ask an expert in that field, however, I do know that the process is circumstantially correct. With twelve years' experience, I have seen a lot, therefore, my gut instinct has never steered me wrong."

"So, your gut instinct is something you use, as part of your profession?"

"It's something all detectives rely on…it's encouraged."

Joe Perry, made a face, indicating to Jimmy that he wasn't satisfied with the answer. There was no way he could argue that the gut instinct was a whimsical phenomenon, not after Jimmy's explanation. The overweight, spectacled, red faced, lump of a man looked down at his notes, before pressing on with his cross examination.

"Explain to me, Detective, what the second phase of the REID Technique entails?"

"The second phase is all to do with theme development. The interrogator creates a story about why the suspect committed the crime. Theme development is about looking through the eyes of the suspect to figure out why they did it. We offer to the suspect, a psychological justification for the commission of the crime. We don't legally justify it, but we offer them a moral excuse."

"Allow me to quote here judge, if I may, "the only thing to do now, to make this better, is to stand up and be a man and say, "yeah, I made a mistake." This would be an example of theme development?"

"One of many."

"Do you have a certain theme in mind when you begin an interrogation, or do you create them based on the suspect's reaction?"

"It's kind of like playing poker."

"I'm sorry, Detective, do you mean you gamble on a confession?"

"No, it's kind of like poker because you don't know what hand you're going to be dealt with, and you have to make the most out of what you have."

"When you have no evidence, such as in the case of Mr. Rivers."

"Not every case has evidence falling directly onto your lap."

"Very true, Detective, can you explain to me please, the third phase of the REID Technique?"

"It's to do with denial."

"Can you explain what it entails?"

"In layman's terms it's about handling denials. If you let a suspect deny the crime, their confidence levels begin to rise. What you need to do is to cut off the suspect as soon as they speak. You tell the suspect they will have their chance to talk, all they can do is listen. You need to cut off any denials as soon as they happen. If there are no denials, and your theme development is working, then you know they're going to confess.

"What if they continue to maintain their innocence?"

"If they keep denying the crime outright, you need to take that into consideration. But generally, we don't begin an interrogation until we're sure a suspect committed the crime."

"As in when you collect all the evidence?"

Jimmy could see where the cross examination was going. Joe Perry was zoning in on the lack of evidence at the crime scene. Jimmy was becoming self-conscious of his own mannerisms and ticks. He wasn't going to let his emotions get the better of him.

"Speak the truth", his uncle always told him, "Just speak the truth, and let the chips fall where they may. Don't beat around the bush, don't put a yarn on what it is that you're trying to say, just speak the truth and you'll be fine."

"Not just evidence," Jimmy replied, "There's witness testimony, timeline, past crimes, criminal record, etcetera."

"Is this the reason why you begin to tell him, "I know you didn't plan to have this happen, it just happened on the spur of the moment, because you were angry?"

"Yes."

"You then went on to say, "We both know this happened, we both know this was a momentary lapse of judgement on your part, that all these frustrations that have been happening in your life build up to the point that you don't even realise what you're doing until you're actually doing it."

"That's correct."

"Anything the suspect may say then, you can tighten your hold, so to speak. You overcome objectives, as you would kindly put it yourself."

"Yes."

"Can you give me an example of overcoming one's objectives?"

"Okay, let's say you're the suspect. We'll put you in a hypothetical situation."

"Okay?"

"You've raped a woman."

Commotion broke out in the courtroom, some people sniggered while others were shocked at the forwardness in the way Jimmy put forth his hypothetical situation. Judge Lyndon raised her hands in the air to quiet the crowd.

"Detective, please tread carefully."

Jimmy ignored the Judge's warning.

"You were out one night, your wife was in a bad mood, you lost your job, you're sitting in your car, drinking beer, you see a young woman out jogging, you're pissed off at the world, you want to take it out on someone who isn't your wife, you think all women are the same..."

"Yes Detective, I see your situation."

"You become our prime suspect in the investigation. I interrogate you and accuse you of rape. How would you respond to the threat?"

"I would say that I could never possibly rape somebody. My niece was raped when she was a teenager and I know how much pain that caused. I could never do that to someone for as long as I lived."

Jimmy saw emotion and anger in Joe Perry's eyes. He wasn't lying.

"I would say to you then, "See? That's good. You're not a monster. What you're telling me is that this wasn't planned, this was out of your control. You care about women, just like you care about your niece. It lets me know that this was a one-time mistake, not a recurring thing."

"You make statements seem like admissions of guilt?"

"If it's done right, yes."

"What happens after that?"

"Procurement of attention. I do everything in my power to make it seem that I am the only friend the suspect has in the world. I move in closer, cutting off any route of escape. I make it hard for the suspect to detach from their situation. I deploy concern, a sense of camaraderie."

"You make up a story about having a wife and a two-year-old son..."

"I create a theme about having a wife and a two-year-old son, yes."

"But the truth of the matter is you've never been married, nor do you have any children, am I correct in saying that?"

"Yes."

"Is that moral, to do that?"

"Morality has got nothing to do with it, as I've said, my job is to create themes, to build rapport."

"Do you realise that my client has an IQ of 80?"

"Not when the investigation first began, but afterwards I did know that, yes."

"Were you aware of my clients IQ when you interrogated him?"

"Yes."

"Yet it didn't cross your mind that my client could have been easily swayed."

"He knew the process when he got in there, he knew that he had the right to speak to a solicitor and he had a right to silence. Nothing about the process was forced upon him. I was well within my legal rights to pursue The REID Technique and he was well within his rights not to speak."

"Your honour, may it please the court to replay a segment of the interrogation, beginning at six minutes and twenty seconds?"

"How long is it?"

"Just a few moments, I would like to clarify something."

"Do the prosecution have any objection?"

The prosecution solicitors shook their heads, they looked bored out of their minds.

"Very well, proceed with the footage."

The clerk dimmed the lights and started the footage from the six minute and twenty second mark. The voices of Jimmy and Sebastian blared through the courtroom, echoing off the walls.

"I've got nothing to say."

"I know that, you're demonstrating the fact that you're a cold-hearted bastard every time you say that."

"I'm only doing what my solicitor told me to do."

"It's a solicitor's job to give advice, Sebastian, but your solicitor is not the person sitting across from me. Your solicitor wasn't there when you shook Ryan to death. Every time anybody speaks to a solicitor, the very first thing they do is recommend that you don't say anything. Let me ask you this, in six months from now, the Gardaí get a tip, about a robbery, let's say, down at the off license, okay? So, the detectives go and look at the investigation and look at the guy who did the robbery, the CCTV is a bit foggy, they never upgraded the cameras there, and the detectives find that the main suspect in their robbery investigation looks very similar to you.

Slicked back hair, pale skin, wearing a red t-shirt and blue jeans. So, let's say they go to your house, six months from now, and they say "how's it going, guess what? We think you did this robbery, so you're under arrest." They take you to the station. Are you just going to sit there and say nothing? You're just going to let them think that you committed the robbery? Or are you going to say, "listen fellas, you made a big mistake. You need to go and speak to Detective Sergeant Jimmy Daniels, because I was with him the day that robbery took place." Is that what you're going to do? A solicitor will always give you that advice, you must decide whether you want to take that advice or not…"

"If you could stop it there, please, thank you!" Perry demanded, shouting to the clerk, who stopped the footage and brought the lights back up to full brightness.

It was fair to say that Jimmy didn't like this solicitor. To be more precise, it was fair to say that Jimmy found Joe Perry to be a pompous, arrogant repulsive human being. Jimmy had been on numerous ends of cross examinations conducted by Joe Perry, who was considered one of the top defence solicitors in the state.

While a lot of law officials worked hard at their job, and did it well, Perry liked to go that one step further. Perry liked to put on a show, a form of entertainment, whether it be in a packed courtroom for a major trial, or a bail hearing with merely the judge and respected parties present. It was a formula that worked well for the man, Jimmy presumed that Perry was a failed actor, everything the man did had to be done with panache. Perry wiped the lens of his glasses with a clean white handkerchief before continuing with his cross examination.

“As you can see, from that piece of footage, and from when we viewed the entire interrogation in length, my client certainly made it clear, on a number of occasions, that he was advised by me, to say nothing, which was met with the continuation of the same method, over and over again.

Each time, my client asserted his position, informing the detective he was advised to remain silent, rather than listening to my client and heeding his advice, the detective went back to square one of his ‘technique,’ and repeated the same refrain.

How is it so, Detective, that this confession

is not coerced, as you so kindly put it yourself, when you keep enforcing the same technique, over and over, to a young man, with a low IQ of 80, who is clearly unsure of the procedure?"

"The suspect has the right to silence, but they don't have a right to be reminded every five minutes that they have a right to silence and even if the suspect asserts his right, we, as detectives, still have license to ignore it. It takes a particularly adamant, stubborn individual to be able to maintain their right to silence.

I have the right to repeat the questions if I may wish to do so and taking a suspect's IQ into accountability doesn't give them a right to get away with murder, especially when the murder victim was an innocent two-year-old toddler."

Jimmy was cooking now. He was getting fed up with the line of questioning, Perry was about to notch up the pressure, Jimmy could tell by the way the veins in Perry's nose were beginning to flare up.

"Explain to me what the alternative question entails."

"Don't you want to hear all nine steps?"

"Bringing the suspect into conversation, the confession and the end process speaks for itself, the people present clearly can see that, also when the suspect enters into a passive mood, what I'm interested in, Detective, is the alternative question, and to what effect this method is used?"

"We offer two contrasting motives for the main aspect of the crime. The first motive has more of a minor effect, so it is less threatening to the suspect. The options as to why the crime is committed is either a motive that it was socially acceptable or morally repugnant. So, let's say in the hypothetical situation that I placed you in, I would offer you an alternative question, did you do it for the money? Or was it just a crime of passion?

"Am I dealing with someone who is a decent person or am I dealing with someone who is a cold-hearted prick?"

The crowd giggled, due to the crassness of the line spoken by the high-class authoritative figure with the posh accent.

"That would be a prime example of the alternative question, yes."

"As we delve further into the interrogation you begin to tell my client, we don't arrest people until we have all the evidence, it's clear you the one who did it. Did you have any evidence, Detective?"

"No." Jimmy replied softly.

"Yet you were convinced of my client's guilt

in this crime, were you not?"

"Yes."

"Can you explain the process in how my client became the prime suspect in this crime?"

"By the process of elimination."

"By hearsay, you mean?"

"No, I didn't say that, I said by process of elimination, I never used the term 'hearsay,' because I'm always conscious about what I say. I'm very careful about the words I choose and how I convey them. The process was conducted mainly through interviews and witness testimonies involving anyone that knew the child. His mother, Casey, was at work, and her parents weren't due to arrive at her home until four, like they did every other evening she worked, to take the pressure off Sebastian having to look after the child by himself. He wasn't able to care for the child. He couldn't cope.

"Yet he is a qualified carer?"

"He received special training due to his disability, he was helped through his exams, that doesn't necessarily make him qualified. Sebastian Rivers has never actually worked as a carer. He refused to go to the reposal and was even audacious enough to not appear at his stepson's funeral. We interviewed the suspect on two occasions, and never once did he ever show an iota of emotion to how this awful tragedy occurred."

"Yet you were aware of the fact that due to my client's disability, he has difficulty registering emotion?"

"That doesn't make him any less guilty. And before you suggest that my team or I didn't look down every possible avenue we had available to us, let it be on the record we had not only Ryan's mother and grandparents under surveillance for the following six months, but also every member of Sebastian's family, to see if they were in any way involved in committing the crime. After we were 100% convinced that Mr. Rivers was our main suspect, we arrested him for second degree murder."

"Am I correct in saying that the goal of the interrogation was to convince the accused in this case, that this fabricated evidence was so overwhelming that he had no choice but to confess?"

"It was to put pressure on him."

To lead him into signing a false confession..."

"You intended to apply pressure on the accused because due to the lack of evidence, the case was in fact weak?"

"Yes."

"Did you or did you not say to my client that if you weren't forthcoming about him shaking his two-year-old stepson to death, and admitting to the crime in question, that you would make sure you would do everything in your power, to portray him as quote, "a peado killer?"

Jimmy mulled over the question. "Well, that depends."

"Depends on what, Detective?"

"On whether I did or did not."

The crowd broke out into infectious giggles of laughter, fully immersed in the spectacle.

"Could it please her honour and this court that the detective answers my question?"

Judge Lyndon took off her reading glasses and glared at Jimmy.

"Detective, might I suggest that you keep your comedy routine down to a minimum when testifying in my courtroom?"

"There's nothing funny about the matter, Your Honour."

"Then may you be so inclined as to answer the question?"

"I will once Mr. Perry asks a question that's not in the form of a paradox."

"We're not in your interrogation room now,

Detective."

"That's precisely my point."

The crowd laughed again. Perry's cheeks turned as flaming red as the broken veins on his nose.

Judge Lyndon rolled her eyes and shook her head in disdain before turning to Perry and saying, "would you kindly rephrase the question in such a way that it is to the detective's satisfaction? A paradox seems to confuse the rationality in his thinking process."

Judge Lyndon's words were spat out with such facetious venom that Jimmy had to mentally refrain himself from making a snarky comment.

"Did you say to Mr. Rivers, that if he did not confess, you would portray him as a peado killer?"

"Ycs."

"No further questions."

Jimmy stepped out from the dock and made his way back to his seat at the end of the courtroom. The judge was silent for a few moments, mulling over her paperwork. The more she kept silent the more fearful Jimmy became. No video evidence meant no trial. To Jimmy, it seemed like the judge was going to end proceedings there and then. Finally, she spoke.

"One does not need a degree in psychology, to understand the psychological and mental impairment that the accused has, an exceptionally vulnerable, gullible individual when confronted with a vastly more intellectual superior being, a top interrogator who was in a position of authority. I am persuaded by the facts given by Mr. River's Solicitor, Mr. Perry, in relation to the charge against his client of second-degree murder.

I am persuaded that Mr. River's will was overcome whilst being interrogated, he simply caved into the pressure that Detective Sergeant James Daniels placed on him. The most effective tactic that the detective had in his arsenal of interrogation techniques, was to create false evidence, to convince Mr. Rivers that he was guilty of the crime, a crime in which I truly believe, after reviewing the facts and lack of evidence presented before me, the accused did not commit.

A re-occurring theme that happened throughout the hour-long interrogation was Detective Sergeant Smith's false claim that the case was already solved, that the evidence against the accused was overwhelming, and that 'resistance is futile. 'The phrase reminds me of a certain classic science fiction show and one can hardly hear the phrase 'resistance is futile,' without being put to mind of the Borg civilisation portrayed on that show. The Borg civilisation were known to overwhelm and assimilate entire civilisations.

In stating their intent, they always declared to any civilisation that they were about to admonish, that, 'resistance is futile. 'To summarise, Detective Sergeant James Daniels lied to the accused, engaged in a relentless monologue against the accused, who wished to remain silent, a wish that was well within his legal rights. The Detective undermined Mr. Perry's advice by suggesting the lawyer was, quote, "completely ignorant," of the evidence against the suspect, when in truth, no such evidence existed. Detective Sergeant Daniels then went onto claim that he was "speaking for the courts," which in my view, translates that the detective was speaking for me, a claim which I find completely irresponsible and highly offensive.

The detective even went so far as to offer leniency in place of a confession. He placed a choice in front of the suspect, confess or be damned, in which innocence, although technically presumed, was not an option. I have no choice but to acquit Mr. Rivers of this crime. May I also suggest that Detective Sergeant Daniel's superintendent and superiors analyse his use of the REID Technique, a technique that has been out of fashion for almost twenty years, and to train him in the more adept lines of techniques used by interrogators in an Gardaí Síochana, such as the PEACE Technique, so an event like this will not happen again and another innocent Irish civilian will not be coerced into confessing and charged with a crime in which they did not commit.

Let this be a warning, Detective Sergeant Daniels, I will not allow this sort of rubbish to be placed in front of me anymore.

#

Once Jimmy stepped outside of The Central Criminal Court, getting a whiff of the cool fresh air that blasted against his face as he opened the door, he was mobbed by journalists, all holding their phones and microphones into his face, shouting questions at him.

"Detective? Are you being suspended for your actions?"

"How does it feel to take advantage of people with mental disabilities?"

"Are you going to quit?"

"How do you feel about the judgement?"

"Is it true you called Sebastian Rivers a retart?"

Jimmy refused to answer, instead he pushed

his way through the sea of journalists, and made his way towards his Ford, which sat in a car park quite a bit away from the courthouse. He saw Sebastian Rivers standing with his family at the far end of the courthouse, he was smoking a rolled cigarette, and Jimmy was almost convinced that he was smiling. He had to refrain himself, that smile was digging right under his skin, mocking his entire method, his profession, and his sense of pride.

As he approached his car he began to jog, the mob of journalists in hot pursuit. He unlocked the car and jumped into the driver's seat, as he turned on the ignition, his car windows became clouded with the faces of journalists, as they thumped their fists on the glass, trying to get his attention.

He had half a thought to gun right through them, to let the car fly bodies around in its wake, but that would be suicide, not only to his career, but to his general freedom, instead, he let the car roll along at five miles per hour, as the journalists ran alongside him, barking out their questions, and the photographers snapped blurred images of him driving away.

He was going to have to go and see the Deputy Commissioner, he hadn't received the call yet but he was as well to get the whole process out of the way. He knew what was going to happen.

There was going to be a committee hearing, all of them dressed in their finest uniform threads, looking like a cheap knock off of "The Last Supper."

Jimmy had no idea how long his suspension would be. This was the first time a criminal profiler was suspended for merely doing his job, the term that the committee would use would be 'indefinitely.' Meaning that they did not have a fuckin clue, they would keep him off work until they needed him. Anything between 3 weeks to six months. Jimmy felt shameful tears sting his eyes as he drove back towards Galway City.

***

CHAPTER 8 --- MYIA

Wesley Harding first met his 'special' friend, Myia Dawkins, five years previously, during Fresher Week at NUIG, when both students were beginning their degree in Law Criminology and Criminal Justice.

Wesley was sitting alone under a tree, on one of the lush lawns that were dotted around the campus, dressed entirely in black, the sun blazing, as he read 'The Communist Manifesto' by Karl Marx. He was trying to be edgy in the way that he looked and in the reading material which he chose for public scenarios, which in truth, bored him to death.

Wesley found the day slow, he had to wait an hour until his next induction lecture and hadn't been able to click with any students that were in his year. He began to wonder would this environment be just like the one he loathed in secondary school? An outsider with no friends.

Wesley was mulling over this thought when

he saw Myia slowly walking towards him, she was dressed in a pair of ripped jeans, which had come back into fashion recently, and a low-cut white vest. Wesley was astounded by the sheer radiance of Myia's beauty. Her face was small, round and perfect in the eyes of Wesley, she had soft brown eyes and a full mouth, which was pierced right at the very edge of her lower right lip. Her hair was a mop of tight blonde curls that flopped down over her eyes. Her snub nose was dotted in freckles, also pierced.

She was small in stature, which made her seem more adorable to Wesley, maybe this was the girl he finally dreamed of dating? Wesley, who was a virgin, still had an extremely high opinion of himself in the style and look of women that he should be dating.

He put the Communist Manifesto into his rucksack as Myia slowly walked by, she was staring into space, not thinking of anything, the weight of the books in her rucksack, which she had slung onto her back, was causing her to walk like a penguin.

"Hello."

Myia looked around to find where the soft sounding voice came from. She found a skinny guy with big eyes and long hair, looking at her innocently. He seemed shy.

"Oh hi, how's it going?"

"I'm okay, kind of bored actually, how are you?"

"Still trying to get the hang of this place, I've gotten lost about three times already this week. Why are you bored?"

"I'm waiting for the Forensic Psychology induction to start and it doesn't start for like, another hour or something..."

"Do you know where it is? I have to be there too."

"Are you studying Criminal Law?"

Myia nodded excitedly.

"Oh cool, me too, yeah I know where to go."

Myia let out a squeal of delight. "Can I hang out with you then, until we go to class? I'm getting tired walking around like a blue arsed fly, and this bag is getting heavy."

Wesley nodded pleasantly, with a hint of a smile on his face. On the inside his heart was palpitating, he couldn't believe his luck. A good-looking girl, who seemed friendly, not like some of the other pompous, stuck-up bitches that he saw around campus.

She was almost nerdy in a way, good looking nerdy barbies were hard to come by, *"wait until the Incel forum get a load of this*." Wesley thought to himself. They wouldn't believe him. Wesley took a breath as Myia sat down next to him on the grass.

"So, what's your name?" Myia asked, in her sweet-sounding voice.

"Wesley."

"My name is Myia."

"Where are you from?"

"Athlone. What about you?"

"Oh, I'm from here, I grew up in the town."

"Cool, so what made you want to study Criminal Law?"

"I think I could be a good prosecutor. Plus, it's very intriguing."

"Isn't it though?"

"There's so much to cover, it's not just about locking up criminals."

"I know! Right?! It's crazy!"

Myia and Wesley were referring to the modules they would have to study in the Criminology section of their Law Degree. The past few days had been a crash course in introducing the young minds to the various aspects of Criminology, it wasn't as cut and dry as some of the students thought.

There was more to finding a person guilty of a crime and locking them up in prison. There were crimes that were not considered criminal, such as smoking in prohibited places and health and safety violations. It wasn't so much a moral study of right and wrong, more of a study of why crimes came to be.

As their lecturer explained to them, Criminology is more about the process rather than the justice. They would have to study about why certain cultures enforced laws that others did not. It was all quite fascinating to Wesley and Myia, who began to discuss the future of their course at length, but neither of them were under the illusion that it was going to be easy.

"I'm actually looking forward to the Forensic Psychology induction. How the criminal mind works."

"Did you see the guest speakers that are coming in?" Wesley asked, as he grabbed his copy of the student handbook from his bag. "There's going to be some pretty big names coming in."

"I'm looking forward to the criminal profiling lecture. That's going to be cool."

There was a minute of uncomfortable silence, Wesley felt he needed to break it. He tried to come up with a question, any question, to keep the conversation going.

"Have you been out much since moving up here?"

"No, I haven't been out at all, I'm renting a room down near the G Hotel. She's a sweet old lady, but I'm looking for a place of my own."

"There's some flats nearly ready down near me, more like bedsits, if you like I can give you the address."

"Oh that would be brilliant, where is it?"

"They're on the Knockmore estate, in Hollywood, near the hospital, that's where I live."

Myia dialed the information into her phone, the screen displayed information on Google Maps. "What's the address number?"

"Well, I'm 128, so try around there, they're across the road from me." Myia found the building and tapped on the map location for information details. A contact number appeared, along with the landlords name, a Mr. Martin McDonacha, she tapped on the listing and called the number.

"You're calling now?"

"No time like the present."

They waited in silence, finally a male voice answered, Myia placed a Bluetooth in her ear and stood up, away from Wesley.

"Hi, I'm calling enquiring about the bedsits you have for rent? I know that...I got your number from Google Maps...Well I don't know why the number was listed...Can I arrange a viewing please?"

Wesley watched Myia pace over and back on the lawn, she'd make a good delegator, she didn't seem the type of woman who took no for an answer easily.

"I can't wait that long. I can wait for them to be ready but I can't wait that long for a viewing...it doesn't matter how I found out, what matters is your number was listed...yes but you will be advertising for them at some point...I'm sorry, I'm not joining a waiting list...You might say my name will be on the top of the list, but that's never the case, is it?...My name is Myia Dawkins...I can come by and view them at your earliest convenience...well this evening then? Mr. McDonacha, have you never heard of seizing an opportunity? Well, I'm all about that sir... I'll come down anyway, I guess you live nearby. No problem...I can find your address in the listings and call down this evening...How does seven pm sound? I think it would make things a lot easier if you just agree, you wouldn't want me calling around every day. Okay...great...thank you. Bye."

Myia hung up the call and smiled at Wesley,

who shook his head at her in disbelief.

"He doesn't sound like he's renting."

"He'll come around."

"And I thought I was a persistent person. That was pretty impressive."

They chatted for a while longer, Myia told Wesley what her tastes in music and film were, and to Wesley's delight she was a major fan of "The Walking Dead" franchise, they talked about their favourite episodes, characters, storylines, and debated over which TV show was the best in the entire franchise. Wesley didn't feel the time slip by, and before he knew it, it was time for them to head over to their Forensic Psychology induction.

"Can I sit next to you?" Myia asked, as they made their way down the main hallway towards the lecture hall which was situated in one of the older buildings down at the back of the campus. "It's just I don't know many people yet..."

"Yeah...I normally sit up the back, but I'll sit wherever you want to sit."

Wesley had never been happier. He had an impulse to gently grab her hand and hold it but thought better of it. He felt it imperative to ask her out on a date, but what if she said no? That was the risk he was going to have to take, maybe if he seized the opportunity, she'd respect him for it.

But what if she said yes? Where would he take her? The 'redpill' subreddit, a dating advice forum for Incels, always preached about displaying an aura of confidence and keeping things low key. The best route to take was to ask her out for a coffee. They made their way into the stuffy, over heated lecture hall that was dotted with students and sat next to each other at the back of the room.

The lecture itself lasted about 2 hours, and Wesley was so comfortable and warm in the presence of Myia that he did not want the lecture to end. It was interesting enough, there was so much to forensic psychology that the lecturer could only give an overview on what was involved and warned that the students needed to work extremely hard to even get a grasp of what the entire field entailed.

Even though they were studying to become criminal lawyers, forensic psychology now played a part in almost every criminal case, and it was up to these young, bright minds to understand the aspects of all concepts involved with the science.

These included everything from custody evaluations, parent alienation syndrome, workplace violence, the psychology of solicitors, the

Disability Act of 2005, right through to evaluations that included insanity pleas and competency to stand trial. Wesley sat half listening to the lecture, whilst trying to get glimpses of Myia, who had a furrowed look on her face, as she frantically tried to write everything down.

Wesley could envision them as a married couple, been comfortable in each other's company, not having to rely on clasping onto one another every two minutes in order for the relationship to work, he just needed to ask her out and he needed to be casual in doing it.

This led to an excitement growing in the pit of his stomach, along with the dread of having the lecture finish. He would have happily sat there next to Myia until the end of time if he was able to.

When the lecture finished, they slowly made their way outside, discussing what they heard during the lesson. Myia was extremely optimistic, while Wesley tried in vain to share her optimism with her, his infatuation for Myia was drowning out any optimism he may have had for forensic psychology.

"So, what are you going to do for the rest of the day?"

"I'm going to go back to my digs, have some lunch, watch a bit of Netflix, study my notes, and then I'll go and meet this landlord and convince him to rent me some digs, what about you?"

"I'll probably play some 'Battlestar' for a while."

"What's that?"

"It's an online RPG."

"A what?"

"A role-playing game, you play online with other people."

"Oh cool, I'm not really into video games."

"That's probably a good thing, it's very addictive."

"Well thanks for today."

"No problem."

To Wesley's surprise, Myia gave him a gentle, warm hug.

"Are you on WhatsApp?" Wesley asked.

"Yeah! Message me, it's so good to make friends this early."

"Cool, I was thinking..."

Wesley clammed up. His head went blank, he knew the words he had to speak yet he could not speak them. Myia looked at him, half expecting what he was thinking about, it was clear by the way she furrowed her brow.

"Would you like to go for a coffee tomorrow?"

"Eh..."

"It's okay if you don't, I mean, it'll be nice to see you again...soon...I mean."

"Where are you thinking?"

"Eh...you know 'Dungeons and Doughnuts?"

Myia laughed, for a second Wesley thought she was laughing at the proposal, and his heart jumped in his chest.

"I never heard of it. That's funny, so it's like..."

"Dungeons and Dragons...yeah...a lot of people play there, plus there's coffee and doughnuts."

"Okay, cool, what time?"

"I was thinking we meet at the tree, at four maybe? And then we can walk down."

"Sweet! All right, it's a date!"

Those three words sent off such a dopamine rush into Wesley's brain that he forgot the fundamentals of speaking the English language.

"Woo..."

Myia hugged him again, and before he could

find his bearings she ran off, leaving Wesley with a big goofy smile on his face. He watched her walk off into the distance before he put on his Spotify playlist and made his way back to his apartment.

Everything in Wesley's universe looked perfect. Everybody and everything he saw was beautiful, everything smelled amazing, he was so happy that the sun was shining in the sky, he loved the sensation of the cool autumn breeze caressing his face.

This would be the last evening for a long time that he would feel this blissfully happy. He didn't skip any songs on his playlist during his twenty-minute walk. Every song he listened to sounded amazing. He couldn't wait to get home so he could go online and tell his friends about the wonderful, amazing, pretty, smart, witty 19-year-old that he had met.

Wesley did something out of character, he smiled at everybody he met, which worked most of the time, almost everybody smiled back, except for one menacing skinhead in a tracksuit who glared at him saying "What the fuck are you smiling at?"

When Wesley got back to his haven, he switched on his computer and logged into his Incel.co account, he was in a group with sixty other men, all virgins, all various ages. Maybe he was better off going onto the redpill subreddit but he wanted to gauge the reaction of his online friends, he couldn't wait to gloat.

WHarding

SOMETHING AMAZING HAPPENED TODAY

So I met this girl and she agreed to go on a date with me. Am I dreaming, are there actually Stacey's out there that are not total femoids? She's clever, sweet, warm, friendly and drop dead gorgeous, and she agreed to go out on a date with me. What do I do? Any advice, I'm so excited that my hands are shaking as they type.

A lot of the responses that Wesley received were negative, which included a lot of passive aggressive jealous remarks of how he was going to fail, that all barbies are the same, that all she's good for is being a cum bucket.

The usual Incel chitchat.

Other men offered their advice by claiming the best path forward was to get sex off her and them dump her, some more accused Wesley of being a fakecel and that he should be banned off the website.

There were some positive messages telling him just to be himself but warned Wesley not to get too ahead of himself, and to brace himself for rejection, just because she agreed to a coffee date doesn't mean that she was sexually attracted to him. One Incel merely replied with the question, 'what happens if you fail?'

Wesley mulled over this for a few moments before replying.

I would probably do something drastic. I'm getting desperate. What would I do if she rejects me? I'll go into my shell and hate her guts. What I would love to do is to buy an AK47 with a few mags, pop one in, load it, walk down to the main street in the city where I live and mow down all the Ken and Stacies I can find. Kill them all. When they are all dead, (and believe me, they'd all be dead) I would place the rifle down a few feet away from me, sit on the ground, and rock back and forth without blinking. I wouldn't speak, I wouldn't say a word. I'd be arrested and brought to the station. I would continue with my trance like state. I wouldn't talk to anyone, I would only answer with 'yes' or 'no' and stare at whoever is speaking to me without blinking, regardless of who it is I am talking to. I don't sleep either, I refuse to sleep. They (the authorities) would have to think in drastic measures to try and break me out of my trans like state. My mother (who is a very influential figure...and a five star bitch who hates me,) would have to be brought in to speak to me. When that happens, I'll break out of my trancelike state and look around panicked, claiming I couldn't remember what happened. They'd have to get a solicitor to defend me, which is fine, because in this country defence solicitors have a hell of a lot more leeway than in other countries, I would have to do psychiatric tests, and eventually, when the case gets to trial, my solicitor would put in a plea deal, and argue every ounce of evidence the prosecutors will have, I'd probably have to spend a good few years in a mental institution, but I'll more than likely avoid prison.

Wesley received hundreds of likes and heart symbols from people who read his post, more than any other post he had ever written in his life.

***

CHAPTER 9 --- DUNGEONS AND DOUGHNUTS

The following afternoon Wesley stood by the tree, waiting for Myia to arrive. When he checked the time and saw that it was five past four, he began to get extremely agitated. This agitation only began to rise inside of him as the minutes ticked by, when the time reached twenty five minutes past four, he was just about ready to make way for home in despair, when he saw Myia approach in the distance. He let out a huge, shaky sigh of relief.

Myia looked nice. She wore a summer dress and had added a touch of lipstick and mascara to her face and lips that enhanced her beauty even further. Wesley was dressed in the same clothes he had worn the day before, he didn't notice the slight look of perplexion on her face upon realizing this when they greeted each other awkwardly.

“So, are you ready to go?” Wesley had asked her after they exchanged greetings.

“Sure thing.” Myia said.

“If you don’t drink coffee, they also do milk-shakes and smoothies.”

“I’ll see how I feel when I get there, are you a big coffee guy?”

“I need at least one every morning, and one after a lecture in the afternoon. What about you?”

“No, not really, I do like the odd cappuccino, but I’m more of a tea drinker. Is it okay if I vape, the mist won’t put you off?”

“No, not at all, what vape do you use?”

“Lemon Kush.”

“You like to get stoned?”

“I fuckin love to get stoned, it’s my most favourite thing in the world to do.”

“Do you drink?”

Myia shook her head as she took a vape from her machine. “What about you?”

“Sometimes, I enjoy a bit of whiskey, but I don’t really like getting drunk, I can’t deal with the hangovers.”

"Tell me about it, I got really drunk on tequila when I was fifteen, ended up in hospital getting my stomach pumped, I'd swore I would never do it again, and I haven't."

"Good for you."

The conversation dried up after that. They walked in silence down past the Cathedral, along by the river, not saying a word until they arrived at the coffee shop on Mill Street.

Inside, they were greeted by a large, heavy-set German with long hair and greasy features, who took their order. Wesley ordered a large coffee and chocolate doughnut, Myia, getting the munchies, ordered a strawberry milkshake and blueberry muffin. Myia bit her lip as they sat down at a small table near the window.

"What's funny?" Wesley asked, smiling at Myia's attempts not to smile.

"No, it's nothing, not being mean, but I've never seen somebody as 'original' as that guy in my life."

"His nickname is "The Dragonslayer."

Myia burst into a fit of giggles, "that's funny, sorry…I'm sorry, I think he looks like a troll, aw man, I shouldn't laugh."

"You have a nice laugh…"

The Dragonslayer appeared with their order,

placing it down on the table, Myia had to hide her face in her hands to cover her laughter.

"Is she all right?" The Dragonslayer asked, curiously.

"She's just stoned is all." Wesley replied.

"Cool, wunderbar."

The Dragonslayer made his way back to the counter, it took Myia a few minutes to get over her fit of giggles.

"I'm sorry, I'll stop now, aw man, these look good."

They began to eat, Myia looked around the shop, admiring all of the dungeons and dragons items for sale in the shop.

"You weren't kidding about this place."

"Have you ever played dungeons and dragons?"

"No."

"It's good, it's a lot of fun. A good way to meet people. Dragonslayer, he's one of the best dungeon masters in the country..."

"What's a dungeon master?"

"He's kind of like the referee of the game, he makes up the story, the quest, and decides the fate of the players."

"Cool. So it's like a boardgame?"

"Oh no, it's like a storytelling game. The dungeon master tells the story, and any obstacles you meet along the way, you have to use whatever is at your characters disposal to get over that obstacle. So let's say, we're playing a game, and we're walking through a forest, and we come across some…evil goblins…"

"So what am I?"

"Anything you want to be."

"So can I be like a pirate queen?"

"Yeah, let's say you're good with a bow and arrow."

"Okay?"

"You tell the dungeon master you want to kill a goblin by using your bow and arrows, he rolls dice, and the dice decides by factoring in your skill level, damage, armour of the goblin, all of that, to decide if you succeed or not."

"Can you die in the game?"

"Oh yeah, we can all die. I took part in this ten-hour game, it was epic…"

"Ten hours?"

"Oh yeah, it was online and there were fifteen of us, and we got separated and had to go on these crazy quests, and then we all got reunited, but when we got to the main dungeon we all fell, one by one, it was the most emotional thing you would ever see in your life."

"Wow."

"It's still talked about, that game, and I was a part of it."

"Good for you."

"Maybe we should play sometime?" Wesley's suggestion came across as slightly pitiful, like he pined for it. Myia just nodded as she ate her blueberry muffin and watched people pass by the window, it was a few minutes before Wesley asked another question.

"So are you looking for anything serious?"

"How do you mean?"

"Relationship wise."

"Oh…no…I've never been in a serious relationship, I mean, I've had boyfriends, but nothing long term. I'm just all about getting into studying and enjoying myself, meeting new people, you know? I'm not looking for anything too serious right now…"

"Oh yeah…totally…I know exactly where you're coming from, I was with girls over the summer, I fucked a few of them, you know? But nothing serious, it was all just a bit of harmless fun." Wesley was completely lying through his teeth.

“Anybody special, anybody who got away?”

“No. What about you?” Myia noticed that Wesley would not break eye contact, it became a little bit unsettling.

“No, but I don’t fret over it, I think the best thing to do is to be yourself and whatever happens, happens. True love could be just around the corner.”

“I wouldn’t say I’m an old school romantic, I think it’s something different, spending quality time and not falling into the trap of what society wants a couple to be. It sickens me.”

“What does?”

“When you see a couple on a bus, or sitting in a pub, or on a park bench and they are publicly showing their affections to one another. It’s horrible, especially when they get up right into your space, and all you can hear are the sounds of squelching as their lips meet, it makes my stomach turn, I’m just so glad you’re not one of them.”

“One of what?” Myia asked absentmindedly.

“A barbie, a dumb bitch, you know? A slut.”

Myia looked at him in horror, her mouth full of blueberry muffin.

“Wesley, I know I’ve only just got to know

you, but that's not an okay thing to say."

"Oh, I'm not trying to offend you."

"I'm sure you're not."

"No, I'm not, honestly, I know you're cool with me saying something like that because you're not one of them, you're different."

"I'm totally against insulting women in any manner."

"But you see my point, you have to, it's why I don't focus on serious relationships, it's because the world is full of air headed barbies who have nothing better to do with their time than to grovel over thick empty headed wankers with big muscles, which I obviously don't have, I mean, I can see the difference in people who are into looks rather than people who are into intelligence and I firmly believe that you're in the latter."

"That's not how it works..."

"Of course it is, I'm just making a valid point, that's all."

"Listen Wesley, thanks for the milkshake and the muffin, but I have to go, I've joined the drama soc and they're having they're first meeting today."

"This isn't because of what I said, is it?"

Myia swiftly stood up and exited, slamming the glass door behind her.

#

Soon after Wesley was rejected by Myia he became more withdrawn from society. The changes in his personality were subtle at first, he signed up to the D&D society where he became an avid player and made plenty of likeminded acquaintances, most of whom were male, cautious in keeping their opinions to themselves.

It wouldn't have surprised Wesley if he had found out quite a number of them were members on the Incel forum. He could tell the men who weren't Incel. They were geeks, but they seemed to be cool geeks, they all had girlfriends who came along to the games and played with them.

They had something Wesley didn't, which was confidence. They oozed confidence. Wallowed in it. They were so self-assured that it made Wesley sick to the pit of his stomach. They wanted their attention all on them, however, Wesley kept his opinions to himself.

The few single women that were part of the society didn't appeal that much to Wesley, except for maybe one who was pretty on the eye, a good player and extremely funny, Wesley could sense all the single guys fancied her. He probably would have too if his thoughts weren't so wrapped up in Myia.

He tried with all his intellectual might to focus on moving on with his life and keeping his thoughts and his mindset positive, but he couldn't shake off the failure of rejection. He would replay the scenario over and over in his head, and the same hurt and emotion would flood his nervous system, so much so that it manifested into physical ailments. His health began to suffer. He began to have crippling migraines and was forever nauseous to the point he seldom ate, only doing so when he couldn't hear his thoughts due to his stomach rumbling.

There was one night, during his first year of college, he was so ill he had to go to the doctor. The doctor blamed it on nervous exhaustion and told him to rest, writing him a sicknote to hand over to administration. It was the nicest, most relaxing week Wesley had ever spent in his entire life. He kept himself busy playing 'Fortnite' online, browsing the Incel message forums, watching classic movies and masturbating to porn.

When the week ended and he went back to his studies, Wesley noticed that his physical ailments would only flare up if he had to go and socialize. So, he stopped socializing. Rather than going to societies and parties, he spent the rest of his time in his small, cramped, dungeon-esque apartment. This was all fine and good, except for the fact that he could not shake Myia from his thoughts.

#

A typical day in the life of Wesley Harding would consist of going into the Tesco Express to buy a coffee, and a breakfast bar, his 'Bad Motherfucker' wallet clasped in his hand. He would have to endure queuing for the express machine behind all the other students who were buying coffee and breakfast bars, feeling awkward and uneasy in the presence of fellow humans.

He would then wait at the traffic lights to cross the road, before taking the long walk through NUIG campus, walking along the pathways of the neat, curated trees and gardens, admiring the 19th century architecture of the gothic buildings, watching his shadow loom out ahead of him.

He would enter the main building and head over to where all the other misfits sat in the cafeteria, a group who would rather study and listen to music than converse with one another, and that was just fine with Wesley, he wasn't a big fan of extraverts, who normally sat around at another part of the canteen, laughing, and joking together.

Wesley thought the extraverts were hypocrites, these jocks and their bitch friends, walking around campus in their designer tracksuits and GAA sportswear, all holding on to bottles of water or glucose drinks like they were a fashion item, flaunting their bodies after being to the gym that morning, eating their salads, and listening to their shite techno music.

These extroverts, they acted like they were happy and content, but they were nothing of the sort. On the rare occasions when Wesley ventured into a student nightclub, he would see them stumbling and falling over each other, half poisoned with alcohol, stinking of vodka and red bull.

Sure, they all played sports, and playing GAA would probably land them a good job, later on in life, when they were finished studying for their 'arts' degree, because that's how it worked, that's how the Irish economy worked, all the jocks looked after each other, but they had nothing to offer in life.

They had nothing to give back to society, besides dumb jock babies that would grow up into tall, lanky trans neutral jocks, and hence the vicious cycle of poser nihilistic ignorance would continue long and arduously into a hopeless, uncertain, more than likely, post-apocalyptic future.

Wesley would normally take this quiet time in the canteen to write down any intellectual musings that weighed on his mind the night previously. He would take out his mini notebook and write a draft on whatever thesis he wanted to post to his class message boards.

Even online he was an arrogant intellectual, and his long ramblings would only result in ridicule from his classmates. Wesley was immune to this criticism, he would read the replies, but generally found them to be inferior to his own vast knowledge.

Wesley's college schedule was normally filled with lectures, there wasn't much in the way of group assignments to divulge in, which was just fine with him, and there were the digital presentations in front of the entire class, which he relished in.

Wesley's presentations normally honoured him distinctions, as did his exams, it was the essays that brought his grade down. They were long, arduous, worthless tasks, and the threat of plagiarism forever loomed over the grammatical layout and general content. The university were getting stricter in their laws each passing year.

Wesley's classes consisted of lectures from law professionals such as judges and high-powered solicitors, and generally ranged from about 9:30 in the morning to 5:30 in the evening, covering all different aspects of criminal law. Lecturers found Wesley to be extremely bright, although the general opinion was that he wasn't studying to his full potential and they got the impression he was trying to breeze by, to get the marks he needed to attain to qualify as a barrister. Wesley didn't care that he was breezing his way through college, truth be told he didn't want his university life to end.

Sometimes, although not very often, Wesley could break his mind from the chains of reality and completely space out. Wesley could think of nothing while his body toiled through the daily routine. He could be anywhere and nowhere at the same time. The feeling he experienced was like being sedated with a cosmic tranquilizer.

When in his mantra like state, Wesley was completely free from any stress or reality. He could even travel from destination to destination without having any recollection of how he got there. When he was able to snap himself out of his hypnotic state, he always felt refreshed and relaxed. He could breathe much easier. His consciousness needed time to recharge to haunt Wesley for days on end with more of its perplexing, negative stream of consciousness.

When Wesley would arrive back to his dungeon, basement apartment, he normally needed to eat, his stomach would rumble from lack of food, he would light the gas stove in his kitchen and pour spaghetti hoops in a saucepan and watch them bubble.

He would look for a plate less dirty than others that were piled up in his sink and when he felt his spaghetti was hot enough, he would pour it onto that plate, grab some bread, make a cup of tea and bring his lunch to eat at his computer.

Wesley would spend a few minutes reading over his study notes, making sure he knew the material before throwing them on the bed. He would then mull over the prospect of beginning an essay he was given the previous week and was due in the next fortnight. Normally, his lesser self-got the better of him, and he would generally decide to wait until the night before when he would then stay up all night peddling together a meek essay with weak arguments, hoping that he would get a passing grade.

He would mull over the thought of working on his manuscript for a while, a fantasy novel about a detective mage, a cross between Gandalf and Sherlock Holmes, set in the fantasy land of Naviera, where dragons and kings ruled supreme. He had about 50,000 words written, and was very pleased with what he had written, but he felt he needed to take his time with it, that when people would read it, he would win countless awards, he felt the public weren't intellectually ready for Wesley to finish his novel and show it to the world. He bragged to anybody that would listen that it would be his magnum opus, a 250,000 word masterpiece that would win him nothing but accolades and be showered in praise. Every time he mulled over it his anxiety would always prevent him from working on it.

Wesley would then brace himself for his daily anxiety attack and try to think about anything other than university, or his manuscript, or how he was a loner, or how he was a virgin, or how uncertain he was of what his future would be, as he patiently waited for his anxiety attack to sweep over and vanish, his face pale, his mind full of sheer terror, not being able to breathe.

He would sit at his computer, looking out one of the few windows that were in his basement flat, looking at the view that consisted of the house apartments opposite him, including the entrance and main window of Myia's ground floor apartment.

Once Wesley was comfortable and calm, he would then turn on his computer and connect to his broadband. He would post onto message boards on reddit about certain topics, before logging onto message boards which hosted in-celibates, self-proclaimed nice guys, to wax lyrical about his hatred for women.

Wesley would then go onto his university account and post a 'theory' to his classmates on the blackboard, in the hopes of beginning an intellectual debate...but, like previously stated, it never did. Wesley thought maybe it was because his theories didn't spark enough debate and began to get creative in his arguments.

From: WESLEY J. HARDING

Sent: Tuesday, May 19th

To: NUIG LAW STUDENT BODY

Subject: Hypothetical Theory – DONALD TRUMP IN EASTERN EUROPE

The following is a hypothetical question aimed at determining one method of political mentality of the student body of NUIG's School of Law. Please take the time to read the hypothetical and respond to it by replying to this blackboard account or at Wesley.harding@gmail.com

BEGINNING:

Suppose it came to public knowledge that DONALD TRUMP, within the past ten years, had been in extensive contact with a covert Eastern European political influencer in the fictional country of Naviera, (A country approximately the size of Russia).

The political influencer, ROSKOLNIK, had become a high-ranking member of a small right wing communist movement, a movement that was gathering momentum and popularity amongst their nationals, with their long-term aim being to replace Naviera's diplomatic laws with doctrines that fa-

voured the writings of Carl Marx, most notably, The Communist Manifesto.

ROSKOLNIK narrowly lost the last Naivierian election to become president, and descending from the Gallen mountains from Northern Naviera, called on his fellow Gallen citizens to rise up with him and dethrone the democratic president in power, claiming voter fraud. Without any proof that there was any such fraud detected, Gallen citizens performed a failed coup de grace in the capital Naivieran city of Okosha, the violence causing thousands of deaths and displacing an entire race for generations to come. The violence becomes so obscene that NATO must step in and offer ROSKOLNIK the position of Leader of Northern Gallen, putting him in a position of power which is on step with that of the democratic president. It is later found out that TRUMP, travelled to Naviera at the tax payers expense, and stood next to ROSKOLNIK for several public opportunities, implying that he supported him, if not funded him, in his destiny to become president of Naviera.

There is also evidence unearthed that American officials had drawn up plans to help in ROSKOLNIK's reign of power, in the form of ethnic cleansing. An investigative journalist for the Irish Times flies to the country and unearths evidence to suggest that corruption did take place, as he is investigating the story, he is captured by Gallen forces and held in captivity at gun point for six months before the Irish Government broker a financial deal to release him and bring him home. When he arrives home he writes a detailed article that causes NATO to investigate and Trump finds himself in court facing criminal charges.

If this hypothetical scenario did in fact, take place, would Trump, irregardless of his empire, have to step down and declare to the public that he was not running for president?

Please explain your answer. I also implore to everybody who replies to be civil. Please do not try to include any personal criticisms aimed at Trump.

COMMENTS (7)

GrammerNazi69: *Irregardless is not a word, why don't you check your spelling before wasting everybody's time with this fantastical bullshit?*

WesleyHrd: *Yes, it is a word. Even though it is not described as a kosher phrase, it is completely fine.*

GrammerNazi69: *I think you mean, 'regardless.'*

WesleyHrd: *I wrote this hypothetical scenario in the hope it would start an intriguing, political debate to help better ourselves as not only law students but as decent human beings.*

Holeefook: *As a citizen of Naivera, I am*

appalled by my country's violence, and I am summoning an army of LGBTAZ dragons to help fight against the ethnic cleansing of these poor unfortunate magic midgets. Their very annoying, not as annoying as people posting crap on a law blackboard which is to help people in their studies, but annoying all the same. I suggest you check your IQ, good sir, as it seems to be only slightly higher than your average room temperature.

P.S. My Nigerian cousin is a prince with bucketloads of money, if you send me 100,000 Euros, today, he will double your money in a week, and promises to send voodoo priests to my beloved country to help in the war in freeing magic midgets.

PoppyZcat22: *@holeefook - Stop racially discriminating magic midgets, what have they ever done against you?*

GrammerNazi69: *They're not their…*

#

Wesley knew that his feelings for Myia were becoming ridiculous, and he blamed it on the fact that she lived right across the road from him. He shut the blinders on his windows for weeks on end, out of sight, out of mind, it didn't work, knowing that she was there didn't make it any easier.

He would lie in bed every night, staring at the ceiling, listening to music, music that he thought Myia would like, music that was more mellow and soft to his ears, just like her sweet-sounding accent.

Wesley preferred death metal which portrayed his awkwardness, angst and sexual frustration better than any other music ever could. When he thought of Myia, he would listen to classic punk/indie romantic bands like Interpol and The National, bands which explored the depths of the human soul, hinting at darker subject matter, with lyrics that had multiple meanings. It was the only music he could listen to when he thought of Myia, and he thought of Myia every night, meaning that he listened to these bands more than any other person on the planet had for the past four years.

What was it that was eating him up? What was it that made Myia's rejection so painful and embarrassing? What was it about her that kept him awake at night? Why couldn't he just move on with his life and get over her? Maybe she wasn't all she seemed to be? Maybe, if he got to know everything about her, maybe then, his feelings would go away.

Or even better, what if he got to know everything about her and changed his personality? Alter his appearance to her standards, make himself the man she wanted, rather than the pathetic loser that he was, pining after her like a lost puppy. He'd have to move slow, be friendly to her but not overly friendly, give her the impression that he had gotten over her rejection and was absolutely fine with it, even though that implication couldn't be further from the truth. He had to seem that her rejection was like water off a duck's back to him.

Wesley resented Myia for this. He resented her for having to put so much time and energy into this obsession. Why was she so blind to the fact that they were meant to be together? Anybody with half a brain could see that Wesley and Myia were meant for each other. Myia became his very own complex puzzle, and he would work on this puzzle until the end of time to solve it, looking for answers that weren't even there in the first place.

It never occurred to Wesley the real reason why Myia rejected him. It never occurred to him that he acted in all the ways a person should never do on a first date. It never crossed his mind that if he in any way, acted like any sort of gentleman, if he had put time and effort into his appearance, if he wasn't in so much emotional ordeal over how he looked, if he wasn't so jealous of the world, if he had any sort of resemblance of normality involving his thinking process and listened to her speak, rather than moan about women in general, then maybe, just maybe, Myia would have agreed to another date with him, if not more.

Instead, he had allowed the venomous hatred rants of members of the Incel movement poison his mind, rather than let a young lady by the name of Myia Dawkins into his life. Myia did like him at first, that was the reason why she agreed to go on a date with him, she was right to reject him after his hateful, spiteful rant about women.

While Wesley spent his five years in University dwelling in his dungeon basement, Myia became an avid member of the drama society, until the essays and exams began to take their toll, and she ended up working more as a production assistant for the society rather than a budding actress, eager to help out in any way possible.

She enjoyed the lectures, and made friends easily, she would see Wesley around the campus and would always make the effort to say hello to him, she felt bad about rejecting him but figured it was the right thing to do, there was something about him that day that made her feel uneasy.

He was always warm and friendly when she greeted him and figured he had put the rejection behind him. As the months rolled into years and the studies increased, she saw less and less of Wesley. She put her life into studying and relished every moment of it. When lectures finished and students made their way back to their rented digs, she would make her way over to the library and study there until closing time.

Myia barely had time to socialize, she had no interest in Galway's nightlife, but she did make time to see her friends. She would meet them for coffee, go shopping, go to the cinema, go to the theatre, and would attend any house parties that were held for big occasions. If one of her favourite musical acts were playing in the city, she would go and watch them perform, but she always made sure she got home in time to do a couple of hours more study before going to bed.

She had fallen into a routine that she enjoyed, but the one thing she enjoyed doing, more than anything else in the world, was getting the train home to Athlone on a Friday evening to see her parents, and her dogs. Myia was a home bird, during her five years of studying at NUIG, She never spent a weekend in Galway City.

This would later become the downfall of Myia, through no fault of her of own, it allowed Wesley to evolve his obsession to the next level.

Myia travelling home every weekend wouldn't have meant anything if Wesley hadn't managed to get a copy of her apartment key.

#

It started on weekends, when she went to Athlone, that's when he would let himself into her apartment and snoop around the place. The idea of stealing her key and copying it only came to fruition when the landlord asked if Wesley could look after the office for the day while he was away purchasing property in Dublin. Wesley agreed to it, mainly because he was paid to sit behind a desk and watch Netflix on his phone all day.

"So what do I have to do?"

"Just take the rent off anybody who calls in, you'd be surprised the number of tenants I have who can't obtain a bank account."

"What about the people who are due to pay and don't show up?"

"There's a spreadsheet on the Mac, but don't worry about it. If anybody calls saying they'll be late with the rent, just leave a message. At the end of the day, put the money into a safe in the back office, all you have to do is roll over the carpet and slide the money down through a hole in the floor, and take a note of how much you received, and copies of any receipts you need to give out, that's it, you think you'd be up for that?"

"Oh yeah, sure thing, no worries."

"Any complaints about maintenance or repairs, or about noise or whatever, just get them to leave a message and tell them I'll get in touch with them when I'm back in town on Monday."

Wesley had no doubt that he would, he was an exceptionally good landlord.

“Anything else, just call me, but it should be a slow day, if you do a good job, keep things tidy, I’ll think about maybe getting you in on the weekends if you want?

“That would be fantastic, thank you for the opportunity.”

It was there, sitting in the foyer of his landlords business, when Wesley’s plan came to fruition. The landlord was right, it was a quiet day, and when it was time to lock up for lunch, Wesley went into the back office to make sure everything was locked, that’s when he saw the keys hanging from the notice board behind the landlords desk.

Wesley liked to smell the perfume and soap that lingered in the air when he let himself into Myia’s flat. He liked to stand extremely still and get lost in his surroundings. Wesley would become a statue, his face pale, his hair dangling down over his unblinking blue eyes. His pubescent-esque stubble making him look horribly demonic, portraying the freak masochistic spirit that lurked inside of him, as he stared at her bed, her photographs. He never touched anything that he did not want and was always extremely careful. Wesley knew Myia’s schedule better than she did herself. He knew when she was at university, he'd read her emails and browse through her Facebook on her laptop, two screens which she always left open to view.

He would watch her through closed curtains, and he would film her leaving her apartment every morning and coming back home in the evening. This began in their second year of studies after their schedules had been altered. Because Wesley didn't get a chance to see her every day, not seeing her just made him extremely anxious...and jealous. He'd begin to think of all possible scenarios involving Myia, scenarios that included places she may have visited and people she may have slept with.

He would make himself sick with jealousy and envy as he imagined her kissing a man, sleeping with a man, fucking a man. He came to a crazy rationalization that if he saw her every day leaving and entering her apartment, that he would have nothing to worry about. He then decided to place a small camera on his windowsill and have it record her apartment across the road, so he knew for sure at what time she left and at what time she arrived back.

Wesley would only enter her place when she was not there, at first, that was a few years ago, after a while the thrill wasn't the same as it used to be. It used to turn him on, his chest would palpitate, he would feel his heart banging in his ears, as his shaking hands would unlock her front door. Food tasted better, porn was better, yet once the rush began to recede, he found his thrills becoming more dangerous and hardcore.

After a few months he would become frustrated at the lack of dopamine his brain was devouring, he began to steal skimpy pairs of panties out of her laundry basket. This was exhilarating, and making them into a mask which he was able to wear as he surfed the web for porn was a day he fondly remembered.

It was when Wesley let himself into Myia's apartment, in the middle of the night, that's when he felt a rush, standing over her bed, watching her sleep. That's when Wesley felt God-like, he felt like he was protecting her. For the next three years, Wesley would let himself into Myia's house in the middle of the night, just to watch her sleep. She never knew he was there. She never woke up when he stood at the end of her bed. Not once.

***

CHAPTER 10 --- THE DISCIPLE HEARING.

Jimmy walked very slowly down one of the winding hallways of the main head-quarters in the city. His preliminary hearing was due to begin soon, in front of a committee panel who had absolutely no experience in psychological criminal profiling.

Jimmy knew this meeting wasn't going to go smoothly, he'd have to argue his point and hope that they gave him a short-term suspension, more to please the courts, there was no such thing as defending your fellow man, especially not with these corrupt fuckers.

At least one of the committee had already suffered a demotion when it came to light that she was part of the cover up in the controversy involving a garda whistle-blower who was falsely accused of child sex crimes.

The whistle-blower had claimed that gardaí

in his constituency had physically beaten accused members of the public and had covered up the murder of a man who was influential in the area, refusing to investigate the murder properly and imprisoning an innocent man who had supposed links with the IRA.

When the whistle-blower came forward, to silence his cries of corruption and violence in the force, the Gardaí big wigs had managed to break into his house and place child pornography onto his computer hard drive, before arresting him on trumped up charges and publicly shaming him using their contacts in the media. If it wasn't for one investigative journalist in the Sunday Independent who managed to uncover the conspiracy, the whistle blower would still be in prison.

None of the commissioners involved in the cover up were sacked, merely suspended without pay for a certain amount of time and demoted, and one of the demotes had managed to wangle her way onto this committee board, that dealt with internal investigations and conduct.

Jimmy was pissed off more than anything else. They would put on a display to humiliate him; his best plan of action was to say little, take the punishment, defend your honour and leave.

He knocked on the door of the large boarding room and was summoned in sharply by a low male voice. He entered and sat down on the leather chair that faced a long table, on the other side of the table were five superiors of an Gardaí Síochána, who sat glumly, with stern faces, glaring at Jimmy, there didn't seem to be an ounce of warmth or friendliness to be found anywhere in the room.

Jimmy noticed another woman, a brunette, wearing a smart business suit, who sat in the corner of the room, taking notes, she looked slightly terrified, but tried to hide her terror behind her act of professionalism.

He nodded to his own superior, who sat on the far left of the table. Deputy Commissioner Helen Deeley nodded back politely before getting her paperwork into order. She was a small slender woman with short blonde greying hair, who wore spectacles on the end of her slender nose. Her official title was Deputy Commissioner of Policing and Security. While she overlooked many of the divisions in the NBCI, The National Bureau of Criminal Investigation, she took a considerable interest in Jimmy's unit, mainly because of their talent in solving crimes using psychoanalysis, profiling, and interrogation.

She never married, had no children, some people believed that she lived with a partner, but it was never certain whether this partner was male or female, she kept her private life secret, much like Jimmy, and although she was a tough nut to crack, and not too easy to please, she was the least corrupt police officer out of the higher ranks that Jimmy could think of.

Jimmy highly respected her for those reasons. Her record was clean, no speeding tickets, no accusations of bribes or criminal cover ups, no drunk or disorderly behaviour, nothing to suggest that she dabbled in the fruits of rule bending, that was so common nowadays with any high ranking, Irish, authoritative figure. It was the reason why Jimmy refused promotion on three different occasions, after becoming head of his Major Crimes Unit. He didn't want to be tempted, and the peer pressure was immense, regardless of whatever authoritative organisation that sat in power, the higher you climbed, the more corrupt you became.

Alongside Deputy Commissioner Deeley, was the Deputy Commissioner of Governance and Strategy, Karen Brady, a heavyset woman, with long black hair and a face of doom and gloom, the demote involved in the whistle-blower cover up.

Assistant Commissioner of Governance and Accountability, Pat Ward, was the most effeminate policeman that was to be had at the force, he had long slender hands that was out of shape compared to the rest of his composure and demeanour. He was proud of his appearance and styled his blonde hair in such a manner it reminded Jimmy of the band, The Smiths, in fact, he could easily pass for Morrisey if he made the effort.

Next to him was Assistant Commissioner of Strategy and Transformation, Michael O Houlihan. More fondly known as Houlihan the Hooligan, a large tank of a man with receding red hair and a beard that would make The Dubliners envious.

In the middle of the table, cutting a Christ like figure, was the top dog himself, the man put in charge by the Irish Government, Garda Commissioner Harrison James, a thin bald man. A Dublin Protestant who rose through the ranks so quickly that many people guessed it was because of his family political connections.

Jimmy fixed the sleeves on his shirt and jacket as he sat, while the Garda Commissioner cleared his throat before he began proceedings.

"Detective Sergeant James Daniels, I know you want to be here less than we do, so let's make this brief, shall we?"

"That's fine by me, Sir." Jimmy replied in a polite tone.

"Because of Judge Lyndon's ruling we've gathered here to decide what the best course of action is to take. But before we get into it, there's a question I want to ask you and I know you to be an honest man, so I have no doubt in my mind that you will be truthful in your answer."

"All right."

"Was it your primary intention to coerce a confession from the suspect, Sebastian Rivers, in order for you to solve the case?"

"No, Sir, my primary intention was to find and capture the person who shook that toddler to death. I used all of the techniques in the interrogation process that were available to me, and I honestly believe I did nothing illegal or forceful in obtaining a confession from Mr. Rivers. I believe Mr Rivers is guilty of the crime, and I thoroughly believe that there was a major injustice in dismissing his case."

"That may well be true, however we are here due to the interrogation technique you used to gain that confession, rather than the media circus that surrounds it and the ruling of the judge. I am satisfied that there was no intention of coercion on your part. However, this REID technique that you use, is far too controversial, and we believe had you used a more appropriate technique, that Mr. Rivers would be behind bars as we speak. The media are having a field day, the government wants you sacked, because they feel that this case puts the entire police force in a poor light. The public see us as bullies rather than protectors of the peace. Do you understand?"

Jimmy merely nodded.

"Good...uh Karen, you have something to say, I believe."

The commissioner of doom and gloom looked sternly at Jimmy before saying...

"We have a way of doing things now, that you have ignored purposely, since promotion to the head of your Major Crimes unit. You have been flippant in how you conduct your investigations, arrogant in the way you go about them, and unprofessional in the reports and memos I am forced to read, due to you withholding information and cutting corners, being 'creative' in your approach, which darkens the lines of legality at best. I am forced to read complaints from your peers, who see you as dangerous, unhinged and careless in your actions and decisions."

Jimmy knew it was Hobbs who was making the complaints. He wanted to point out to the commissioner that her opinion was like the pot calling the kettle black but thought against it. "I beg to differ." Came the polite reply.

"As is your right, Detective, however this is the straw that broke the camel's back. In all of the shenanigans you have pulled throughout your career, this one takes the biscuit entirely. I am upset that you had to lie in order to get your confession, you fabricated evidence, now the commissioner might see this as perhaps a glitch in the method that you use, I see it as a false, slanderous, illegal…"

"It's not illegal."

"Let me finish, please. I must look at this technique that you use, and I really need to consider the legality of this technique. Nevertheless, I have advised the commissioner and your superiors that you partake in a three-week course to give you the sufficient training you need to maintain running your unit."

"What kind of course?"

"A programme!" Houlihan shouted. Jimmy noticed that his beard shimmered as he spoke. "You are to partake in a special programme that we are to utilize to all new Detective Sergeants in dealing with interrogations, so a stunt like this will never have to cross our paths again!"

"It's a specialist programme," Ward continued on, even the way he spoke was effeminate, "It's designed to introduce radical new interrogation techniques that fits the criteria that an Gardaí Síochána are trying to achieve. It's for old and new detectives alike. It's a pastiche of the PEACE Technique, adding in elements of other techniques that we feel are quite useful. We are evolving, Detective Daniels, long gone are the days when you could rough up a suspect..."

Jimmy almost chortled, but kept his composure, this seemed like the kind of police officer who would have trouble roughing up a piece of wet tissue, never mind a suspect...

"And while the technique you used may have been relevant or cutting edge, say, thirty years ago, now, it's dated, we need to keep up with the evolvement of judiciary law, and we've come up with a revolutionary new training programme that will achieve great success if utilized properly, and will banish any dismissal rulings in our judicial system."

"Hold on...sorry, just give me a second here, does anybody think that maybe the judge is to blame here and not the technique that I use?"

Nobody replied, Jimmy looked at Deeley, who seemed like she wanted to give some sign of agreement, but if there was one, it was too subtle for Jimmy to notice. "Because you sure as shit have never complained about it before. A technique I've been using since I first became a detective, a technique that has never failed me, not once..."

"Detective Sergeant, you would be strongly advised to take this matter into serious consideration." Harrison James said, bluntly.

Jimmy got that sense, the same one he got

in the courthouse. The blades of light that were cutting through the window, reflecting off the tables and the people sitting before him, made it seem like Jimmy was in the middle of an old film noire of the nineteen forties. He had gotten a similar eerie feeling when sitting in the courthouse, this feeling of grandiose authority, the blades of light had the same necessary effect when he was cross examined by Joe Perry.

The way the shadows fell on the walls and on the furniture, making everything seem like German expressionism, he felt it once again, this noir feeling of expressionism in the rules and procedure. No matter where Jimmy looked in the room, he felt deprived of any sign of freedom. It was like a physical manifestation of the existential crisis, what the great writer, HG Wells put so fondly once as, 'the cinema sheet that stares us in the face, the sheet which is the fibre of our being.'

Jimmy received more signs of humanity from hardened criminals he met than from the people sitting before him today. These people would suck your soul dry if they were capable of doing so.

"What happens if I don't comply with this… request?"

"It's not a request." Karen Brady seethed back. "And failure to comply will leave us with no other option than to dismiss you from service."

"So if I don't go back to school I'm sacked, that's the bare bones of it, really?"

"I'd advise you see this more as an opportunity than compliance." Houlihan said. "See it as a way of enhancing the many talents that you have at your disposal."

"Okay, when do I start this...programme?"

"The programme will begin in the late May. Until then, you will be suspended indefinitely with pay, and we will consider when your suspension ends once you begin the course. Any other questions?"

"Who's that lady?" Jimmy asked, pointing to the young lady in the corner of the room.

"That is Detective Linda Ní Gorman. She has just completed her doctorate in psychoanalysis, so you may call her Doctor, you may call her Detective Ní Gorman..."

"Just don't call me on Sundays." Linda said, chortling. Nobody laughed, not even when she went "bud dum dum tish!" In a panic she stood and walked briskly over to Jimmy, with her arm extended.

"Hello, Linda, nice to meet you." She said, shaking his hand warmly.

"The pleasure is all mine." Jimmy replied, before turning his attention back to the committee.

Linda stood next to Jimmy, it took her a few seconds to decide to either walk all the way across the room, back to her chair, or to stand next to Jimmy with her hands clasped in front of her. She looked like she was in two minds before she corrected herself and stood next to Jimmy, she hoped it wouldn't be for too long, she didn't like wearing high heels and could feel her baby toes were getting crushed up against the casing of her shoes.

"So let me guess," Jimmy said, waving his hand to Linda, "you're assigning me a babysitter."

"It's up to Dr Linda Ní Gorman to make sure that you follow the new protocol, and to report back to us with her findings, she is an expert into the delving's of the criminal mind, it is of my opinion that the good doctor here will become an essential member of your team, and the time you're on suspension will be sufficient for her in getting to know everything about your unit."

"Is that it?"

The commissioner merely nodded.

"Linda, nice to meet you." Jimmy said, shaking Linda's hand again. "And I'll see you…whenever."

"Oh, I'll be seeing you at the training program, I need to take it as well."

"Wonderful!" Jimmy cried, before exiting the room, Linda wasn't sure was he been sarcastic or optimistic in his response.

Before anybody could say anything further, Jimmy was already down near the end of the corridor about to take the main elevator. As he stepped inside and let the doors close, he put his head in his hands and let out a big cry of frustration. Things were going to be different now, and Jimmy did not like change.

***

CHAPTER 11 --- THE LONDON OPENING

Jimmy arrived home in an awfully bad mood. He could not remember any time in his professional career when he felt his mood as devastating as it was now. He wanted to hit something, break something, anything to dial down the thunderclouds that were forming in his brain. He entered his warm, plush apartment that had a wonderful, picturesque view of the Galway City docks. The apartment had some very white furniture, with a white and black checkered decor that screamed modern bourgeois, full of the latest gadgets and home theatre technology. It was Jimmy's haven.

He fixed himself a Baileys with a shot of brandy and lit one of his trademark cigarillos. He didn't feel like getting stoned yet, perhaps later on in the evening when he had less on his mind. He switched on his collection of LED monitors that were fixed to the walls in his living room.

Jimmy liked to be surrounded in vision and sound. He tuned one monitor into the Newstalk podcast, another to the 24-hour news channel with muted audio, the 10th game of The World Chess Championship played on a third monitor. It was no surprise to Jimmy, that he was the main headline on the news. He sat down in his recliner in front of his custom-built chessboard, a gift to him from his uncle on his 21st birthday and began to study the position.

The game had just started, and they were still only on their sixth move after fifteen minutes of play. Magnus Carlsen was white, and the new chess prodigy Nihal Sarin was black. Jimmy set up the position and settled into figuring out what Magnus's attack would be. He liked to think five moves ahead, to give him a chance of guessing if he was right with his tactical analysis. There were as many chess moves as there was stars in the universe, an infinite amount of attack plans to choose from, and if Jimmy was close to guessing the moves that the great Magnus Carlson was going to play, he knew he'd be in a better mood come evening time.

It looked like Magnus was going for a variation of the London Opening. A bold move considering they had drawn the previous nine matches. Jimmy was now guessing if Magnus was going to build his pawn structure and set up his defenses, or set up his major pieces in a group formation behind the queen.

Jimmy relaxed into the game, switching his brain off as he zoned out on the board, visualizing all the different moves and attacks he would play if he were in the same position. When Magnus would make his move, Jimmy would then swivel his board around and look at black's position. Every so often, he would glance up to the news monitor, to see if they had moved onto a different subject, but it was always repeated footage of Jimmy fighting his way through an army of journalists on the steps of the Central Criminal Court.

The Newstalk podcast were debating whether Jimmy should resign from the police force over his debacle. The news really had a way of painting you as the villain if it suited their needs. One person from Galway called in with the theory that Jimmy did his job correctly and that the judge was wrong to dismiss the case, only to be ridiculed by the D.J. and his 'so called' expert, a journalist from The Irish Times. Jimmy couldn't remember the journalists name, and he couldn't care less.

After gaining an immaculate school record, and a clean career with offers of promotion, with not one black mark to his name, society was now deeming Jimmy to be an enemy of the people.

Jimmy tried to keep his mind on the game.

He moved his king side bishop down to the H1 square, guessing that was part of Magnus's attack plan. This match wasn't going to be a draw, after 20 moves one chess player would be pulverizing the other. Sarin was playing the Nimzo-Indian Defence. Jimmy had more trouble figuring out black's position. This whiz kid was setting up some kind of bizarre counterattack, he was going to alternate his defence at some point but Jimmy couldn't figure it out, but this was why Sarin was a prodigy, it was going to be an intriguing game.

Jimmy wondered what he'd do to while away his time while he was on suspension. He could start writing his book, a memoir of his professional career, he'd been planning on doing that for years, his work was intriguing enough to be a popular read. He could go on holiday, but he didn't like going places on his own. He'd probably just end up reading and listening to music, maybe head down to the chess club and have a few games, anything that didn't involve murder and violence. He could always head down to his local pub, but he didn't enjoy going there unless there was a pool or darts tournament.

He was only on suspension for five minutes and already he was at a loss as to what to do.

After about two hours following the chess game, and having roughly a 60% success rate in guessing the next move, he turned off all the monitors in the house, opting to play some music instead, making sure to record the chess match when it resumed the following day. He needed time to think, he couldn't opt between Dylan, Rodriguez or Prine. After some deliberation, he opted for Rodriguez. 'Crucify Your Mind' blasted from the stereo speakers, it's haunting lyrics fitting Jimmy's mood to a tee.

Thinking was Jimmy's main hobby. There was nothing he enjoyed more than sitting in his recliner chair with the lights down low, thinking.

Jimmy always needed to think for a few hours every evening. He would think about his work, his life, his career. Jimmy knew from a young age that thinking things through about every aspect of life was a major part of who he was.

The major problem he had was how in the world did he let Sebastian Rivers get away from him? The other main aspect in his life that was troubling him was if this Linda Ní Gorman was going to attempt to sabotage him and steal his job.

The last thing he needed in his profession was having to jump through political hoops when he was chasing down killers and rapists every day.

Jimmy was about to go down some deep dark places in his psyche, places where even angels would fear to tread. Jimmy thought about calling headquarters to check in, but decided against it, there were no major cases in the pipeline, Hobbs and Rodge were working on a case that involved a stalker preying on females, and Jimmy's team were inducting Linda into the group, there was a mountain of paperwork to get through, plenty to keep them busy. He'd wait until they called him. It wouldn't be long until a murder case dropped on their laps.

He thought about his current predicament, and wondered what advice his Uncle Jed would give him if he were alive today. Jed had died eight years previously, after suffering a massive stroke. There wasn't a day when Jimmy never thought of him. His advice would be typical advice an elder would give to a loved one, such as, "keep your eyes on the prize", or "don't let your ship sail off course." Jimmy closed his eyes and began to think.

#

Jimmy Daniels was an only child, who was adored by his parents until they perished in a car crash when he was eight years old. A drunk driver had collided into them at high speed, killing them instantly. Jimmy remembered the reposal vividly. He had to stand next to the coffins, and shake hands with people who lined up telling him how sorry they were.

Jimmy couldn't understand why they were sorry. They didn't kill his parents. He remembered his uncle Jed, his father's brother, being a rock of support throughout the entire ordeal. Jed was the only family that Jimmy had left. He remembered that he tried to cry at the funeral, but he was unable to do so, it was only in bed at night, when he was alone, that's when the tears came. Seeing his parents lying in their coffins was the first time Jimmy had experienced death. From then on, he had developed a fascination for it.

Jimmy had few memories of his parents. His father, John, was a professor of philosophy at Trinity, tall and skinny, a pure intellect. He remembered his mother, Maggie, to be beautiful, black hair and green eyes with a smile that could stop traffic. He remembered how warm she was, when she cuddled him, and how she always smelt nice.

He could remember everything about the reposal, sitting next to the coffins, looking in on his parents. How peaceful they looked. Their faces were heavily caked in make up to cover the cuts and grazes from the accident. He remembered wondering where his parents were, he knew they weren't in their bodies anymore, and was convinced their holy spirits had gone to a better place.

He could remember how warm the living room was from the amount of grief and sorrow, and wondered if there was a heaven, like the one he was taught at school, or was it different? Was there one God or many Gods. Why would God take his parents away? He got the sense his parents were still with him somehow, and that comforted him. He could still feel their loving, ever glowing presence long after they were buried. Jimmy often wondered if his parents hadn't died so young, so tragically, would he be in a different line of work altogether?

Jimmy was raised by his Uncle Jed and his wife Betty, and tried to make their lives as easy as possible. His Uncle was a solicitor, and Jimmy wanted to follow in his footsteps, so he studied hard, he was never told to do his homework. He never missed a day of school. He enjoyed the company of his classmates, and loved playing all manner of sports.

His childhood was safe, uneventful, and happy, and he was well looked after. The greatest gift his uncle gave him was teaching him how to play chess. Jimmy fell in love with the game straight away, he played many a game with his uncle after school, never winning, but always learning. He became fascinated with the game.

Another fascination that Jimmy was never able to shake off was his fascination with death, what motivated certain people to take another human life? This led to a young Jimmy studying the human condition, while other teenagers browsed dial up porn and watched video nasties, Jimmy would spend his free time researching unsolved murders, treating them as puzzles.

He envied people who had the capacity to kill. Most notably famous serial killers. He admired their intellect, their creativity, their tenacity. He envied the freedom and power serial killers felt when taking a life. Jimmy was willing to delve deeper into their mindsets than many people would feel comfortable with. It was no secret that killing and death was a morbid fascination with many people. The ratings of true crime shows and films on streaming platforms only proved there was a market for stories about rapists and murderers, as long as the stories weren't too specific on gory details, what people in the media would call 'Hollywood Gloss.'

Jimmy preferred knowing all details, especially the gory ones. His fascination became so great he felt he could help do good in society, which led him to completing his Garda training at Templemore, and becoming an officer of an Gardaí Síochána.

Jimmy remembered the very first time he

found a dead body as a uniformed Garda, the first of many he would find throughout his career, the first ever face that would haunt him in his dreams and give him many a sleepless night, now when he closed his eyes he saw a crowd of dead faces, but that first one, the most memorable, was always in the forefront.

He was on patrol, in the vast area of Co. Clare countryside, when he got the call to go and investigate a farm that was situated out in the middle of nowhere. There was no word from the occupant, a bachelor farmer who lived alone, from any of his family or friends.

Jimmy was partnered with a young garda who was herself fresh from the academy, a pretty young blonde by the name of Nancy Whelan, and remembered the look of terror that was etched on her face as they stepped out of their patrol car to investigate the farmhouse and surrounding area.

There was a real gothic horror vibe coming from the house, and the only sound that could be heard was the whispering of the trees. The front door was locked, and after ringing the doorbell and knocking loudly for minutes on end, they decided to look around the house for clues to the farmers whereabouts.

Walking around towards the back of the large two-story house they noticed that the back door was wide open. A trail of muddy footprints was seen entering and exiting the house, going down through the fields that were situated next to the large industrial sheds.

As they followed the footprints, Jimmy could sense they were about to embark on a grizzly discovery. He could hear Nancy behind him struggling to control her breathing, which was shaky and uneven. They both knew the back door being wide open was a bad sign, there was no intention of the occupant coming back.

Through the fog and the darkness, illuminated by their vest torches, they saw a large oak tree in the distance. As they neared closer, they could make out the outline of something dangling from the tree. Jimmy turned around to see that Nancy had stopped dead in her tracks.

"Call for back up and get an ambulance out here. I'll go in for a closer look."

She nodded, regaining her composure, she radioed for an ambulance.

He was barely aware of Nancy's nervous tone and the crackling of the radio as he edged ever closer to the tree. He could make out the shape of a large, heavyset man in the moonlight. His face was bloated, to Jimmy, the farmer looked like he died with a smile on his face, happy to end his life on his own terms. Jimmy saw the thickness of the rope, and the injuries inflicted from the hanging. Jimmy decided to get a sharp knife and cut the body down. There was no point leaving him dangling the way it was, it just seemed inhumane.

He ran back through the fields, with Nancy in hot pursuit, when they got back to the farmhouse, he ran in through the back door and began to rummage his way through the drawers and cupboards, looking for a sharp knife. He found a Stanley knife in the top drawer. He told Nancy to wait out front for the emergency services, to which she gladly obliged, and ran back out into the darkness, as he approached the body hanging from the tree, he could faintly hear the sirens in the distance.

He climbed the tree towards the thick branch and began hacking away at the rope with the Stanley knife. The more he hacked, the more the branches began to creak and moan. His hands lit up with pain as he dangled from the branch with his legs, and slowly cut his way through the heavily knotted rope.

Finally, the rope broke free, and the body crumpled to the ground below with a sickening thud. The last thing Jimmy could remember from that fateful night was vomiting as he sat on the branch, making sure not to projectile any of his stomach contents onto the body itself. Seeing the body that night, and cutting it down in that forceful manner, much to the dismay of the coroner, only amplified Jimmy's belief in him realizing his dream of being a detective. The fear and shock from losing his parents at such a young age, helped him manifest this morbid sense of belonging with the dead.

He wanted to be a comfort to those who lost a loved one. He wanted to look evil in the face and lock it up. He wanted to be a comfort to both the living and the dead.

Suicide, that was a different animal altogether. Suicide was invisible, you couldn't see it, taste it or smell it, yet it ate through a person until their only escape was death. There was too much evil in the world, and Jimmy felt a responsibility to put a dent in it, to try and help make the world a better place.

This evil that he was faced with now, that came in the form of Sebastian Rivers, was something new to Jimmy. He began to think through his career, the criminals he had put away, wondering if his technique had caused him to make mistakes in the past. The more he thought about the REID technique, how it was vital in getting a confession from Sebastian Rivers, the more he became convinced he was right in how he executed the interrogation. It was society that was changing, not him, PC culture was so rampant now that excuses were made for cold blooded killers with disabilities.

He began to reminisce through all of the killers he had sat across from in his career. He had seen them all, the people who killed out of desperation, because they felt they had no other choice. The hardened criminals who lived by a code, some of them more honest and loyal then certain members of the police force. The ones who killed in self defence.

Then there were the sociopaths, psychopaths, and narcissists, the possessed, the satanic, the ones who killed merely for the power and the pleasure. Jimmy knew whether a person was innocent or guilty as soon as he stepped into an interrogation room, just from reading their body language. If a person was innocent they sat forward and protested profusely, as if they had nothing to hide. There were also clues in the pitch and tone of a suspects voice, the length of their answers, their overall demeanor.

Did Sebastian Rivers know that he was evil? It seemed that when he was confessing, it came across like he was bragging. He was falling into the same trap as everybody else, he was letting Rivers autism block him from witnessing his pure evil. Was there anybody else who came across with that same sense of evil? Not that Jimmy could think of, nobody had River's aptitude for evil.

***

CHAPTER 12 --- INSTANT KARMA

Opiate – Part 2
(The Gaping Lotus Experience)

Wesley, after two months of painful therapy at Novalis, hadn't gotten to the point yet that he could have full on primals in front of his fellow peers, he was able to do them in private, but even the one-on-one sessions he did with Polly were now becoming repetitive and fruitless.

During group therapy, he would merely sit in the middle of the room and scream his head off. While the rest of the commune were able to tap into their deepest, darkest memories, some of them leading directly back into their time in the womb, Wesley just screamed his head off, he felt better every time he did, but Primal Scream Therapy wasn't just about screaming.

Primal Scream Therapy was all about tapping

into your fears, trepidations, anxieties, the stuff that you pushed way back into your mind and deep down into your soul, and facing it head on. That scared Wesley, that was some real breakdown shit that Martin Sheen did in 'Apocalypse Now.'

Wesley didn't feel he was at that level yet. Any of the private sessions with Polly merely involved meditation, yoga, and tapping into your birth primal, which was difficult for Wesley, considering he had already confessed to Polly about not being able to cry as a baby.

Bringing up, what Polly called, 'The Birth Ritual,' only caused Wesley to feel dizzy, light headedness, and nausea, and he always managed to cling onto this overwhelming power of sleep, he couldn't keep his eyes open, he couldn't do anything without having a nap first and letting that feeling wane off. Polly reckons that was part of the primal, that being knocked on the head like that, with that amount of pressure, was like getting hit in the face with a sledgehammer, and that was the reason why Wesley was so shy, and introverted, the reason why he chose to be in his own company.

"You don't become a loner because the whole world hates you." She remarked, "you become a loner because you choose to be one, it's as simple as that. What you need to do is to confront your parents, your mother for not loving you and your father for abandoning you when you needed him the most. That's why you wallow in this self-misery, it's because you enjoy it. It's like a protective blanket against the big, bad world outside.

You can sit there with your imaginary safety blanket around you and call out all of the what ifs, buts and maybes that you want to, because for everything bad that happens to you, for every day that you endure loneliness, all you have to do is pull off the whole, 'woe is me,' angle, which is a cop out from you being able to stand up and take responsibilities for your actions."

Wesley had stormed out of the session and went and locked himself in his room, and lay on the bed, half asleep, letting Polly's speech play over and over again in his mind. He caught a nap for a couple of hours at dawn, and was wide awake, fully washed and dressed, sitting at the end of the bed watching the torrential showers batter his window when he heard the rest of the commune stirring downstairs to receive their breakfast. Wesley wasn't hungry, the group therapy was going to start at nine, and he'd wait until then. There was no hurry.

Wesley thought back to his anxiety riddled mornings waiting until it was time to get ready for Uni and it dawned on him that he didn't feel that way in the mornings anymore. This realisation caused him to smile.

What day is it anyway? He thought to himself. *It feels like a Saturday.* It was a Saturday; Wesley was picking up on the free energy that was vibrating around the convent, that feeling of it being a weekend.

There'd probably be a party tonight, and some weed, and some good times to be had. The only thing that troubled Wesley now, was how spot on Polly was in her character assassination the previous evening. He spent his entire life trying to fix his issues without having to face them, or hope that something, some cause, some force out there, could fix it for him, that some kinetic force could map out his life journey without him having to do anything.

Wesley leant on the windowsill, and watched the summer traffic plough through the puddles as they passed left and right. He saw vans and cars carrying surfboards and all sorts of beach equipment attached to the roofs of their vehicles, and campervans who crawled along at twenty miles per hour, trying to take in all the scenery, even though it was foggy and you couldn't see two feet in front of your face.

Probably one of the worst days of the summer and the place was packed with tourists, a bit of rain wasn't going to stop them having fun on the beach and surfing, the bad weather always brought great surf this time of year.

Wesley checked his watch, it was two minutes to nine, he couldn't hear any more echoing in the hallway, so he decided to join everybody downstairs in the common room for the daily primal group therapy.

When he entered the room, everything seemed different. Instead of people sitting and standing at random points around the room, everybody was sitting on the floor, forming a semi-circle around Gideon, who sat in an armchair smack bang in the middle of the room. The curtains were all drawn shut, the video that normally helped them get into their headspace wasn't being used at all, it was a strange sensation walking into the room at this time in the morning, with no sunlight coming in, candles lit, and with all of the televisions switched off.

Wesley snuck down to the group and squeezed in next to Bonnie and Polly.

"What's going on?" He whispered, not wanting to ruin Gideon's concentration.

"Gideon has had a breakthrough, he's going to open up to us," Bonnie whispered back, "so listen to what he has to say."

Gideon cleared his throat and opened his eyes, already there was a teardrop rolling down his right cheek.

"Hi everyone, eh…you all know me, my name is Gideon, but a lot of you, well…you don't know why I decided to come here, except for Polly of course, who's been great, but I know you see me, being all quiet and stuff, wondering why I sit by myself all day, well, I've come to terms with everything, all this shit that I had rolling around in my head, so I thought it be best to just tell you my story, why I'm here, and what I hope to change about myself while I'm here."

Gideon paused briefly as he took a deep breath and composed himself.

"I'm not really sure how to start this story, Polly said to be yourself, so here goes nothing."

He scratched at his beard, pondering what to say next, he let out a couple of groans, almost like he was about to speak but changed his mind just as his vocal chords kicked in. He was wearing a Metallica Hoodie and a pair of knock off Adidas sweatpants and trainers.

He had his hood up over his head, which shadowed the top half of his face, all anybody could see was his thin, wiry, beard, large red cheeks and his crooked thin mouth. Finally, after covering his face in his hands and letting out a loud cough, he looked at all the members of the house one by one, and said:

"The reason why I'm here, was that I was so hooked on LSD, I was convinced that aliens were after me. I swear to Christ, when my mother found me, I was sitting in her bath tub with tin-foil on my head, because I came to the scientific conclusion that, if I wore tin foil, they couldn't get into my head and brainwash me into doing their bidding, or else, fry my brain like an egg. That's why I don't drop LSD with you guys, it's not like I'm anti-drugs or anything, I just don't trust myself."

He paused for a moment, the group remained silent, captivated by his story.

"Jesus, this has to be the most difficult confession I've ever had to…well…confess to anybody in my entire life.

But that's the jist of it, I was taking so much LSD that I was convinced there was a species of aliens who could pose like humans on earth, and that they were using me to gather intel so they could take over the planet, and it has taken quite a while, and quite a few sessions with Polly to help me see that these were just hallucinations that I was having. She thinks now that if I go back enough, that I'll be able to hit a primal, so here goes nothing."

He grabbed a glass of water he had prepared on the floor next to his chair, and he took a big gulp out of it before returning it to its place.

"I first took LSD, at a house party, about six years ago, this was when the happy hard-core scene was coming back in, night long parties on ecstasy and speed and shite like that, and I was at a warehouse party one night, and my mate said, 'here, take this.'

And it was LSD, a little tab, like it was on this tiny piece of paper, blotted on, and I took it, and for the next eight hours I went on this nasty trip, like really fuckin nasty, so my girlfriend at the time, she had to physically carry me home, cuz I could hardly walk, and I had to sleep at her place, well lie down at least, no way could I sleep.

But yeah, all the faces at the party, they all sort of morphed into these demonic like faces, and it freaked the fuck out of me, not to mention the walls started melting because there was so much body heat from people dancing, I was convinced, that I was in hell. I came around a bit in my girlfriend's bedroom, she kept talking to me and feeding me water, but I never, ever would wish a nasty trip like that on anyone, not even my worst enemy.

So things were sound for a while, I was studying Arts at UCD and was studying hard and playing hard, the typical student lifestyle, I kept boozing, kept snorting speed, but I wouldn't touch the acid again, I swore to myself I'd never, ever take it again, easier said than done yeah?

But at the time, the trip I had was so bad, if I hadn't had met Tommy, I probably wouldn't be sitting in front of you all today, I'd still have my job, my career, my apartment, up in Dublin…"

Wesley looked around the room, absolutely captivated by the look of captivation etched on everybody's face as Gideon continued his story. The thought of having to get up there and do the same thing was daunting, Wesley was never one to be honest and open, he began to feel nervous, envisioning what it would be like, as he listened to Gideon continue his tale. Having a breakthrough was a revelation in the House of Novalis, they seldom occurred.

"I had a job, I had this great fuckin job, I was manager in the 'ComicZone' up in the city, you know the one, near the Hay Penny Bridge, and my job basically was to order the comics, made sure the shelves were stacked and up to date with new releases, and any and all paperwork and accounting shite that went along with it.

All I did was talk comic books, all day long, and there were large periods in the day when I did sweet fuck all, everybody smoked joints, so we'd use my office to smoke in. That was around the time Tommy started showing up. He was a mate of one of the lads in the staff, somebody who I had a lot of time for, somebody who I considered a close friend, Gizmo.

Gizmo got his nickname because he was obsessed with video games and was amazing at fixing gadgets, and super friendly, and handsome, all the women loved him, but he stuck to the one woman, for the time I knew him, her name was Natasha…I think…pretty sure her name was Natasha.

Anyway it was Gizmo that brought Tommy into the shop, and he started introducing him to everyone, and the first thing Gizmo said to me was, "Here, Giddy, this lad here, has some proper gear, if you want to…you know…check it out. So we went into my office, all of us, I left the rookie on the desk in case any customers came in, and we shared this fat joint, and we all got stoned off our balls, I mean it was the most powerful weed I ever had in my entire life.

I honestly thought, there and then, especially after hot boxing the office, that I was going to pass out, I had never pulled a greenie before, but once the sudden impact wore off you felt fuckin amazing, and the best part of it is the buzz lasted a good few solid hours, not like that soapbox shit we got off the knackers down at the Quays, this was the serious stuff.

I thought Tommy was a nice guy, English, but not a really distinctive kind of accent, come to think of it, I'm not entirely sure where Tommy was originally from, he claimed he was Irish, but it was hard to know, and man, was this fella out there, or what?

Of course, Gizmo loved him, they were best mates for years. He could talk about anything under the sun, conspiracy theories, proof of alien life, ancient history, the new world order that are secretly governing the entire planet, man he was a great story teller, and there wasn't anything he didn't know about comic books, so I'd turn a profit cuz he'd know what comics to sell, just by knowing, let's say, who the writer was, and because I'd know the story, then the lads, I mean the staff knew, which comics and graphic novels to push.

There was a weekend Gizmo wanted to go camping in the Wicklow mountains, and asked me if I'd come along. I thought that was a sound idea, as I hadn't been out of the city for a long time. When we were setting up camp, he said a few of his mates was coming along, and Natasha, there ended up being about seven of us, four boys and three girls, and Tommy was among that group.

We were sitting around a campfire one evening, drinking cans and smoking joints, when Tommy pulls out a baggie full of tabs and proclaimed that this was the best shit he had ever dropped in his life and I was saying to myself, Aw, feck this, I want to enjoy myself, not lose the fuckin plot completely.

I explained to Tommy about the bad trip I had, and he turns around to me and said, "That shite that you had, that was fuckin poison, they put rat poison in it to fuck with people, this is the good stuff, this stuff will make you feel you are at one with nature and want to hug everybody, there's a real love buzz off this, don't worry, we'll all be feeling the same way, I can guarantee there will be no bad trips from this."

I was reluctant, but I don't know, call it peer pressure, call it not wanting to be the odd one out, because everybody else dropped a tab, so I said, "fuck it, give me one too."

"Coming up on it was nice, what made it amazing though, was when I felt like I was one with the nature all around me. The grass moved, I could see power lines of electricity running through the ground, the trees, the whatchamacallit, the bark, on the trees, were doing these amazing, zig zaggy kind of patterns, I could even see where the roots of each tree lay, underneath the ground, I could see mother earth feeding the trees! It was the most amazing experience I had ever gone through in my lifetime.

Then...then I did something stupid. Gizmo and Natasha were, clutching each other closely, and Tommy had pulled another one of the women in the group, I didn't fancy the third one, and the other fella, I got a strange vibe off of him, and I guarantee you, to this day, to this very day, I couldn't tell you their names, even if you put a gun to my head as if my life depended on it, I can't for the life of me, remember what their names were.

I remembered Natasha alright, cuz she was fuckin weird. Very quiet, too quiet, you couldn't hold a conversation with her, you'd ask her a question and she wouldn't reply.

I must have spent hours in the woods, I felt like a God of nature. I felt indestructible, I felt like I could make shit start to grow out of the ground just by laying my hands over the dirt. I was miles from the camp, walking, with nothing but a torch for light, laughing away to myself as everything jiggled and waved around me.

I felt like the trees were saying hello to me, and then this thought hit me, and I wished I never thought it, but once I did, the thought overpowered the rest of my emotions entirely. I thought to myself what if I get eaten by a bear? I managed to frighten the fuck out of myself, and I started running..."

"I'm pretty sure there aren't any bears in Ireland." Tara said. "Sorry to interrupt, but are there bears?" She looked around at everyone, who gave a slight shrug of their shoulders.

"No, there's not, I looked it up afterwards, there hasn't been bears in this country for thousands of years, but that night, I was convinced there was a big black bear after me, wanting to shred me to bits and eat my balls for breakfast. I was so convinced I wish I had a gun with me, I shit you not."

This got a big laugh from the group, including Wesley, whatever else could be said about the story, it was highly entertaining. Nobody had moved, or stirred an inch, since Gideon began his story, Wesley could feel pins and needles in his left leg, from awkwardly sitting on the floor, but he chose to ignore them, the story was too good to let comfort get in the way of it.

"So after running around like an eejit, I found my way back to the camp, they didn't even realise that I had left, they saw me sweating and shaking, and told me to drink a beer to calm my nerves, so I did, they asked me what was wrong and I was too afraid to tell them, not that there was an imaginary bear in the woods, but by just saying anything about bears or wild animals, would have them all paranoid, so I kept my mouth shut, once I drank a beer and smoked another joint to take the edge off the high, I was golden.

I never had such a magical trip, we had brought a ghetto blaster with us, those old school boom boxes from the eighties, and we played The Cure all night long, I actually ended up riding that bird I didn't fancy in my tent, that was...profound, connecting with somebody I wasn't normally physically attracted to, in that way. I laid there, beside her, thinking about...life...what was the point to it all?

That night changed my whole mentality to LSD. We started dropping it at work, I sold my little apartment, and moved into a rented house with Tommy, Gizmo and Natasha, and some Dublin Chinese bird that Tommy was seeing, her name was Cathy Lee.

Nice girl, lovely face, really sound, down to earth personality, it was gas to hear a thick north side accent come out of this five foot nothing Chinese woman, she'd have you in knots every time you spoke to her, she really did have a great sense of humour.

We'd smoke weed every day and night, and we fell into a routine of dropping acid three times a week, normally three days in a row, from Thursday to Saturday night/Sunday morning. It was all going amazing, really well, then things started to change, Tommy started to act differently, not to mention I woke up one morning and found someone had nicked my wages, so I accused Tommy, which upset Cathy, that upset me because over time I had developed feelings for

Cathy.

I knew Gizmo wouldn't steal from me, and Natasha, despite being strangely quiet, did a lot around the house, she liked to cook and loved to clean when she was tripping, so the house was always spotless, a nice buzz always came off her when we were tripping together, I felt like I didn't need to talk to her.

Tommy on the other hand, that was a different story altogether.

He'd be our pilot, that's to say, when we would go tripping he'd be our grounding, if things got out of hand we'd use him as a gateway back to reality, because he was the most experienced, but after a while, I could see a darkness, in his soul, and instead of piloting us, he'd try to fuck us up, try and make us believe whatever scenario we were going through, and this vibration would start resonating off of him. And he'd be a real arsehole at times, you know?

"What kind of vibration?" asked Polly, "was it like something you could see or was it more like something you felt?"

"Definitely more like something you felt. Plus I could hear this buzzing noise that went along with it, it happened everytime he was in the room.

It was difficult to get away from each other

living under the same roof, and all of us on the welfare. Yeah, I missed so many days and started losing custom, so I got the sack, I think it was one of the lads who ratted on me, cuz they didn't give a shite about the weed, the lads who owned the place they were pure stoners altogether, naw I think they got wind of the LSD, somebody must have snitched, and I have a fair idea who it was, there was only about three or four people in the entire staff that didn't smoke or do anything like that.

I'd say this person must have thought that if they stitched me up and got me the sack, they'd get my job, thinking that anybody who dropped LSD would get the sack. But joke's on her. Gizmo got the manager's job, and he quit the LSD then. I had no resentment against him for that, he told me he wouldn't take it if I was anyway uncomfortable with it, I told him don't act so daft.

Anyway, after a few weeks of constantly dropping I had to leave the house, not move out, just leave for a while because Tommy was freaking me out. There were a couple of trips where he tried to convince me that I was dead and nobody loved me..."

"How could you let someone treat you like that, and still call him your friend? I'm just wondering, please don't think that I'm accusing you of being weak or something, but I'm just curious as to how you could let a person try and manipulate you like that." Oscar was getting visibly upset at his own statement; he began to rock back and forth on his spot, pulling at his curly hair. "I always let people manipulate me...but this; you could have walked away after the first time, and said, no thank you, so I'm just wondering...how? Do you see what I'm trying to say? Do you see what I'm trying to get at?" Tara crawled over next to Oscar and put a loving arm around his shoulders.

"Try and hold off on having a primal until Gideon has finished telling his story, Oscar, and then you can let it out."

"Sorry."

"Don't be sorry, we all know somebody like that...anyway Gideon, keep going, it's good you're telling us this story, it'll help us all with our primals."

"The problem with Tommy was, he was a very charming person. He was full of energy and jokes, he was an extreme extravert, full of boundless joy, but on LSD, it was like he was using me as an experiment so that he could manipulate people into doing his bidding.

I mean, we all enabled him, anybody who knew him enabled him with drugs, and money, and gifts. He made me question my own sanity, he made me question the decisions I made in my life, he was getting to the point he would question my actual existence.

Like, take one night, for instance, whatever tabs he got, they were extremely heavy, they'd warp your mind completely, and he kept talking in my ear, even though he was high as fuck as well, although, saying that now, I'm not so sure was he even tripping at all sometimes. But I got so high, I felt like I was floating above time and space itself, and Tommy kept telling me to let go, let my spirit leave my body, and then a few hours in, the buzzing noise got louder, and I felt weightless.

I saw myself above Earth, and began to scream from a joy mixed with a sudden terror, I kept asking Gizmo was I dead? Was I fuckin dead? But I was laughing so much he didn't understand the question so he wouldn't answer, I think at this point he saw what was going on, and he was just smoking joints, he was beginning to see through Tommy.

I was starting to see aura's around people, and different people had different coloured aura's and I kind of knew the sort of person you were just by the colour of your aura. Tommy's was brown, which meant that he was not a good person. Not a lot of people can see through him. He's not that handsome, but he is handsome, he's not that magnetic, yet he's able to sleep with any girl he meets, he's an odd mixture of heavy charisma, and ruthless intention, and if he doesn't like you, he can get everyone in his circle, to turn on you, and when that happens, you come around and you realise that you have nothing, and he has everything. Bastard…"

Gideon was about to say something else, but he stopped himself before he made a noise, and began to frown. Wesley was the only one to pick up on it. He kept quiet, intrigued by the story.

Bertie was the one who spoke next, his effeminate gestures and squeaky voice as opposed to his fat, manly appearance, was something Wesley was still getting accustomed to and there was a particularly strange odour emanating off him today.

Wesley couldn't place the scent, he was surprised nobody had pulled Bertie up about his hygiene and appearance, and Wesley, more than anybody, knew what it was like to be self-loathing, he promised himself that he wouldn't point out his flaws to Bertie, but nobody did, and it was seriously starting to take the piss.

"So the aliens, when did you start to believe that aliens were trying to brainwash you? I have an interest in aliens myself, so…were they, like, a certain kind of alien, did they have a name? What galaxy did they say they were from? Like, did they ever give you that information?"

"It was a hallucination," Polly said, "Making out like they were real won't help Giddy face his demons, Bertie."

"Well who says they had to be a hallucination?" Said Bertie, delicately pushing his glasses up on the bridge of his nose before sniffling, he then took a dirty old snot rag out of his pocket and blew his nose.

Bertie made the most horrendous sound when he blew his nose, it was as if you could hear the warm snot leaking out of his nostrils onto the tissue, Wesley had to close his eyes and look away as Bertie went about wiping his snotrag up and down the nostrils. "Am I fair in saying that, Giddy? Just because you thought that it was all a hallucination, doesn't mean that interplanetary aliens don't exist."

"You can believe whatever you want, I don't care, to me, they seemed very real. They called themselves Arcturians, I was so out of it that I thought they could communicate with me through a telekinetic device called a Nortek, and if I told anybody of their existence that they'd incinerate anybody I had ever known in my life and enslave me on their planet.

But it didn't start off like that; it was just this humming sound. I moved to the Wicklow mountains, and rented this run-down cottage in the middle of nowhere, and I had an old Ford Fiesta for getting out and about, I'd spent weeks just meditating and painting, trying to decide my next move, and weekends I'd invite friends, Gizmo and Cathy and people like that, and I'd drop acid with Cathy and a few other mates at my gaff at the weekends.

The first few trips with them were magical, there was one in particular that I will never forget for as long as I live, well, the same can be said for all of the trips I had, but this one in particular, was special, I thought God was in me, than I believed that I was God. I was all seeing and all knowing, I understood the meaning of existence..."

This sentence grabbed Wesley's attention, up until then he was listening, sitting on the floor with his knees up and his arms resting on his knees, his head down in between his arms, once Gideon said, "the meaning of existence," his head shot up, he was at full alert.

"What is it?" Wesley asked.

"What's what?"

"What is the meaning of existence?"

"That's quite hard to summarize..."

"Give it your best shot."

"It's very hard to describe, especially on the spot..."

" Are you saying it to be dramatic, or do you mean it?"

"I mean it, I could feel it."

"Feeling it isn't the same as knowing it."

"I know it.."

"Well then, what is it?"

"It's gonna take a while to explain."

Polly took control of the situation; she placed her hand gently on Wesley's arm.

"Maybe, after this session, you and Gideon can go for a walk and discuss it. Would you be happy with that Giddy?"

"I have no problem doing that at all…no."

"See? There you go."

"Are you telling the truth?" Wesley asked him directly, giving him a steel cold gaze.

"Yeah man, always, I'll do my very best to explain it to you."

"Cuz…it's been bothering me, you have no idea the amount of hours I've spent, wondering what this all meant."

"This is what I call the beginning of a

breakthrough, Wesley, you do realise that?" Polly smiled gently as she spoke, sounding very re-assuring, " I'd advise you to let Giddy finish his story, it's very important to him that he does so, we're breaking barriers today, but I want to tap in to that topic, that topic that troubles you so much, in private, would you like that?"

How could Wesley say no? He was invested now, there was no turning back, it was this or death, he was afraid to know the truth, he wanted there to be meaning to existence, what scared him was if it all meant nothing. Polly was so re-assuring, soothing him with that sweet, motherly tone of a voice that she had, that all Wesley could do was nod his head in agreement.

"Brilliant!" Polly exclaimed, "We're doing so much work today, keep going sweetheart! You're so close, you're so close to getting to the root of your primal, please, don't lose focus, don't stop now, we all want you to do it, isn't that right guys?"

Everybody sitting on the floor, including Wesley, began clapping and cheering for Gideon, encouraging him to get deeper into his past experiences.

"Well like I said..." Gideon was re-composing himself, there was a bit more throat clearing and a bit more shuffling around on his chair, before he continued, "That trip was fine, the problem was the trip right after that."

"It was a week later, and we dropped some tabs, I forgot to mention, I had a shitload of tabs, that I...well...let's just say confiscated would be the best term to use, I confiscated Tommy's tab collection. That was another part of his genius, somehow he managed to convince people he'd sell their product for them, and when he got said product, he had a way of twisting things and make it seem like they should be thanking him for taking the product to sell, and not get a cut of the sales.

All the money went to him, nobody came after him, he could manipulate people, he could get people to doubt themselves so much, they were convinced the Gardaí were after them and would get so spooked they'd go into hiding, or give up dealing altogether.

Anyway, I digress, the problem with the next trip was...the buzzing sound, the negative sonar waves came back, only, this time, Tommy wasn't around, so I knew then for certain that he wasn't the cause of it, then there was this kind of rumbling sound, like there was some force field between my eyebrows. I started to feel this strong pull of energy, and there were times I heard rumbling noises, instead of buzzing noises, like the kind of sound a truck would make. Because Tommy wasn't around, I somehow managed to convince myself that I was working for the UFO people,, some secret organization, from another dimension.

There was another weekend Gizmo came up to the house to visit and he brought with him a book about UFO sightings and experiences, and I read it cover to cover and what freaked me out were the accounts of people who met aliens telekinetically.

They all talked about knowing when the aliens were nearby because they let off this frequency, sort of like a buzzing noise, and there were these sonic waves that blasted through the air. I couldn't believe what I was reading, these were accounts from people all over the world, interviews with photos, and I became paranoid, thinking the aliens were after me next, or were attached to someone who I knew and I could feel the energy waves coming off them.

I had to know, I had to be sure that this was happening to me and me alone. So I booked a hotel room in Dublin, away from everybody I knew, I can't remember which hotel it was, but I booked a room and stayed there dropping acid for four nights, only opening the door to get room service, breakfast or dinner, whatever time it was, I was never hungry on LSD but I knew I had to eat to keep my strength up.

The whole time I was there, in that hotel

room, the sonic waves never left me, and they became stronger and stronger, so did the buzzing noises. It was scary, I didn't know what to do, I figured I'd stop dropping LSD because this was all a pure hallucination.

For the next few weeks, I was fine, I began jogging, eating the right foods, I even quit smoking joints for a while. But then, the buzzing got louder and I began to hear voices, this was when I was fuckin sober!

So I had to go to the doctor, I was diagnosed with Bi Polar, and they wanted to put me in the psych ward to help me, they said they had pills that would make me be normal again, but I didn't trust them. I convinced myself they were a front for alien operations, for aliens to brainwash people into doing their bidding.

I did what any insane person would do in that situation, I stole a car and fled. I drove anywhere I could think of, hoping the aliens wouldn't get to me. I started smoking weed again, I lit one joint and found that when I was stoned the buzzing noise would fade out, and the noises would stop, for a while, so I kept getting stoned, really fuckin stoned, I mean, so stoned I didn't even know what to do with myself. So I kept driving, and at night I'd camp by the side of the road, or sleep in the car, or rent a cheap room."

"How were you surviving?" Oscar asked,

"how were you making money, was it all just the dole?"

"I was selling tabs where I could, I'd charge like a tenner a tab, and when you go to so many towns you start to meet the same kind of people in each town who all want the same thing, so it was easy to sell, I'd just find out where a rave was going to be and stood outside and shouted that I had tabs, there were never any coppers around, it's like a fair trade market for drugs at the raves, the Gardaí don't have a clue."

Wesley was invested in Gideon's story now, forgetting that Polly's warm hand was still resting on his lower arm. He was fascinated by the fact that somebody's life could be torn apart by drugs, and jealous that he never thought of doing it himself, the fascination of going crazy on drugs, never sure of your surroundings, not trusting reality, bending your mind to break the laws of this planet, and exploring the inner depths of your psyche. He was riveted...

"Was it ever fun, or was it always a nightmare?"

"It was always a nightmare."

"I'm not sure I believe you when you say that."

"Why would you think that?"

"Because if every trip was a complete nightmare, why keep taking it?"

"It was better than reality."

"So you were hiding from reality?"

"You could say that, although, I don't know, I've thought about that myself. I convinced myself for a while that if I took LSD it would keep the aliens at bay, then there were times I took LSD and broke reality, and felt like God, as I've mentioned before, the problem was it didn't happen every single time I took LSD, and I began to wonder why not? Then I was convinced there were aliens amongst us the entire time regardless of whether I dropped or not. So I'd rather be high than sober knowing the truth is out there."

"How many tabs would you drop in a day?"

"It started off with just one, than the more I became immune to it the more I needed it. It was getting to the point I had to drop four maybe five tabs to get high, to lose the filter and see things for what they're truly are. This is what Wesley wants to know, why if it was such a nightmare, did I keep dropping?

Because in the end I wanted to know the truth, nothing else mattered.

I spent my days surfing the internet, browsing pages on the unexplained, reading reports involving the new world order, the eight dimensions, endless conspiracy theories involving the CIA and the KGB…and of course, aliens, how they can communicate, sightings, gurus who were experts on different planets and different galaxies, it was a nightmare because I couldn't stop, I couldn't help myself, I would have been happy dying on an overdose believing I was God. The nightmare is losing self-control, and trusting no one or nobody. That show what's it called? 'The X Files,' that doesn't even scrape the surface of what's out there.

I was so paranoid I couldn't stay in my house, I had to sit in public places all day because I figured they wouldn't let them be known to me in public.

I ended up going to my mams' home; I didn't know what else to do. I spent days driving around the country, I'd drive one hundred miles in one direction then I'd make a sudden u turn and drive two hundred miles in another direction, hoping that I could lose them, so they wouldn't track me.

I convinced myself that was working for a while, but then, it was getting to the point I could hear the buzzing sound all the time, no matter what I did, I couldn't shake it off.

Things got to a breaking point, at my mams house; I'd sit in the bathtub all day, with tin-foil on my head so they wouldn't melt my brain. Then, one night, I was in bed, and I saw these bright lights through my window, and I knew right there and then, that they were here, they were going to abduct me, and the wall started to collapse, the buzzing noise got louder and louder until it was so loud it drowned out any sound completely.

Then I saw them, little fuckers, about five feet high with green skin. They claimed their planet is on the Milky Way, outside of our solar system, they claim to be the most intellectual beings in the universe, and they had chosen me to study the behaviours of the human race, and they abducted me, or I thought they did.

I remember they were doing experiments on me, and then I woke up, in my own bed, the wall was intact, I knew then I needed help, they had made contact, and I was either going completely crazy or those little green fuckers were going to brain wash me completely or incinerate me.

I rang Gizmo, Cathy was there, she had left Tommy, Tommy was nowhere to be found, I asked Cathy did she know of anybody who could help me with my problem, I told her that I couldn't tell what was real from what was fake anymore, and I started to cry over the phone. She said she had a friend who's niece was getting Primal Therapy, off...Tara here."

Gideon laid his hand out in a gesture towards Tara, before clapping, a slow clap, encouraging the gang to join in. She got a massive ovation; Wesley could see tears spring into Gideon's eyes. *Giddy was crying. So it was okay for men to cry, so why the fuck can't I do it?*

"I drove to Mayo to meet Tara, who was living in Westport at the time. And I was really scared, like shit scared nervous. Tara, was able to calm me down straight away, I told her my story, and there was no point where she said that she didn't believe me, or that I was hallucinating, all she did was listen.

I stayed in Westport, and met her a few more times, this was in the stage last year when she was packing her things and moving here to Novalis. I had a really bad day. I was super paranoid. Anytime I was in town I felt like everybody was watching me, I felt like they were all in on this little secret and I was the only one left out of the loop.

The buzzing and rumbling sounds were becoming unbearable. Every time a car honked a horn I was convinced it was the aliens trying to send me a message, to let me know they could harvest anybody's energy and take over human forms just to honk a horn at me, to let me know they were watching me.

I explained this to Tara, who was so understanding, and then she asked me to do something which came completely out of left field, she asked me about my parents, what were they like?

I said my father left home when I was young, and was still technically married to my mother, even though they have been separated for years. I wasn't close to my father, but I didn't like to think about it because it just brought a lot of emotional pain. And Tara said, in order to get rid of these hallucinations, in order to overcome my fear of UFO's and anything related to aliens and UFO's, that I would have to be myself, I would have to confront the feelings of bitterness, of hatred, of fear, of the resentment I had towards my father. And just like that, like I am doing now, I started to cry, and I've been crying ever since."

Gideon began to bawl. He sat on the floor and curled up into the foetal position, he cried and cried. Every so often he'd let out a wail, it was hard to make out what the hell he was screaming about at first, Wesley couldn't make it out, eventually he was able to piece it together.

"Why dya leave me daddy? why the hell did you leave me? I needed you and you weren't there for me. I felt so much pain, you put me in so much pain, not anymore! I don't need you anymore, do you hear me? I don't care if you're dead or alive because you're not important to me anymore. You caused me so much pain, I'm not going to let you ruin my life, YOU'RE NOT GOING TO RUIN MY LIFE!'

Wesley looked around at the rest of the women, they were all strangely quiet, Bonnie, Lulu and Ruby hadn't said a word since this session started, Ruby in particular, looked grief stricken and very sympathetic, for a woman who barely spoke Wesley found himself liking her more and more each day.

Bonnie, well Bonnie was a drama queen, and Lulu was great fun. Ruby was something different altogether. She was a mystery; still rivers ran deep in her.

Polly and Tara went and sat on the floor next to Gideon. This was standard practice for a member going through a vicious, primal breakthrough. Polly placed a hand on his feet whilst Tara kept his head propped in her lap, they comforted Gideon with soft lilting and hushing, waiting for him to get through his primal.

There was always a worry with a primal that the patient would become so overwhelmed with emotion that they could go into shock, or have some sort of seizure, Polly would always say that although these seizures were uncommon, they did happen, and if someone was going to have a primal, they had to do so in a controlled environment.

Other risks were physically scratching yourself, cutting yourself, swallowing your own tongue, or accidently knocking yourself unconscious from the amount of rocking and shaking during the process.

Both Polly and Tara had first aid training and were proud to mention it to anyone, even if they weren't prompted to do so. It was essential to have first aid if you were to run a primal scream commune.

Gideon eventually began to calm down and gather his bearings. He sat up, cross-legged, as he wiped the tears from his eyes, while Polly and Tara placed their head on each of his shoulders, rubbing his arms in comfort.

Nobody said anything for quite a few minutes, nobody wanted to break the silence, they all wanted to digest the information and were fascinated in how Gideon was able to open up and have his breakthrough in front of the rest of the group.

Lulu was the one to break the silence. "Well done Giddy, that was fuckin brilliant, you do know we're all here for you, don't you? This is the first day of your new life, the end of the beginning, and I'm so proud of you, it takes bravery to open up to us the way that you did. "

With that, Lulu began to clap, and everybody,

including Wesley joined in.

Gideon stood smiling and hugged Polly and Tara. Then, one by one, everybody in the group gave Gideon a supportive hug, Wesley was the last to do so. Even though he was never a hugger in his life, thinking it was an effeminate gesture, he was finally seeing their worth and was beginning to enjoy offering and receiving hugs.

Without prompting, without any kind of direction from anybody in the group, they all found themselves in a circle; Wesley had Lulu on his left and Oscar on his right. They began to sway in unison, laughing at the spontaneity of it all, then out of nowhere, Polly began to sing John Lennon's 'Instant Karma,' and everybody joined in.

Wesley Harding joined in, he sang and he swayed and he danced with the rest of them. What Wesley Harding was pondering at that very moment, was if he confessed to Novalis about taking another human life, would cleansing his soul help him in having his own breakthrough?

***

CHAPTER 13 --- ODYSSEY

Historians and scholars would have you believe that Wesley's odyssey into becoming a notorious cult leader began the day he set foot on Achill Island, in fact, his odyssey began on the day of Myia Hawkin's death.

Wesley had not slept well the night before. Every time he closed his eyes the faces of strangers would form in the darkness. They had immaculate features and were so real that Wesley wanted to reach out and touch them. They would drift towards him, ever closer, until Wesley found their presence so unbearable, he would have to open his eyes in order for them to drift away.

At one point, in the middle of the night, right before the dawn, the face of a demon appeared in front of Wesley. The face was wrinkled, he had the eyes of a sheep and a monstrous evil grin.

It looked terrifying. Wesley kept his eyes closed for as long as he possibly could until the demon opened his mouth as if to swallow Wesley whole.

He had to get up after that with a dry mouth and a headache, mainly due to the lack of water he had drank the day previously, lying in bed was only making things worse for him.

He was bone tired, but he didn't feel like trying to sleep knowing there was some evil fucker of a hallucination lurking in the darkness wanting to swallow him whole. He felt pains rocket throughout his entire body as he stretched. He had some god forsaken creak in his neck from whatever awkward way he was lying in bed. He felt like a piece of elastic band, wound by something in his brain so tightly, it was on the verge of snapping. No matter what way he sat in his sofa, he felt uncomfortable, uneasy and extremely restless.

He had no appetite the morning of Myia's death, even thinking about food made him nauseous. He spent the entire morning lying on the couch, drinking coffee, listening to Nirvana Albums, even the John Peel sessions. He willed himself into getting ready for Uni. He started tricking himself into thinking that having a shower would refresh him and make him a damn sight better than he was feeling now, both in the body and the mind.

The effort it took Wesley to stand up and walk the mere twenty steps to the bathroom, felt to Wesley like a monstrous task. He was as well-off climbing Mount Everest, especially with the amount of willpower and energy it took to motivate himself to get off his arse and get ready. Once he made the great journey across the hall and into the chilly bathroom, he did his morning routine of sitting on the toilet and putting his head between his hands.

He didn't...feel right. Every morning to him was a challenge, but this morning in particular made him feel completely disjointed from the world. He felt like his eyes were merely a pair of camera lenses, filming the information but doing nothing to him emotionally, he felt like his body was a machine that belonged to someone else.

Everything felt lifeless and numb. His penis was wrinkled and flaccid. He tried to give himself an erection, just to see if he could, but nothing stirred, no matter what sexy thoughts he could muster up in his brain. He had to touch it and grab at it to feel that it was still there. He could feel it; it just lay there, as shriveled and hopeless as Wesley was feeling.

He turned the shower on, at least he was able to turn something on, and let the water build up heat and pressure. He stood naked, breathing deeply, letting the cold chill of the morning air creep into every pore of his skin.

He closed his eyes and tried to control the panicked shuddering of his chest. He envisioned all of the aggravating dull aches in his body as unwanted energy and tried to breathe that energy out of his system as he listened to the steady stream of hot water drum off the basin.

Whilst he pulled at the roots of his hair, he massaged his skull and began looking at his own reflection in the bathroom mirror.

He dove into the large black pupils of his blue eyes staring back at him. He drowned in the morning shadows of the bushes cascading through the bathroom window. He wallowed in every pale aspect of the bathroom, everything from the dull blue paint and the chilliness of the atmosphere to his skinny, bony, naked body, to the rising damp that was seeping in along the ceiling, to the toothpaste stains spattered along the metal taps.

It was all becoming crystal clear, horribly clear. He was all alone, and there was nobody around to help him. There was no reverence, there was no salvation. There was no future, nothing to look forward to.

He screamed as loud and as long as he could at the top of his voice. He screamed the house down. He felt his voice soar and hit the rafters of the roof, scaring away the ghosts and demons of his tormented shy childhood. Then, out of nowhere, he stopped and the silence deafened him. He became drenched in tiredness; it was like he summoned up Novocain to alleviate his dull aches. He felt better. This breed of tiredness was new to him. It was something that felt pleasurable, relaxing.

He could now float through the rest of the day without worrying about returning to the depths of his depression, he could put off sinking and exploring the depths of his deep dark psyche for the day.

He got into the shower, he had screamed for so long there was no hot water left in the tank, but he persevered with his task. In the end, the water didn't feel cold enough, Wesley ended up turning the heat down to feel the icy cold water zap refreshing life back into his body.

#

Wesley was informed by his friend Calum that there was going to be some standup comedy showcase taking place in the Cellar Bar in the city that evening. Callum's first cousin was performing stand up, and Callum was going to support him. He said that the event would start at about seven, but probably would wait until people got there around eight before they would actually start.

Wesley said no at first, but he changed his mind when he found out he was on a half day in his study schedule. He needed something to keep him occupied, something to get him out of the house. He was very upset upon hearing the news that Myia was moving back home to Athlone. So, he found the cleanest dirty hoodie he could find, doused himself in Lynx and let himself out into the fresh evening air. He turned on his Spotify account and let a playlist of 90's rock music blast away into his earbuds.

Wesley considered waving down a taxi, or ordering an uber, but then he envisioned himself in a car having to force a conversation with the driver, which put him off the idea. Instead, he made his way towards the bus shelter at the end of his estate.

There were several people at the bus shelter when Wesley arrived, all of them looking to be transported into Eyre Square. Wesley didn't want to acknowledge their presence, so he stood next to the shelter, away from all the people who were crammed underneath. Even though he had his music playing at the highest volume, Wesley could still faintly hear the small talk between the strangers floating nearby,

"Ooh, it's nippy enough today, isn't it?"

"I hear it's going to get better later on in the week."

"Did you hear the rain last night? It kept me awake so it did."

A truck rattled by the bus shelter, whipping the hair back on everyone's head. The entire scene made Wesley feel anxious, and his anxiety was becoming abhorrent.

The bus pulled up in front of Wesley, fifteen minutes late, Wesley had to hold his breath from the diesel fumes which came wafting from the engine as he stepped on the bus. He sat in the front row of seats that lay directly across from the driver.

The bus made strange cranking noises as it filled up with passengers, and Wesley wondered was the bus deemed worthy to be on the road at all. He could feel the alloys and suspension were shot to hell, meaning that everybody on the bus would be careered a foot into the air after hitting every pothole on its journey.

The bus took an eternity to get to Eyre Square, what normally took around ten minutes, took closer to forty with the amount of traffic and people that got on and off at every single stop along the route. Wesley studied the people that boarded the bus, people that came from different backgrounds, ages, race and colour.

Some of the passengers were quiet and unassuming, happy mutes who were quite content browsing through the web on their phones or merely gazing out the window.

Then, there were the rowdy teenagers who sat down the back of the bus. The noise level which generated from them alone made Wesley grimace in disgust. They got so loud that an older passenger, who was seated about halfway down, had to stand up and yell at them to 'shut theeee fuuuuck up!!' at the top of his voice.

About halfway through the route, when the bus loaded on another five passengers, the vehicle was about to pull away from the bus stop when a female voice shouted 'wait!' at the top of her lungs.

The automatic doors creaked open and on stepped a young woman, in her early twenties, with short bleach blonde hair and blue eyes, who was out of breath from running for the bus as she rummaged around in her purse for her ticket. Wesley thought she looked like a pixie. She turned and paused as she scanned the bus for an empty seat before flashing Wesley a polite smile and sitting next to him.

Her hair smelled like apples and berries. Wesley could get the sweet scent of chewing gum off her breath. The warmth that she emanated caused Wesley to flush red. 'Cherub Rock' by The

Smashing Pumpkins began to play on the Spotify playlist. Wesley adored this song, he thought of it as one of his absolute favourites. He turned in his seat slightly to catch a glimpse of the pretty lady sitting next to him and turned away quickly when she glanced back and flashed another polite smile at him. Fear, anxiety, anger and shame began to override Wesley's nervous system.

Wesley felt himself beginning to sweat. He worried so much about sweating that the worry only caused him to sweat. He willed himself not to sweat, but to no avail. She smelled so good.

He wanted to say something to her. He wanted to be friendly and begin small talk because he knew that this was something a normal person would do. He decided against it, he was too concerned coming across as creepy. Fuck his shyness anyway.

The bus journey took another five minutes, the length of 'Cherub Rock.' To Wesley, it seemed a lot longer. His job was to stay invisible. Everything from the way he smelled to his composure had to be solid as to not give off the wrong impression.

The only way he felt he could achieve this was to remain completely still. His composure couldn't prevent his cheeks blazing a violent shade of red. He could smell the freshness of the evening air every time the doors opened. He hated blushing, and was furious at himself every time it happened, he thought blushing made him look extremely ugly.

Every time the bus hit a bad patch of road, Wesley and the young lady were lifted out of their seats causing her soft, warm denimed thigh to brush off his own.

Her warmth was a pleasant sensation. Wesley had to fight away the sexual, devious thoughts that began flooding his mind. All he kept thinking was how good it would feel to have her sitting on his lap. Her warmth was something that Wesley could envelope himself in, both spiritually and sexually.

Wesley tried in vain to think of something to say to her, but his head kept firing blanks. He knew later that evening, when he got back home, all the ways of beginning a conversation with her would come easy to him. Hindsight really is a wonderful thing.

Eventually, the bus fought its way through heavy evening traffic and pulled in at Eyre Square, the final stop on the route. The young lady shot Wesley one last polite smile before stepping off the bus and disappearing into the crowd. He watched her walk away and wondered where she was going. She was probably going to meet her boyfriend, or her girlfriend, or whatever, she was too pretty to be single.

Wesley shook away the thought, no point in overthinking when he was going to have to go and socialize and mingle with other people. He waited for all of the other passengers to disembark before he turned his Spotify playlist back on and stepped off the bus, without any acknowledgement to the driver, and began to dart through the human traffic on Eyre Square as he made his way towards the Cellar Bar.

He walked as quickly as he could, he hoped there wouldn't be a large crowd at the event, he wanted to find a good place to sit. He hoped that his friend Callum was already there, because he was always really good at finding seats. Neither men fancied having to stand in the middle of a packed crowd all night.

A sudden downpour of rain pelted off the stone cobbled pavement and the roofs of cars as soon as he made it to the entrance of The Cellar.

Wesley entered the venue, taken aback by the amount of people that had already gathered to see the stand-up comedy. To his dismay there were about 100 people packed into the venue, all chatting, drinking, while some darkened figure of a DJ played some god-awful type of futuristic techno music.

Wesley couldn't see anybody that he knew.

He checked the time and saw that it was ten to nine, he frowned, he hated having to wait on people. The show was supposed to start at eight, and he purposely arrived late so that he would only have to endure some of the show rather than all of it.

He made his way to the long bar at the back of the cellar and frowned again when the barmaid asked him for four Euros for a glass of ginger ale with a slice of lime. He purchased the drink by scanning his watch on the machine before standing by a large, mirrored pillar that was situated in the middle of the venue.

He spent a few minutes there, in silent turmoil, pretending to check through imaginary messages on his phone. When he checked the time again it was ten past nine, he looked around the tables in the dark corners of the venue, trying to place anybody that he knew…anybody, he didn't care if they didn't talk to him, he just wanted to sit with people and not look like so much of a lone…

Wesley did a double take, he could have sworn he'd seen Myia kissing a boy. He took a few steps closer to where the couple were sitting, he could make out that she had blonde curly hair that was quite similar to Myia's. The problem was, Wesley couldn't make out her features, he wasn't 100% that it was Myia shifting this fella, a large guy with slick black hair. He had to wait until they came up for air.

Wesley didn't want to look, he was repulsed by what he saw, yet he had to know for certain if Myia had broken his heart. He had to know for sure if that was her small, lily white hand clinging to the back of his head as she sucked his tongue.

When the couple eventually pulled away from each other, his heart sank to the pit of his stomach. It was Myia, in all of her beautiful glory, gazing at her beau in such a manner that Wesley had spent the last five years yearning for. He wanted to projectile vomit onto all of the vermin that crawled around him, humans with empty souls, all thick and soulless. He wished he was carrying a loaded gun so he could blow his brains out, right then and there in front of Myia, to prove his love to her.

He wanted to shit, cry, vomit, and scream. He wanted to pull every strand of hair violently from his skull. He wanted to die and float in the blissful ignorance of eternity, where green eyed monsters could never catch you, never devour you with the sweet sickness of want and lust. He couldn't let Myia see him. Letting that happen would be more painful than rubbing salt into an open wound.

He turned for the exit and ran, salty tears

stinging his cheeks. He needed fresh air. He needed to feel the sensation of hail stones burn and batter his face as he fought against the tide of paying patrons cramming their way into the venue.

***

CHAPTER 14 --- THE CAT AND THE SEAGULL

Who the fuck was that? What the fuck made him so special? Why wasn't he blessed with a six-inch dick and a six pack. They were all the same, all of them. Myia was no better than the rest of them. She'd broken his heart. Seeing her kiss another person was an image that was never going to leave his brain...unless he did something about it. What could he do? How could he make this sweet sickness go away?

Wesley stopped dead in his tracks as the hailstorm rained down on top of him. He was already halfway home, standing near the cathedral, he must have been walking at a furious pace. The revelation wasn't so much a thought that sprang to mind rather than a sensation that ricocheted throughout his entire body.

The revelation was so strong it knocked the breath out of him, causing him to keel over and place his hands on his knees. It was the answer to all of his problems, realizing the revelation caused the sweet sickness to wash away from his stomach. The permanent solution. He felt numb all over, he could breathe easy.

Out of nowhere, the hailstorm subsided and Wesley floated home in soaking wet silence. He felt like an immortal ghost, absolutely sure of his cosmic path. The clear night sky came like an approval from the universe.

As he turned into his estate he watched a seagull peck at an empty plastic bottle, absolutely determined in his task to peck as many holes as he could, more than any other seagull has ever done in the history of seagulls pecking holes into plastic bottles.

What made the scene even more surreal was the small, black cat standing next to the bird, watching him hard at work, meowing his approval as if he were shouting praise and instructions.

As Wesley walked by, the animals continued on their relentless task.

Peck peck peck peck peck peck peck peck meow! Peck peck peck peck peck peck peck peck peck peck peck peck peck peck moewawawahwahhh! PECK PECK Peck peck peck....the animals faded behind Wesley into the distance.

The pecking noises stopped.

Wesley turned to find the cat and the seagull both staring at him. It was like they knew exactly what Wesley was about to do. They were observing Wesley the same way people observed animals at the zoo. No condemnation, simply observation. Wesley walked a few metres, stopped and turned again. The animals continued to observe him. They could sense the animal instinct raging inside of this human, and it was the first time in Wesley's entire life that anybody or any animal had taken a unique interest in him.

He sat on his couch, wide eyed, thinking of nothing, as he stared out of his window, over towards Myia's flat, waiting for her to come home. If she ended up spending the night with that empty headed ken, that dumb jock dickhead, he'd wait until morning. He had all the time in the universe. He felt like a hunter, waiting for his prey.

Minutes turned to hours. He didn't notice the time pass by at all. He was above space and time. What he needed was to have music blasting from his stereo, to hear music in thunderous, godly vibes. Music that resonated the cry of his tortured soul trapped in this worthless body. He switched on his Spotify account and hit the random button on his massive playlist, letting fate decide what song should accompany his blackened mind. “Sober” by Tool reverberated off the walls.

The music was so loud that Wesley didn’t care if it woke the neighbours. He was in the zone. He was in the moment. Nothing was going to break him from his godlike trance. He stared at the sole light that illuminated Myia’s doorway.

The next thing Wesley knew, he was standing outside Myia’s front door. Myia was inside, Wesley was hoping that she was fast asleep. He couldn’t remember her coming home, but she must have, why else would he be standing outside her front door in the middle of the night?

He ever so gently placed his key into the lock of the door and slowly turned the key until he heard the door unlock with a satisfying click.

He strolled silently into Myia’s apartment, letting the familiar scent of strawberry, lemon kush, shampoo and soap hit his nostrils. She smelled so clean…

So pure.

He walked directly towards her bedroom. Full of purpose and poise. Breaking his nightly ritual of touching her belongings.

She looked so peaceful as she lay there sleeping. Wesley stood at the foot of her bed, silently weeping. Feeling pure sadness and sorrow for what he was about to do. He couldn't let anybody else have her, she was his, and his alone.

He crawled onto the bed. He knelt over her, his thighs straddling each side of her body.

He went hard against the lustful sensation of her hot warmth.

Myia stirred awake.

Puzzled, her eyes full of sleep.

"Who's there?"

Wesley firmly gripped her neck, his pathetic, white, long fingers jolted Myia awake as they began crushing her windpipe.

She tried to scream, but all she could do was croak.

"Wesley, what are you doing? Get off me..."

Wesley howled like a wolf in anguish, as Myia choked.

He felt her straining, fighting for her life. Scratching, clawing at his face, his eyes. Convulsing, twisting, turning...

"I'm sorry, I'm so so sorry!"

He blubbered through his tears. He genuinely meant what he said.

Murdering Myia Dawkins was far more violent than he had envisioned. Where Wesley saw it as something out of a Greek tragedy, to Myia, it was a full blooded horrific nightmare.

He didn't account for her pretty BROWN eyes dislocating from her sockets.

He didn't account for how long it took for her to lose consciousness and die.

He didn't account for how painful her torturous death would be.

He didn't account for her face turning a vicious shade of purple.

He didn't account for how viciously she had fought him. How often she had successfully scratched him and clawed at his eyes.

He didn't account for how physically tasking it was to strangle a person to death.

Most of all…

He didn't account for how powerful and horny he felt as he strangled her, resulting in him climaxing into his jeans and boxer shorts. He came like a baby gorilla, on top of Myia's lifeless body.

It was his greatest sexual thrill.

He spooned her, feeling joyful and fulfilled as he cradled her, making sure her purple face and dislocated eyes lay away from him.

Time passed by slowly and ceaselessly.

His hands hurt, he had a sickly sensation of sawing through flesh and bone, but he couldn't match any image that went along with this sensation.

He couldn't remember leaving Myia's.

Wesley wasn't sure how he felt about everything, not at first, at least. He couldn't think anymore, he felt numb. The voices in his head had fallen silent, which came to him as a blessing. The crime that Wesley had just committed would be quite perplexing to most people, the burden of taking somebody's life would be too heavy a burden to carry. Wesley wasn't like most people.

Did he wash his hands? He did, he looked down and saw that he was wearing different clothes. He smelled like bleach. He felt clean. Heavenly clean.

He sat on his couch, feeling above the law. After the whole process of being questioned and interrogated by the Gardaí and knowing they would have to let him go over lack of evidence, his main concern was what his next step was?

How would his mother react to him being arrested? She probably wouldn't even care.

His end goal was to find out what the meaning of life was, once and for all, before ending his own. Now that he was capable of murder, and the power and liberty that came along with it, Wesley felt like he was capable of anything. He wanted to die knowing absolutely what the truth was. He didn't want to throw away the gift of self-awareness for nothing. He needed solid proof and clarification before pointing a gun to his head and pulling the trigger.

Wesley tried to practice grieving for the loss of Myia. He knew he had to put up a front of sorrow and grief when she would be reported missing to the authorities. He was her neighbour, there was no doubt in his mind he would be questioned about her whereabouts, but no matter how hard he tried, he couldn't make himself cry.

Wesley felt content sitting in this strange, distilled atmosphere. Without the noise of heavy metal blasting off the walls and the thick fog of melancholy in the air. The morning was stretching out long before him. Shadows began to creep along the walls. The greyness of the morning sky distilled all colours with its radiant beams of light that shone in through the window. The greyness made everything around him seem distant and meaningless. Wesley felt like he didn't belong in this place anymore, which gave him the positive anticipation of not knowing what was going to happen next.

He wondered was it dangerous to feel any hope for the future? Was he cursed? Did killing Myia break that curse?

There was no doubt in his mind that it was the putrid, black lump of consciousness that lay on his brain, the demons that whispered to him were the reason why he felt so lazy and entitled. It was the demons that made him a murderer, but so what? Would it not be more relevant to just let life lead you where you wanted to go?

Wesley knew he had to hatch a plan to either get out of the country or at the very least, get out of Galway and stay off the main grid, away from suspicion, but there was a time for planning later. Right now, Wesley just wanted to sit in silence and enjoy not having to hear the voices anymore, or the faces of demons haunting his dreams.

***

CHAPTER 15 --- THE INTERROGATION

There was something off about this kid. He was extremely talkative early this morning, he said he was willing to help in any way he can. He was extremely friendly and courteous, was well spoken and intelligent, and seemed to know a lot about Myia, who at this point had been missing for a week, the kid claimed they were very close friends. They had talked for a good long while, in the interrogation room, and the more they talked the more Hobbs realized something was amiss. Wesley was...cocky, and Hobbs didn't like cocky people, if you were cocky it meant you had something to hide.

There was also the long scratch he had on his nose, and when Hobbs asked him where he got it, Wesley naturally proclaimed a wild, feral cat scratched him. This only caused Hobbs to ask him more questions about the scratch, it wasn't a cat scratch, Hobbs had two cats and knew a cat scratch when he saw one, Wesley's scratch was long, it ran down his face, like somebody was trying to push him away and ended up digging a fingernail in under his eye before dragging it down to his mouth. As soon as the scratch was pointed out to him...Wesley turned...funny.

"All right, I just need to ask you a few more questions, is that all right Wesley? You don't have any questions, do you?"

"No."

"What's wrong, what's the matter? You know I'm Detective Hobbs, right?

"Yes."

"Do you remember...put your hands on the table where I can see them...please, do you remember us talking, earlier on today? Do you remember that? Because I do remember that, I remember that we had a good oul chat, didn't we Wesley?"

"Yes."

"We sat right here, and had a nice cup of tea, and chatted for a while, you do remember that, right Wesley?"

"Yes."

"Okay. Now Wesley, I need to know about this girl, right here, you see, I have this photograph of her, right here, do you know her Wesley?"

"Yes."

"Who is that?"

"Myia Dawkins"

"And she lives across the road from you?"

"Yes."

"When was the last time you saw her?"

"Two...maybe three weeks ago, something like that, I didn't see her around all the time."

"Hmm...and you were friends with her, is that right?"

"Yes."

"Wesley, pal, I need you to look at me, look at me when you're talking to me, can you do that for me?"

"Yes."

"And you were friends with her?"

"Yes."

"Close friends?"

"We...we were good friends."

"So, you **were** *friends."*

"Yes."

"And ye were both studying at NUIG, ye were both studying law, ye went to all the same classes together, you're studying to be a solicitor, am I right in

saying that Wesley?"

"Yes."

"What kind of law do you want to go into, criminal law?"

"Yes."

"Civil law?"

"Yes"

"Which one is it Wesley, civil or criminal, which law do you want to have a profession in?"

"I don't know."

"You don't know?! Well, you had five years to figure that out, didn't you?"

"Yes."

"And you don't know which law you want to work in?"

"Yes."

"Well surely, by now, you know which law you want to work in, what about criminal law?"

"Yes."

"So, you **do** *want to do criminal law?"*

"Yes."

"Well make up your mind, which one is it Wesley, yes or no?"

"Yes."

"So you want to be a criminal solicitor."

"Yes."

"Defense or prosecution?"

"I don't know..."

"I get it, you don't know, okay... and you're almost finished?"

"Yes."

"So, you don't have that much more to do right? You'll be graduating in a few months..."

"Yes."

"All right then, and when you go looking for work, are you going to go to Dublin...or Cork...or Belfast...or are you going to stay here in Galway?"

"I don't know."

"And when you were working, you worked at the courthouse? You did your work experience at the courthouse?"

"Yes."

"So, you're on our side."

"Yes."

"Good to know...eh...Wesley...good to know....and... did you like it when you were down there?"

"Yes."

"And you got along with everybody when you were working there."

"Yes."

"Okay, and you've lived next door to Myia, for quite a while, haven't you Wesley? In fact, you found the place for her, didn't you Wesley?"

"Yes."

"When you both first started your studies, she couldn't find a place to live, she was renting a room near The G Hotel."

"Yes."

"Do you know where Myia is...Wesley?"

"No."

"See this photo of her here, have you ever seen her with that dress on?"

"...No."

"You have no idea where she could be?"

"No."

"Wesley, just tell me what happened."

"I don't know."

"Well, where is she?

"I don't know."

"Right now, Wesley, right now, I need your help, and you're not helping me, I'm a detective for An Gardaí Síochána, I'm doing my level best to find this girl, and you live next door to her, and you claim to be friends with her, that you studied together, that you both did the same degree in university and I don't see any co-operation from you at all, whatsoever.

The way you're behaving, Wesley, the way you're behaving right now, sitting there like a zombie staring at me, only makes me suspicious of you, and the last thing you want, Wesley, and I think you know this all too well, studying to be a solicitor… and all that craic…the last thing you want to be, at any point in your life, whether you're guilty or innocent, is to be investigated by us, because it fucks up every aspect of your life. Even if you're only under suspicion, Wesley, being investigated by An Gardaí Síochána, it fucks up every aspect of your life, and you don't want that, I know you don't want that, do you Wesley?"

"No."

"So where is she…Wesley…help me with this, can you help me with this, where's Myia?"

"I don't know."

"C'mon Wesley. Tell me what to do, has anybody else asked you for help today?"

"I don't know."

"You need to help me out, Wesley, can you do that?"

"I don't know."

"What...you don't know what? You don't know if you can help me?"

"I don't know what you mean."

"I mean...I need to know where Myia is."

"I don't know."

"When was the last time you saw her."

"Two or three weeks ago."

"Did you **see** *anybody over at her place the past few nights?"*

"No."

"If you knew where she was...would you tell me?"

"Yes."

"What do **you** *think happened to her?"*

"I don't know."

"Do you even care, that nobody can find her? Not her close friends, or her family, or her relatives, do you even care, in the slightest, that nobody can find her?"

"Yes."

"I don't believe you…Wesley …I think you know where she is."

"I don't know where she is."

"Do you have a girlfriend?"

"No."

"Did you think Myia was your girlfriend?"

"No."

"Did you fantasize about Myia being your girlfriend?"

"No."

"Is anybody else in your family a solicitor, or working in law?"

"My mother."

"And what does your daddy do?"

"He's…not around"

"What did he used to do."

"I never knew him."

"What about your mother, what does your mother do?"

"She's a judge."

"I hear she's one of the best in the country."

"Yes."

"She's very successful, your mother."

"Yes."

"I bet she'd be very upset that you are being investigated here today?"

"Yes."

"She'd be crying, just about now."

"Yes."

"I'd say she's very proud of you."

"Yes."

"Proud that you're nearly graduated as a solicitor."

"Yes."

"A lot of studying. Do you have any brothers or sisters?"

"No."

"Any nieces or nephews?"

"No."

"Okay, so Wesley, tell me, what's up with all of them pairs of knickers we found under your mattress, it was a...mask of some kind...some kind of mask made out of knickers. Do you steal knickers Wesley, and cut them to make them look like a mask?"

"No."

"Oh, I think you do Wesley, I think you stole those knickers, and when we get the results back on who those knickers belong to, I bet you my house and car and mortgage that those knickers belong to Myia."

"No."

"I bet you stole Myia's knickers, made them into some kind of mask, something like in them "Freddy Kruger" films or something, you cut them out and made them into a mask and wanked off to Myia and you wearing the mask, smelling her knickers, cuz they had a certain...odour...to them, didn't they Wesley?"

"I don't know."

"Yeah...I think, if I was to steal knickers and make them into a mask, if I was a sick twisted little puppy like you, Wesley, I'd say the knickers would have to be from the fine bit of gear with the fine big arse on her, who lived across the road from me. The fine-looking sexy woman that's way out of your league."

"I don't know."

"It's okay Wesley, I've seen your search history on your computer, I've seen the porn you were browsing...my main concern right now, Wesley, is the safety and wellbeing of Myia. I need to find Myia, Wesley."

"I don't know where she is."

"How many times are you going to say, 'I don't know?'"

"I don't know."

Linda watched along on the screens with fascination, next to Detective Sergeant Abed Sayeed, a charmer with brains to burn and a heart of gold. Brady, the commissioner of doom and gloom, was there as well, her arms crossed, there wasn't even a wrinkle on her uniform.

The final member of the team, the West Indian Wise Arse, Detective Sergeant Kiki Reynolds, was at the potential crime scene, conducting interviews and gathering evidence along with the East Side Unit. Detective Sergeant 'Rodge' McGuire was Hobbs partner on this, nobody could remember his actual first name, so they just called him Rodge, because he looked like the arse-faced puppet that used to be on the telly. He was looking through his case file before heading into interrogation to play the role of the bad cop. Linda turned and stared at her boss, much the same way Wesley was staring a hole into the detective.

"Why don't you just give him his keys back and let him walk right out of here?"

"Ye of little faith detective."

“He knows you have nothing on him. There’s not a shred of evidence from the scene. Let me in there, just give me a couple of hours…”

“And force a confession out of him?”

“I was going to say, to let him sweat. Let him doubt his words, if I put on enough pressure, he might let something slip.”

“Any more cracks detective, I’ll send you home.”

“You’ve only got four hours left!”

“I’m well aware of the time, Detective. No stone has been left unturned, this has been greenlit by all of the experts, I don’t feel I need to explain myself any further, I’m fully confident…”

Linda snorted out a laugh.

“Is there something witty you wish to share with me?”

“I wouldn’t call Mary O’ Hora an expert in anything…” Linda was referring to the hippy dippy life expert psychoanalyst, assigned to oversee the intensive course of interrogation training. She spent the first two minutes of her lecture attempting to blow hair out of her face, as she frantically waved her arms around in comic fashion.

The course was a disaster in how not to interrogate a suspect, how a suspects feelings must be considered, and how you must interrogate the suspect in a friendly manner, happily letting them reply with 'no comment,' implying that any kind of grief and pressure on the suspect could result in civil lawsuits.

She then got detectives to roleplay interrogations, it was more like an acting class than anything else. Jimmy could only last an hour before storming out of the class.

Linda lasted until near the end of the day, until O'Hora began insisting that gender pronouns be considered, how not abiding to a suspects pronoun is deeply insulting and offensive. Linda had to insist on leaving, quietly and politely, repeating the phrase "no" as her heels gently clicked out of the room.

Linda got into trouble for that, hence the reason why Brady was prissy with her. O' Hora, the fuckin hippy dippy know it all, didn't have a clue, and Linda wrote a recommendation to the committee advising to cease the course immediately, due to, what she considered, 'a complete and flippant disregard to the criminal mind and the suffering of victims, especially rape victims.' Sex crime was no joke, O' Hora was giving rapists a 'get out of jail free' card by teaching detectives to be all soft and cuddly with them.

The one good thing that came out of the course was that she clicked with Daniels. She liked him. She especially liked his intelligence, and was looking forward to when he returned to active duty, better late than never, judging by how badly this interrogation was going.

The golden boys, Rodge and Hobbs were assigned this interrogation, due to them passing the course with flying colours.

They silently watched on the monitor as Rodge entered the room, throwing his weight around, trying to unnerve Wesley, who still kept his psycho gaze fixed on Hobbs.

"You said you don't know where Myia is, right?"

"Yes."

"You claim to be good friends?"

"Yes."

"How would you describe the relationship?"

"She was my friend."

"She was your friend?"

"Yes."

"Did you do favours for each other, did you go out for pints together, did you go to the cinema together? What was it, that was so special for you, that you two were such good friends? What did she do for you, that you could brag to us that you two were such close friends?"

"We talked."

"What did you talk about?"

"The news."

"The news! Sure, I talk the news with the cleaning lady here every morning, that doesn't make us best buddies now, does it?"

"I don't know."

"Let me put it in a simpler fashion. How many times did you hang out with her over at her place?"

"I don't know."

"If you had to guess, how many times would you guess you were over there?"

"Maybe a couple of times."

"A couple of times? Now I know you're talking shit, because I know, if someone asked me that question, how many times I was over at my best friend's house, I wouldn't be able to harbour a guess it was that many times, I would have lost count. If I had only been somewhere twice, I'd remember that."

Linda rubbed her eyes in frustration and tried not to let out a groan. Brady picked up on the negative body language.

"What are you moping about now?"

Linda looked at her boss, almost flabbergasted.

“He had a way in, and he blew it. He could have worked on that angle; it was a good angle. It would have gotten him to open up, and then amp up the pressure, it’s like he cheats in his exam and then he shows his teacher how he cheated…”

“Well, I don’t see it. I think he’s doing a fine job.”

Linda wearily collapsed onto Abed’s chair and laid her head down in between the mountain of paperwork piled on his messy desk.

“Mark my words, he’ll be eating his soon enough.”

“All due respect Ma’am, but why do you have it in for Detective Daniels? You know he’s right, don’t you? If he was here he’d…”

Brady turned from the monitor.

“When you live as long as I have my dear, you’ll see why. We need to move with the times, his way is done, out of fashion. Need I remind you of why I assigned you to this unit in the first place?”

“What are you trying to say?”

“What I’m saying is, when we charge young Wesley here, with first degree murder. You’re both done.”

“What if you don’t charge him?”

"Oh, we will.."

Linda fell silent not wanting to force the issue any further, as Brady gladly looked on at the interrogation. Linda didn't want to look, she turned her head away, her eyes half closed, listening to what was being said over the speakers, watching the grainy texture of the screen make shadows off the dark office walls.

Linda knew just from listening that Rodge was going in for the war of attrition technique to make Wesley crack. Rodge was about to sit right next to Wesley and try and outstare him. He was following the rules by the book all right, Linda knew it was too early for Rodge to make such a move.

If she was in there she'd build a profile, make him comfortable and then try and make him slip up, if that didn't work she'd pretend like he did confess and congratulate him on being so brave to do so, which would have him all up in arms.

Except she wasn't in there, she was lying on Abed's messy desk, making mental notes to put into her report which she'd have to have on Brady's desk by end of office hours, the following day. God, she was tired. How she was tired.

"Me and you both know when you were a small child, and you reached your hand into the cookie jar and you got caught red handed by your mum, after

she told you not to get that cookie, so that whenever you tell a lie, you feel bad about it right then. With every lie there's a chance that you're going to get caught. It becomes thrill seeking behaviour, every time you get away with it, it weighs on you, because you know you did something bad. Am I right or am I right?"

"I didn't do it." Came the eerily calm reply from Wesley.

Abed grabbed his wallet from his messy desk and made a bee line for the exit.

"Where are you going?" Linda asked.

"I don't know what it is, but I've suddenly got this mad craving for cookies."

"Oh my god, you're hilarious!"

"Do you want anything from the shop?"

"It depends which shop you're going to."

"I was thinking the one around the corner."

"I'm all right."

"What's wrong with the shop around the corner?"

"Nothing, it's just Centra is bigger and has more."

"I'm not going all the way to Centra, it's pissing from the heavens out there."

"Get me a hot chocolate."

"Cool, I'll get some cookies for this dickhead as well." Abed said, pointing to the figure of Rodge on the screen. "He's going to need a pick me up as soon as he is done fucking everything up."

"Don't worry, I have it all in the report."

"That's my girl, you could have been a contender, you know?!"

Linda listened to Abed's shoes echo down the hallway and pondered why all the good men were married. An arranged marriage no less. Then she wondered why Jimmy wasn't married. She pondered on that thought for some time, before shaking her head back into reality, and focusing back on her work.

"You didn't take the cookie?"

"No."

"You smell like bleach, like you've been using bleach to clean up. I know what that smells like, my wife smells like that every time she does clean the house. She does ruin her clothes with the amount of bleach she uses. Have you been using bleach?"

"No."

"So how then, does your place get clean? Does your mam come in and clean for you?"

"No."

"So how does it get cleaned?"

"I clean it."

"When was the last time you cleaned?"

"I don't remember."

Linda flicked through the pages of the heavy case file until she came across the freshly printed shots of Wesley's basement apartment. Nothing seemed out of place, it was an absolute pigsty, but there was nothing to suggest that a body had been stored there. Linda frowned. This case was getting stranger by the minute. She called Kiki, hoping she was still around the crime scene.

"How's my soul Sista?"

"I'm okay, this interrogation has gone to shit."

"Wha ya say?"

"I said it's not going well."

"I can't hear ya woman!"

"I have to talk low, Brady is here, She's up standing near the monitor, I said, it's not going well, it's gone to shit."

"Of course it has, because we're not doing it."

"I admire your confidence."

"What technique is he using?"

"The Cookie Jar Technique."

"Pshh, you use that when someone steals cookies, what the fuck is he playing at?"

"Oh, you should have seen the pair of them... just because their leading, they think they own the place."

Linda was so wrapped up in the conversation she didn't see Deputy Commissioner Helen Deeley enter the large office space and sneak her way down to the back, where Kiki's desk was situated. There she stood, watching from the shadows, as quiet as a mouse.

"They thought they were the proper dogs bollix when they went in, thinking as soon as they were done, he was going to breakdown and confess. He's playing them like a fool. I've never seen anything like it, he's...unshakeable. How are things down there?"

"Everybody has come out of their homes, seeing what's going on. The journalist, pretty young ting, she's going around asking everybody about what they saw, or heard. She's doing my job for me. We searched Wesley's apartment from top to bottom. No weapon. No blood. Forensics have gone over the place with a fine tooth comb. Nothing. Nobody has seen Myia all week."

“What about Myia’s place.”

“Nothing out of place, it’s like she walked outta door and just vanished”

“When do you think you’ll be finished there?”

“Not for a while. The child has so much stuff stored away that I’m convinced he thought that zombies were going to eat him or something. We’ve been looking through everything, and we’re only halfway done.”

“Okay, talk later.”

“Chin up woman, there be no time in fearin now.”

Linda hung up and threw her phone on the desk. She began to take deep breaths now as she focused all of her attention back on the interrogation. The footage was becoming to feel more eerie, like something out of a horror film. She tried not to cry. Hobbs was out of the interrogation room and was sitting back at his desk.

“What makes you think you’re going to find this girl?”

“He’s guilty, it’s only a matter of time. He was in love with her. He has her stashed somewhere. He’ll crack.”

“Big words for a big man.” Abed said, returning with a tray of hot drinks and a packet of chocolate chip cookies. “Why don’t you have a cookie?"

"Why don't you go fuck yourself?"

"Hey tough guy, how about I shove this cookie up your arse?"

Hobbs went to get up from his chair.

"Relax, the both of you!"

Abed merely shrugged as he took the lid off his coffee and started dumping in sachets of sugar.

The three detectives were done communicating with each other. They watched on, as Wesley continued to make Rodge look like an absolute fool of a donkey.

"You used to spy on her. You used to watch her come in and out of her apartment, didn't you?"

"No."

"You see a gorgeous babe like this, and come on, admit it, she is a gorgeous babe. You never once looked at her and thought, 'She looks good.'

"I don't understand."

"What? Don't be naïve. You never saw a sexy girl walking by and thought to yourself, "I'd love to ride her like a pony?"

"Yes."

"You never thought that about her?"

"Yes."

"You mean to tell me you can watch hours of porn on the internet every day, but you never once looked at Myia and thought about doing the no pants dance with her?"

"Yes."

"Yes what? Yes, you have?"

"No."

Abed started laughing as Hobbs's face flared red with anger once more. "I'm sorry, but he got schooled. That was too funny."

"Any better ideas?" Hobbs barked back. Abed could see he was losing his composure.

"Loads, but it's not like you're going to listen to them."

"Give me one. As an example."

"I'll give you two. Get me and Linda in there, become very compassionate and understanding, and then play him at his own game. Whatever answer he says, keep him to that answer. Get him to trip up. Maybe stop playing the yes no game show and ask him some proper questions?"

"You're right, for the first time, Abed, you're right, I'm not going to listen to you."

Abed muttered something in Arabic under his breath, Hobbs glared at him, but left matters at that, it was times like this he wished he learned Arabic, because he guessed that whatever Abed said was an assassination of his character.

"There's blood in your apartment, Wesley, you didn't get it all. Not to mention your hair was found in her place. The blood is faint, but it's there, Wesley, we used lumisol to light up your living room. We could see her blood spattered all over the walls, The whole room lit up like a fuckin Christmas tree, Wesley. We know what happened..."

"STOP THE INTERVIEW!"

Linda, Abed, Hobbs and Brady jumped an inch out of their skin, they turned to find the booming command coming from the tiny frame of Helen Deeley, who emerged from the shadows.

"What, why?" Brady demanded.

"Because your detective just made an absolute cunt out of himself!"

Before Linda knew what the hell was going on, Deeley had burst through the exit, and was running down the corridor towards the interrogation room. The detectives and Brady followed in hot pursuit.

"Wait, what the hell are you doing?" Brady shouted after her.

"Just you wait right there and don't you

fuckin move!" Deeley had reached the door and was now straightening out her uniform and fixing her hair, catching her breath, making herself as presentable as she could after breaking the 100 metre dash world record in high heels.

Linda watched as Deeley rapped on the door and poked her head in. Linda could just about hear what she was saying.

"Detective, a word please?"

"But…I…"

"A word!"

Linda watched Rodge exit, looking as confused and as bemused as the rest of them.

"Somebody will be with you in a moment Wesley, do you need a coffee, or anything?"

"No."

Deeley had already slammed the door shut to Wesley's reply before pointing at everybody to march their way back toward the bullpen. They all complied except for Brady, who was now seething with rage.

"Just who do you think you are?"

"I'm a respected deputy commissioner of An Gardaí Síochana who has just witnessed her colleague threaten her own career for a second time."

"But I..."

"You do realise there is a difference in a detective building rapport, building a motive, by claiming they have false evidence, yet not implying what kind of false evidence there is against a suspect, for reasons of legality...and the stunt your detective pulled just now?"

"He's in your unit..."

"I'm not having this discussion in the hallway, walk with me, please?"

Linda bit down hard on her lip trying not to laugh, trying not to pee herself with the excitement of watching a woman she loathed get an absolute ear rollicking.

They all converged into the bullpen, Deeley pointed at Brady to walk into Daniels's office, before entering and slamming the door behind her.

The detectives all waited until the door was firmly slammed shut before they all snuck over to listen in.

"I have never seen such incompetence in all my time working here, fuckin trained monkeys would have done a better job!"

"Watch it!"

"No, you watch it! I get it, you're throwing your weight around, you're insecure, so you compromise by acting like a thundering cunt, there's a reason you almost lost your job in that whistleblower fiasco, now! After preaching to my best detective about ambiguous morals and shady legality, suspending him indefinitely, forcing him to partake in a course that he could teach blindfolded, you turn around and do something ten times worse."

"He was following the course green lit by us!"

"By you, you dozy twat, I voted against it, it was you, Hooligan, Harris and that other gobshite. But I stood by it because it was my job to stand by it. But I'm not going to stand by and watch as you completely fuck up a unit I have come to respect and admire. You've just set a murderer free! He's going to walk out of here! After preaching to him about stealing cookies and then lying to his face. You do realise he's a fuckin law student! Even if we try to hold him any longer...do you realise who his mother is? I've been holding off anybody with a phone trying to contact her until we knew, for sure... we could press charges. Now! He doesn't even need her!!!! Just give him the key and tell him to walk right out the door, why don't ya? Give him a coupon book and a stamp for every woman he assaults, maybe after five you can give him a free blowjob."

"You can't talk to me like that!"

"Like what? sure we all know the only reason

you kept your job is because you give good head."

"That is way out of line."

"And where did you find that fuckin air-headed hippy? That O' Hara, or whatever her name is. I read the report on how that fiasco went. How in God's name is she qualified in dealing with monsters, and murderers and rapists!!"

"We have to move with the times..."

"Enough with that shit. You don't break something that's already fixed. If this gets out, if this gets leaked to the press."

"It won't."

"I'm going to have to go into that room and tell him, with a happy face, that he's free to go, and to thank him for his time."

"He was going to con..."

"TO THANK HIM FOR HIS TIME! Why would you greenlight an approach like that? Sure any gobshite with a brain cell would know there was no blood in his apartment. And...AND...the girl is still missing..."

"We can still charge him."

"LINDA! GET YOUR ARSE IN HERE! And I'm telling you something now, woman, if that girleen is dead, I'm blaming you. I don't care if she's been lying dead in a ditch for the past week,

I'm blaming you..."

Linda politely knocked on the door.

"JUST GET IN HERE! Tell the rest of them to get back to work!"

Linda entered as Deeley watched the others scarper back to the desks behind her.

"Doctor, is it all right if I call you doctor?"

"Yes Ma'am."

"After spending a reasonable amount of time with this unit, do you feel that the Detective in charge is more than capable of leading this unit?

"I do Ma'am."

"Do you think he should be on suspension?"

"No Ma'am, we need him here." Linda saw that Brady was in floods of tears.

"Right answer. Can you call him and tell him to get his skinny arse down here? We need him back. Tell him we need to start this investigation over."

"Yes Ma'am, right away."

Linda didn't bother waiting around as she ran to her office to find her phone.

"Now, Deputy Commissioner Brady, I think myself and yourself need to bring this matter in front of Commissioner James. Don't you agree?"

***

CHAPTER 16 --- O.C.E.A.N

Jimmy was exhausted. The case had taken any goodness that was left inside of him and incinerated it all with the sadness, terror and grief that was associated with a missing persons case, especially that of a young woman.

He was glad to be back at it, truth be told, he had spent a lot of his time reading while he was on suspension, it was a long couple of months, but he got through it all right. He was an avid member of the chess club, and when that lost its appeal, went out to darts tournaments, pool tournaments, poker... any tournaments that were on down at his local. Those only happened a couple of evenings a week. By the end of his suspension, he was frequenting the local on a daily basis, having the odd whiskey, sitting with the oul fellas checking the form sheets on the gee gees.

The only difficulty he was facing with his suspension was how long it was going to last, the uncertainty loomed before him like a never-ending highway. This uncertainty caused him anxiety, and anytime he felt it coming on, he'd close his eyes and meditate, dropping deeper, ever so deeper, to the point he felt like he was on another realm, warm and peaceful and happy, letting any colours and lights flash around him, his chest barely breathing, every muscle in his body completely relaxed.

Patience was his greatest virtue as his phone lay dormant. It dawned on him, that when he wasn't working, his phone never rang. It became such an obtrusive device with it's constant belling and whistling, that Jimmy was glad of the peace and quiet, although it did trouble him to some degree that he had no friends outside of his work.

The phone frightened the bejesus out of him when he least expected it. He was dozing in his recliner, listening to John Prine, dozing to the point he was dreaming the lyrics, until the phone tore him back to reality. When he saw that it was work, he immediately snapped awake, clearing his throat as he answered.

"Hello?"

"Hi…Jimmy?"

"Linda?"

She sounded breathless, almost excited. It sounded sweet on Jimmy's ear.

"Deeley wants you back, Jimmy."

"What happened?"

Linda re-counted everything with great gusto and enthusiasm. The terrible interrogation, the great blunder, the ear rollicking given to Brady by Deeley. Linda sounded like a schoolgirl with the hottest gossip in town.

"He lied to the suspect and said they found blood in his apartment?" Jimmy asked, perplexed.

"Deeley was so quick, we all missed it." Linda was now gushing over the phone.

"Did that O' Hora one have anything to do with this?"

"It was all constructed by her."

"What was the approach?"

"Well, it was the PEACE technique, and good cop, bad cop, and then...let me think...there was the War of Attrition technique...followed by, the Cookie Jar technique.

"Fuck." Jimmy was glad he walked out on that stupid training course when he did. Saner heads had prevailed. He was never a fan of the PEACE technique, or the 'no comment' technique, as he liked to call it. This life therapist, or whatever she was, was convinced that in order for a suspect to confess, you kept them to minimal answers until you came to the big crescendo, Jimmy knew now what that crescendo was, it was one thing claiming you had false evidence, it was another describing the false evidence you had.

"They tried to stitch him up, didn't they? Guilt him with the cookie jar mindset and then hit him with such an outlandish lie he'd be up in arms and confess to the whole thing."

"Deeley called Brady out on that, called it double standards. You should have seen the way she tore into Brady, why would they punish you and then turn around and green light an approach like that?

"My speculation is they were convinced the guy murdered her at his place. They felt 100% sure he'd confess."

"Yeah, well now Deeley is pissed and she's on the warpath, she want's you in ASAP."

"She didn't mention my skinny arse by any chance."

Linda giggled, she had a nice giggle.

"Okay, let me get showered and freshened up,

I'll get my skinny arse in as soon as I can."

#

The case was tainted alright, nothing could be used in evidence. They'd have to start from the beginning, which meant canvassing the entire area, and because Jimmy was playing catch up, him and the team would have to find any reports and evidence that wasn't tainted, retype them, and add them to the new case file. Bureaucracy in a nutshell.

The nice thing about being back in the office was that the team were all glad to see him. He could tell that although Linda was added to the unit as a mole, she was becoming a vital member of the team. Jimmy needed all hands on deck. He'd have to inspect every photograph, re-trace Myia Dawkins steps leading up to the disappearance, but before he could do any of that, he was going to have to build a profile. He couldn't look at the interrogation, he had to be completely unbiased when performing his evaluation.

The disappearance of Myia Dawkins was a baffling one. She had vanished without a trace. There was no suspicious activity relating to her bank account, no reported sightings of her anywhere. What was most baffling was there was no sign of forced entry, no sign of a struggle, if she was abducted, it had to have been out in public?

He was only in the office a few hours when the call came in, another case, another missing girl, 12-year-old Stephanie Madden, who was missing for 24 hours, last seen leaving school. Jimmy had to think quick and act quicker. He was going to have Hobbs and Rodge work the Dawkins case, while the rest of them focused on Stephanie Madden.

"What?! Seriously?" Hobbs had asked.

"I need you, both of you. You know the case inside and out. The only difference now is that you have me back, we need to re-write everything, re-interview everyone, add anything we may have missed."

"It's just, we thought, after, you know?"

"After what?"

"After our...blunder, we'd be transferred or worse."

"Why the fuck would I do that? How long have we known each other, Hobbs?"

"A long time."

"That's right. And that...clerical error...or blunder...or whatever you want to call it...that wasn't your fault. I don't blame you for what happened, none of us do, you were following orders. That's it. The only thing I ask of you is look at this fresh, I need a blank face if I'm going to build this profile. Okay?"

Rodge and Hobbs both nodded gleefully, before they all hugged each other and gave each other the heterosexual number of slaps on the back.

There was no time to waste, they needed the bullpen, and they needed to build two profiles. They gathered and got to work, with such clinical speed and accuracy that Linda was in awe. When they were working the Dawkins case the first time around, it was each to their own, before any information was sent to Brady and O'Hora, now, it was like a scene out of the TV show 'The Wire.'

People were frantically writing on whiteboards with blue markers, pinning photographs of the missing victims to the large noticeboard, along with maps, anything that could prove relevant in solving these cases. Everything was all neat and organized as they all ran in a flurry around her. Abed was making phone calls, getting task forces ready in the search for Stephanie Madden, while updating the task force who were searching for Myia, putting out an A.P.B to all other units, the coastguard, even the Navy.

Finding both victims needed a lot of manpower. The Major Crimes Unit would have to overlook the entire police force of Galway City as they went about collecting witness testimony, performing roadblocks, not to mention, the realms of paperwork that had to be filled out and phone calls that had to be answered. Every lead had to be followed up, every tip had to be looked at. There used to be a time in Galway you'd get a mysterious case in the space of a year, now, there were two in a matter of months.

Linda was flapping her arms, not knowing where to start, looking like a babe lost at sea.

"What do you want me to do?" She asked Jimmy.

"Psychoanalysis, anything you think worthy write it on the whiteboard, headings and subheadings."

The team were lighting quick, it was obvious that this wasn't their first rodeo. By the time Linda had gotten her thought process in order, Kiki, Hobbs and Rodge had neatly written out different headings related to the cases, leaving blank spaces underneath for additional information.

The headings they so neatly scribbled included, background information of victim, underneath were the subheadings, social conduct, employment, hobbies, family relationships, physical condition, reputation, domestic setting and weather conditions.

Linda couldn't stop smiling at the level of

co-operation that was to be found. It wasn't the same unit she joined a couple of months ago. It made her think about social media, how a tool that could band people together to cure cancer, Ebola and HIV, was instead used by the masses for virtue signaling, trying to destroy the reputation of people they didn't like just for their own self-gratification.

Hobbs had managed to download arial photographs of Galway City off google maps, before pinning them anywhere on the walls he could find space. While abed was nattering on the phone, the receiver clamped between shoulder and chin, he was frantically typing out new case files, getting them formatted in such a way, that anything relevant could be added quickly.

Linda stood next to Kiki, as she drew lines under the sub headings.

"What about victim risk?" She asked.

"Well then write it down, woman" Kiki replied.

"Aayyy! We accept her one of us, we accept her one of us, gooba gobble, gooba gobble..." Abed was singing the tune from the classic film 'Freaks,' much to the bemusement of the person he was speaking to on the other end of the line.

"Spot on." Jimmy said gently. "We can place that next to background information."

Linda went to a fresh space at the board and neatly wrote out the words VICTIM RISK in large, bold, capital letters. Underneath she wrote the sub-headings – Abduction risk, personal stresses, emotional maturity.

Kiki ran around the other side of Linda and wrote out ESCALATION in large scrawling letters, before adding the phrases, time factor and location factor.

"We need your witchy sense, your psychological whatchamacallit." Kiki said.

"Now that," Linda said as she began to write, "I can do."

Beginning at the top of the whiteboard and working her way down a left-hand side of the board, Linda wrote out the letters O, C, E, A, N.

"What's that?" Rodge asked, looking interested.

"In cases such as abduction or kidnapping, in order to build a sound psychological profile of any and all potential suspects, you can't go wrong following this acronym. Working on this..." Linda said, pointing to the acronym," answers your questions to all of these." She concluded, waving her hand at the whiteboards. She then proceeded to fill in the blanks.

Open to experience

Conscientiousness

Extroversion

Agreeableness

Neuroticism

"Compare these to the profile of the victims, their risk, the offender's risk, and you have a pretty solid understanding of the psychology of your suspect, when you connect all of these, then Bob's your uncle and Billy's your aunt."

It took them two days to come up with their criminal profiles. Days that included long hours, a lot of hair pulling, cheap fast food, gallons of coffee, manic laughter, grouchiness, arguing, shouting, dead ends, and eureka moments. Linda loved every minute of it. She was even impressed by the input given by Hobbs and Rodge, their total recall of anything related to Myia Dawkins from their first investigation was jaw dropping.

Jimmy didn't think the case of Myia Dawkins was related to the case of Stephanie Madden. She wasn't from Galway, and she was much older, so the age profile didn't fit. This information came much to the dismay of his superiors, who gathered in the large office space, the bull pen, to hear Jimmy's reasoning and to lay out the criminal profiles of the suspects.

"In the Stephanie Madden case, we're looking

at a white male, between 25 and 35. He has an average appearance. We know he is local, as he would not look out of place in the area."

"How do you know he's white?" Houlihan demanded. The room was so packed with officers and suits Jimmy found it difficult to breathe with all the heat.

"Serial murderers tend not to cross racial lines, normally in cases of crimes such as this one, it takes about ten years to manifest this kind of psychosis, that's why we're saying 25 to 35, however, I wouldn't put him much older than 30. He's progressing...this is probably his first time, if he was say...ten years older, we'd have a full blown serial killer on our hands.

"Right?"

"He has below average intelligence, meaning he is unemployed, on the dole or on disability and if he is working, it would be in menial labour. He is sexually inadequate, has a large pornographic collection on his hard drive. This isn't a man who is rejected by women, this is...morbid curiosity. Because of the location of her disappearance, I'd be confident in admitting they lived close to one another. This is a man with possible mental health issues. I think there was an accomplice, a younger woman, a teenager perhaps, he would date younger women if he dated at all, because of his limited intelligence, his only conquests in dating, would be with these young, vulnerable, women, more than likely somebody from a broken home, with a drug habit, as he is able to dominate and control relationships in those types of situations."

"Do you think this second accomplice is involved in helping commit the crime?"

"She definitely helped abduct the victim, there's no way she'd get into a car driven by a man much older than her, unless she was coaxed. Victim risk is high, because of where she was abducted, her size, her age, we don't think she's alive...unfortunately. Our suspect is a recluse. He's malnourished. He would be an ectomorph. If he has a car, it'd be messy, he has no form of organization. This idea, however, has been brewing in his mind for some time, he's been building up to this level of violent behaviour. He has a criminal record."

"Why isn't Myia Dawkins related to this case?" Brady asked. Jimmy's superiors were beginning to sound like journalists. They were all gawping at him in fascination. He felt like The Elephant Man John Merrick.

"The age profile doesn't fit, neither does the criminal profile, not to mention her place is spotless, bar the hair samples that were found, that belonged to several people who visited her at her home, there are no other signs to suggest that any kind of malice took place. We've gathered another profile for that case, we're looking for two, if not three, killers."

"Can you give us your profile on that case? Just out of curiosity."

"The only thing the two profiles have in common are their age and race, after that, they skew off in two completely different directions. Our prime suspect in the Myia Dawkins disappearance is highly intelligent, and somewhat organized, maybe not so much in his habitat. His state of mind portrays his living environment. Dr Ní Gorman can fill you in more on his psychological aspects."

Jimmy needed to sit down before he fainted from exhaustion. He was pulling sixteen hour shifts since these cases began, only getting two hours sleep every night. It was enough to keep him going, but everybody at work could see the strain on his face, the bags under his eyes, the redness of his eyeballs, the dirty stubble that was growing on his face. Jimmy was normally clean cut and well presentable in all manners of life, clean shaven, in stylish suits, his hair well kept... now...his clothes were crumpled, his glasses were kept together with tape, he was a mess.

Linda cleared her throat and checked her notes. What Jimmy liked about Linda was in matters of professional courtesy, she made sure she was 100% right in what she was about to say before the words flowed out of her mouth.

“In order for us to build the criminal profile, we had to look at the OCEAN acronym.”

“What’s that?” Houlihan demanded. Jimmy wondered was Houlihan a big cuddly teddy bear in private and the thought made him smile.

“Open to experience, conscientiousness, extroversion, agreeableness, and neuroticism. It seems like he subconsciously prepared for the crime but couldn’t go through with it, not until some major event pushed him over the edge. We’re thinking due to the timing of her disappearance and speaking to her family, it was because she was leaving Galway and moving back to Athlone.”

Everyone nodded and hummed, not taking their eyes of Linda, who began to feel extremely self-conscious from the amount of attention she was receiving.

“Suspect seems to have a high level of openness with experience. He lives in a fantasy world of his own creation. He has high conscientiousness, and comes across as a very dependable, reliable person. He’s a notorious introvert, a misanthropic with grand ideals. Agreeable with no history of violence, and is very in control over his actions and emotions. His behaviour aligns with paraphilia along with cluster A personality features. We believe he may be part of the ever-growing incel movement."

"How did you get to this conclusion?"

"The lack of a crime scene, the comparison of records to archived crime scenes, all fit the profile. He has Schizotypal Personality Disorder, believes in odd ideas and magical thinking, obsessive ruminations without inner resistance, somatosensory illusions, overelaborate thinker, I mean the list goes on. This is a suspect who was so infatuated with his victim that he couldn't let anybody else have her. What is most troublesome, is that he suffers from occasional transient quasi-psychotic episodes with intense illusions, coupled with delusional ideas, normally occurring without any kind of external provocation. The disorder is known to run through chronic courses with fluctuating bouts of intensity."

"Meaning?"

"Meaning, it will take a person, a place of interest, something that peaks his attention, to trigger him off again. Not to mention the fact that now, if he is alive, he feels above the law, which will only make him supremely confident in any action he takes in the future."

Jimmy stood again, next to Linda, he wanted to wrap this charade up and get back to work.

"The differences between the two profiles are ying and yang. We have a pair of disorganized killers and one extremely organized killer who is very careful not to leave any evidence. That's the bare bones of it…now let's go out and catch these fuckers."

A large round of applause thundered through the bull pen, ending the profiling session, which seemed to rejuvenate everybody, giving them motivation into bringing these prime suspects to justice.

***

CHAPTER 17 --- THE PROBLEM WITH STEPHANIE

The problem with Stephanie Madden was nobody had seen hide nor hair of her since she skipped out of school on a Wednesday evening a fortnight ago. Once her classes were finished for the day, she had walked out with her classmates, excited about going to her friends birthday party.

Her teacher, Ms. Lopez, watched Stephanie walk to the end of the playground and wave at a young lady, before Stephanie approached the young lady and began chatting. Ms. Lopez then watched the young lady take Stephanie by the hand and walk out of the school gates, down the garden path by the river that led to the cathedral, disappearing from view. Her teacher assumed it was her mother, or an older sister, and was distraught when she was told one of her students went missing.

She stated that she saw a slender girl with long brunette hair but couldn't make out her features. She was wearing a tracksuit, along with a pink jacket that had a large hood. Ms. Lopez assumed somebody had come to collect her and never thought anything more about it until the Gardaí came knocking at her door. It left the woman a mess, and she had to quit her teaching position due to the guilt she felt. Jimmy couldn't help feeling sorry for the woman.

Even with all of the technology that Jimmy had at his disposal, they couldn't keep track of Stephanie's whereabouts. They had CCTV footage of her walking with the suspect down the lane towards the cathedral, but there was a blind spot along the wall of the cathedral, next to the old hospital, where large coaches would collect students on a Friday afternoon.

Out of all the CCTV footage that they could grab from anywhere around the city, that camera, situated in the trees along the stone wall, directly across the road from the cathedral, had been out of service for two years. The council never got around to fixing it.

Jimmy came up with a theory that there was a car waiting for Stephanie at the cathedral, and the suspect had bundled her into the back seat and driven away.

Jimmy and his team canvassed the whole area where Stephanie disappeared, they questioned everybody along the route of the cathedral, but nobody had seen anything out of the ordinary. They even went about the entire university campus, questioning lecturers and students, but Jimmy found students to be about as useful as a pair of tits on a bull when it came to eyewitness reports, they were so locked away in their own little dreamworld that when they walked to and from that university over the bridge towards the courthouse, they couldn't make out one day from the next.

The area around the university, cathedral, courthouse and theatre bustled so much with people and traffic that seeing a young lady in a pink hooded jacket walking hand in hand with a young 12-year-old girl didn't seem out of the ordinary. Students with any wits about them or who had any agenda with authority and the government, refused flat out to speak to any Gardaí personnel involved in the disappearance

They searched every CCTV of every bus that drove along that route, from the time she disappeared until an hour after her disappearance, but there was nobody that boarded or exited the buses that fit Stephanie or the young woman's description.

After 17 days and no leads, it was decided

by Deeley that they should go on the television show CrimeCall to appeal to the public to come forward with any information they had, and Jimmy was the patsy that had to appear in front of the camera. This would be his first time in the public eye since his infamous interrogation of Sebastian Rivers.

The problem was, the Irish public didn't forget any authorities' mishaps in a hurry, and he knew the media would have a frenzy as soon as his mug appeared on television.

Jimmy had to push his ego to one side and face the grilling of the media and the public with as much grace and professionalism that he could muster in order to find Stephanie. So, he went on CrimeCall, and spoke about the case, showing the CCTV footage of Stephanie leaving the school with their prime suspect, asking the viewers at home to call in if they had any information, no matter how minor the details.

Social media was in a frenzy the following day, and Jimmy's face appeared on all major newspaper outlets, he became a trend on twitter, and the general public had no problem dragging his name and reputation through the mud. He was tagged with the moniker 'crooked Jimmy,' portrayed in memes that depicted him in conversation with Sebastian Rivers with phrases such as, 'confess baby shaker.' And 'I know you're a good guy when you're not killing babies.' Ridiculing his interrogation technique, implying that you were guilty in the eyes of Jimmy Daniels. Even if you had nothing to do with the crime, Jimmy Daniels would make you confess.

Jimmy had received so many messages on Twitter ridiculing him that he lost count. He skimmed through them, trying not to emotionally react to the messages. One message did catch his eye, which he found witty, even though it was horribly dark and distasteful. The message came in the form of a joke and read 'Why doesn't #StephanieMadden have an Xbox Series X? Because I have a PlayStation 5 (wink emoji face.) #jimmydaniels #dirtycop #stupidpig #fuckthegardaí. The tweet was sent by the profile Art Vistas.

Jimmy knew his prime suspect wouldn't be as stupid as to leave a message of such disregard on a public social media platform. But he was in a bad mood, so he tracked the message IP address that lead to a computer in a call centre that sold insurance around the Ballybrit area. An armed Garda unit burst into the offices to arrest the shocked hipster employee, with conspiracy and aiding and abetting in a kidnapping.

They brought the self-proclaimed, nongender, antifascist to the station and held him in a cell overnight, grilling him for details. Jimmy watched the government hating socialist break down in tears and swear to the heavens and back that he knew nothing about the disappearance.

"But which one was it Art? Was it the Xbox or the Playstation?"

"It was just a joke!"

"What games did you buy her? C'mon, tell us, I mean, how would you know something like that? What is it the kids play these days anyway, Fortnite? Or something? Does she have an account online Art? Did you make her the account? That's what it is isn't it? You're keeping her occupied when you're at work."

"I swear, I don't know! I don't know anything! I'm sorry! Please, just let me go."

Jimmy showed mercy and released the hipster to the prying hounds of the media, who were camped in front of the station. After that incident the trolling died down on social media and five days after Jimmy's Crime Call appearance, there was a breakthrough in the case.

After sorting through many anonymous tips that the hotline had received, most of them being bogus, they managed to come across one that held ground. A male heroin junkie, who didn't wish to be named, stated that on that day, he had seen a young woman by the name of Britney Robertson, walk hand in hand with a young girl down along the river where he was sitting, monging out with his girlfriend.

He stated that Britney was wearing a tracksuit and a pink jacket with a large hood. The man also said he knew Britney because he bought drugs from her. The Junkie recalled shouting out to Britney, asking if she was holding and getting no reply. Britney kept her mouth shut, zipped up her hood around her face and continued walking. When he asked if there was a reward for his information, and was declined, he hung up shouting the phrase 'typical fuckin pigs,' before the line went dead.

Another tip came from a woman who was collecting money for a 'charity' in front of the cathedral, who also did not wish to be named, leading Jimmy to believe that she was scamming money from people. These charity cons were common around the city, all a person needed was a large white bucket, a yellow vest and a fake laminated badge showing what bogus charity they were collecting for.

The woman had stated that around the same time of Stephanie's disappearance, she had seen a woman in a pink jacket pick up a girl when they were crossing the road at the cathedral and bundle her into the backseat of an old manual Silver Audi, before speeding away. She claimed that she couldn't see who was driving, but guessed it was male, due to the size of his shoulders and the way he wore his baseball cap, down low, over his eyes. She also asked was there a reward for her information and when asked what charity she worked with, said "I have to check my pictures," before hanging up.

The silver Audi was a good tip, and the timeline matched the one of the junkie's description, along with the time of Stephanie's disappearance.

They ran through various digital footage of manual silver Audis who happened to be driving around the city at that time. Because Tesla had become so popular and affordable, and with impending laws banning people from driving manual vehicles, there weren't that many silver Audi's driving around, the remaining belonging to either speed freaks on the Westside who liked to race each other, or by people refusing to give up their old ways.

They spotted three that drove around the city at that time, and one in particular, which could be seen heading past the theatre, down through Terryland, and out towards Tuam past Bóthair Na Mór, before the city CCTV lost track of their vehicle.

They spotted a male driver, who wore a baseball cap that covered his eyes, but no sign of Britney or Stephanie. They tracked the car as far as they could, it was seen stopping at two different locations. The small android security robots situated outside Supermac's in Ballintubber had footage recorded of a silver Audi stopping, and a woman in a pink jacket clambering out of the back in an awkward manner, using the automated paying system with her watch to pay for food, collecting the food from the dispensary machine and then leaving.

Another camera spotted the Audi pulling up at a Woodie's DIY in Castlebar, again the young woman clambered out of the back, headed inside, ordered black bin bags and a claw hammer from the digital input system, paid with credits, and collected her items at the collection desk a few minutes later.

After that, there was no sign of the car, or where it went, although it was spotted arriving back in the city that night, the investigative team had a tough time tracing their whereabouts when leaving the town of Castlebar.

Mayo was a big county, and like in all parts of the country, it was forbidden to track all movements of citizens, after The Freedom of Information Act was seriously altered, thanks to successful campaigns by the public that it was a violation of their basic human rights to be monitored at all times.

The Gardaí still had a right to search where

you had been and your activities by obtaining search warrants, for your home, vehicle and any digital items that belong to you, but they needed probable cause, they couldn't just delve into a person's activities without first speaking to a judge. Thankfully, Jimmy had probable cause.

The last known tracking of Britney's credit watch was on the ground of an alleyway that ran alongside woodies, smashed to smithereens, along with two phone batteries. *'Cute fuckers.'* Jimmy thought to himself. There was no way of knowing where they drove to next, manual cars did not have built in trackers, and the suspects were savvy enough to know that the gardai could track their movements via satellites from their phone coverage.

Mayo was full of vast fields, bogs, wild landscapes, large lakes and mountains, and the government never bothered upgrading the road system, not like they did in what they considered important counties, such as Galway, Cork, and Dublin, where they forced families to relocate from desolated rural areas into bourgeois cities that ran along the main highway network.

Counties like Mayo still had the same road system it had in the early noughties, which meant that there was still many backroads a car could take, that weren't registered under official mapping Satnav guides, where someone could easily disappear if they wanted to commit a crime or vanish without trace from the authorities.

Jimmy, Linda, Kiki and Abed spent hours meticulously reaming over cctv footage of the Mayo highway that led into Galway city. Hobbs and Rodge were working on the disappearance of Myia Dawkins, following up leads as to where she might be.

The four detectives gaped at monitors for hours on end, pulling up any vehicle that looked like their suspects silver Audi, seeing if the license plate matched. They had to make sure the entire day's footage was searched, not wanting to leave any inconsistencies a defense team could later challenge in court. So, they tracked every car that looked like the car they were searching for, even though their timeline showed the suspects to be driving around Mayo at that very same time.

Finally, after much muttering by Linda, rotten dry jokes by Abed, and constant swearing and dramatical exclamations by Kiki, they finally found the car driving into Terryland, the time stamped on the footage shown was 11:23 pm, on the same night young Stephanie had disappeared. The silver Audi could be seen, waiting at the traffic lights near the shopping centre, the road slick with rain. Whatever they had done, whether the little girl was dead somewhere or still in the car with them, they could now track the car to its primary destination.

"I found the fuckers!" Kiki had shouted in her thick Galwegian, Haitian accent, and the rest of the detectives all clambered around her monitor screen. The car registration was under the name of Britney Robertson, now, they had to find out who the male suspect was.

"Abed, you been eating them cheesy snacks again? Please, give the woman some space."

"I always said you'd make it as a varsity athlete." Abed replied, smiling, he was in the midst of watching the classic TV show, The Sopranos, for the first time, at Jimmy's recommendation, and was now quoting famous lines from the show any chance he could get. Quoting them wrong, but quoting them none the less.

"Kiki, see if you can pull up the footage from the hospital, near the traffic lights." Jimmy asked, peering down through the end of his spectacles.

"What are you thinking?" Linda asked, as she gazed on admiringly. It was no secret that Linda had a crush on Jimmy, something which always amused their colleagues. Abed popped a fresh mint in his mouth, before winking at Kiki, who tried not to laugh. Abed couldn't help but joke around, even in the most stressful of situations.

"How is my breath now, Kiki?"

"Back to your usual, sweet smelling aromatic self." Kiki replied, returning her concentration to her monitor screen.

"Like an angel shitting in my mouth, eh?"

"Shh." Jimmy was frowning now; he couldn't see the Audi go anywhere near the hospital.

"Jimmy?"

"Hmm?"

"What is it you're thinking?" Linda asked again.

"I'm thinking he's heading to Westside, but he's not taking the main route. Unless...Kiki, pull up the cameras to the back entrance of the hospital gates."

Jimmy was referring to the small road the ran through the hospital grounds and ended at the dual carriageway that ran all the way through Westside.

"There he is!" Kiki exclaimed, pointing a well-manicured index finger at the screen.

The Silver Audi could clearly be seen stopping at the traffic lights, indicating it was turning left to head down through Westside.

“Can you freeze the image and enhance it please?” Jimmy asked patiently. It took Kiki mere seconds to get a close up of the figure in the driver seat.

“Shit.” Jimmy couldn’t see a face, the figure looked masculine, well built, with a baseball cap shielding the features of his face.

“Young male, late twenties to early thirties, Let’s see if this fella has any distinguishing marks or tattoos.”

“Where is Britney?” Linda asked. “The passenger seat looks empty.”

“Beats me, unless she stayed with the victim.” Jimmy responded.

Kiki zoomed in on the image as much as she could, first on the darkened face of the suspect, then on the knuckles gripping the driver’s wheel. With the advancement of digital technology, and the effort by the station to have the best possible technological devices available to all of its officers and detectives, the zoomed image looked as clear as the original footage, with barely any pixilation.

Kiki grabbed the image of the face and the image of the knuckles and placed them side by side on a split screen before running a deep 360 degree scan to pick up any minor details on the image.

Jimmy had trained his team never to get emotionally attached to any case, and rather than rushing to a judge for a search warrant, they kept investigating, trying to piece in together any new bits of information they could find on the screen.

"Kiki? Would it be possible to do a 90 degree swing to the side of the car?" Linda asked, softly.

"Yeah, they have good cameras at the hospital, they can shoot from all angles."

"Great, can I get a view of the backseats of the car, looking down into the vehicle?"

"What are *you* thinking?" Jimmy asked Linda as he took off his spectacles and rubbed the tiredness from his eyes.

"I'm thinking, bags, items on the backseat, anything that looks suspicious..."

Linda was cut short by the rapidness of how quickly Kiki managed to get a close-up view of the rear passenger seats of the vehicle. Something odd caught her eye, there was no back seat whatsoever. It looked shadowy and dark, but empty.

"Can you zoom in on the space behind the passenger seat?" Linda asked, circling the area on the screen that she wanted enhanced with her pinky finger.

Kiki enhanced the image by another 60%.

"Empty, it's empty, what about the driver's seat, check in behind there?"

Kiki rapidly enhanced the image directly in behind the driver's seat.

"Do you see something?" Jimmy was now looking at the area closely, but he couldn't see anything out of the ordinary.

"I thought I saw...an outline of something... there...Kiki...zoom in there. Bring up the contrast and brightness if you can."

The enhanced image showed a bulk of pink, shadowed in blackness.

"A pink bulk, it could be Stephanie wrapped in something."

"Or Britney is hiding in the back seat, she could be hunched on the floor, and that's the back of her hood, but why would she hide?"

Abed studied the screen. "Because they had Stephanie hiding in the back, and Britney was sitting on the floor, beside her, comforting her, making sure she wasn't scared. That's why we couldn't see Stephanie in the car when she was abducted. This was pre-planned."

"In what way?"

"Well, my guess is they stripped the back seat

beforehand, in the anticipation of kidnapping a little girl."

"But how could they know Stephanie was going to be on her own?" Kiki asked, turning her head away from her work, looking almost innocently at Abed, like she knew the information but needed clarification, like she needed somebody else to say it to her out loud.

"I really don't think they gave a shit what she looked like, as long as they found somebody, young, vulnerable, and on their own."

"Let's see where he goes." Jimmy said, encouraging Kiki to play the footage further. She tapped the screen and brought up cctv footage from various cameras along Westside and down into the estates, a multitude of mini screens appeared on the monitor, and Kiki highlighted the Audi on each of the clips.

They tracked the car driving all the way through Westside, until the car got to the roundabout and kept driving out west into more countryside, Jimmy knew where they were going. There was a large council estate up there, known as Forest Green, originally built for the middle class elite, but after the housing crisis, the council had no choice but to move people who were on the housing lists, a lower common class of people, into the estate.

Because of this, over a ten year period, the people who bought properties sold them back to the council, not wanting to associate themselves with a certain manner of class who were comfortable in waiting for the council to give them a brand new house and a subsidiary payment every week.

This made Forest Green a lower class haven, a rough estate. The kids that lived on the estate, ran in gangs, sold drugs, mugged people and had managed to break every CCTV camera that was on the estate. Jimmy knew that the silver Audi was going there, because there was nothing past that, end of the line. It was also where Sebastian Rivers lived...

***

CHAPTER 18 --- CRY ME A RIVER

"The problem you got is you're going to have to make people believe that you were only a few feet away from that car, but you're like the monkeys, see no evil, speak no evil, hear no evil, you're saying you're just a few feet away but you're saying you didn't see how Sebastian got blood all over his face and his clothes, and how Stephanie is nowhere to be seen.

You said that you didn't want to see it, but that doesn't change the fact that you saw it, no matter how much you were willing it not to happen, no matter how much you pleaded with Sebastian not to do it, no matter how much you turned your back to what he was doing to her, that doesn't change the fact that you saw it. You need to speak the truth Britney, and I know that's hard to talk about, I know that anything that happened after you grabbed Stephanie from the school is hard to talk about, but the most important thing right now, Britney, are you listening? The most important thing right now is that you tell me the truth."

"But I didn't do anything!!" Britney sobbed, her eyes full of tears, swiping her way through a box of Kleenex on the table, wiping her eyes and blowing her nose. She was being overdramatic, playing the innocent victim. Three times she had asked to go home, and Jimmy got the impression that if she sat in this interview room long enough, and cried for a couple of hours, she would get her wish. Jimmy had seen this act performed countless times from female suspects he interrogated, he nicknamed it the 'boohoo' technique, and knew exactly what to say next.

"The thing is Britney, you've been quite honest with me since you came in here with me today, and I really do appreciate that Britney, okay? I really do. But there's stuff you're not telling me."

"I just don't understand why you muhmegorralladis..." Her voice trailed off in a flood of tears.

"What?"

"I said I don't understand why you're making me go through all of this, it's horrible!" Britney finished the sentence with an extra dose of sobbing, tears and loud sniffing. There were streams of tears running down her cheeks, mixing in with the watery snot that was pouring from her nostrils.

"Because it's important, because it's my job. So what I need you to do is to take a deep breath, gather your thoughts, and tell me what happened."

Jimmy patiently waited for Britney to finish her crying fit and calm down. He knew that if he waited long enough, she'd stop, it would become awkward for her to keep up the crying charade with nobody giving her any understanding or support.

Jimmy needed to cut out any denials and keep her confidence low. As Jimmy remained seated, he rolled in his desk chair closer to her, blocking the entrance at the far side of the room, making her feel like she was trapped, making her realise there was no chance in hell she was going home.

"I've been telling the truth; I haven't bullshitted you or anything like that..."

"I know."

"I couldn't watch but I couldn't help it, that's why I kept turning away, it was all in bits and pieces. It's like when you see a cat get hit by a car, and it's all mangled like, flattened, and you don't want to look but you can't help it. That's what it was like when Sebastian had Stephanie on his lap. I didn't want to watch, even though he tried to make me, and I could hear her crying, she was calling my name!" Britney broke down again, this time, the emotion seemed genuine.

"Tell me what happened?" Jimmy said, his voice coming across like a cool breeze on a summer's day.

"I went for a walk, it was all wilderness, I didn't see one car pass me on the road, and I did some kind of mad loop and found myself back at the car and I saw bin bags laid out on the ground, next to the car, I couldn't hear Stephanie, she wasn't crying anymore..."

Britney's voiced gargled as she grabbed more Kleenex, whatever part she played in this horrible crime, she was seeing the full brutality of it all as she recounted what took place.

"Anytime I walked back to the car, it was to hear if she was crying, because I knew if she was crying she was still alive, but I couldn't hear anything, and I knew right then that she wasn't okay, that she was knocked out, or something worse..."

"I don't care about what you heard; I want to know about what you saw. I know you didn't want to look; you kept your back turned, you walked away from the car and all that craic. But you said so yourself, you found it hard to look away. I need to know everything you saw."

Britney covered her face in her hands, weeping, shaking her head, refusing to comply.

"You know how I see things like this? I meet people all the time, it's part of my job, and I have to hear all manners of stories, all the time. Nothing you say is going to shock me because I've heard it all. I've concluded over the years from doing this kind of work, that there are two ways of telling a story that you don't want to tell. It's kind of like when you cut your hand and you need to wear a plaster.

One way is to do it slowly, have it pinching and hurting you as you try to peel the plaster off, another way is to pull it off quickly, and trust me when I tell you this, to tell me this story now and do it quickly, rather than me having to coax it out of you all night until morning, will emotionally hurt a lot more, and make no bones about it, if I have to keep you here until morning, I will. Better to just pull the band aid off quickly now and be done with it."

"He hurt her!"

"Go on."

"He kept kicking her in the ribs, I couldn't see everything at this point because I ran to the other side of the car, but I could see her little feet sticking out down at the tires. He kept kicking her, and I heard her moans get softer and softer, and then he put a bin bag on her head and started suffocating her. I could hear her gasping for breath…"

Britney couldn't continue and began to whoop with sadness, she had nearly gone through a full box of tissues by this point.

"Okay? What happened after that."

"He used a hammer…"

Britney's voice trailed off; Jimmy leaned in closer to her.

"You're going to have to speak up."

"I said, he used a hammer!" Britney grabbed the Kleenex box and threw it against the wall, past Jimmy's head, Jimmy didn't flinch. Britney wasn't boohooing anymore. Jimmy could see she was slowly morphing into the role of innocent bystander rather than culprit.

"Where did he hit her with the hammer?"

"On the back of her head. That's why there was no blood on the car, because he put a bin bag over her head, and wrapped it up tightly, and he belted her with the hammer, over and over. Fuck knows where he got the bin bags, he had them in the backseat."

This was a lie. The surveillance footage from the DIY store showed Britney buying the bags and hammer, not to mention the fact that there was no back seat in the car. Jimmy let her ramble on, anything she said now he could contradict later on.

"He kept tearing more bin bags off the roll and began wrapping her up in them like a mummy and tying them together with rope. Then he got another bin bag and put her feet in that one, and tied the bag shut. And that's the last time I saw her, it was when he was hitting her with the hammer, next to the car." Britney tried to compose herself, her face was red from crying, her hair was frizzled from the dry atmosphere in the room. She blew her nose with the tissue, before leaning her arm on the table next to her and resting her fist underneath her chin and closing her tired weeping eyes.

Jimmy wasn't buying it.

"Britney?"

Britney opened her eyes and looked at Jimmy.

"Okay, we're nearly at where we need to be. You did a good job at yanking the band aid off, now you need to tear off the last bit, you know the bit that dangles from your skin? The very edge of the plaster that's very sticky, and you need another yank just to get that last bit of plaster off? That's where we're at now."

Jimmy leaned in ever closer, his face barely a

foot away from Britney, who was seated right up against the brick wall.

"You didn't leave her there. You collected everything, the bin bags, the hammer, the rope, and you took Stephanie with you as well..."

Britney tried to convey shock at the accusation, but to Jimmy, it came across in a rather comical fashion.

"No, I would never do that!"

"Britney, listen to me for a second, okay?

Britney crossed her arms and sat in a defensive manner, pouting like a brat child.

"What you said doesn't make any sense."

"But I never..."

"It...doesn't...make...any...sense. Why would he bother going through the effort to wrap and tie her up in bin bags and just leave?"

"No, Stephanie didn't come with us, I'm like, 1000% positive on that."

"I don't know why you don't want to tell me, but you need to tell me the truth about where that girleen ended up."

"I haven't been lying..."

Jimmy cut her off, stopping the denial.

"She didn't stay in that field, if she did, we

would have found her by now."

"Yes, she did."

"She didn't!"

"Yes, she did! I don't know what else I can tell you..."

"She didn't!"

"Yes, she did!"

"It doesn't make you any more guilty not telling me where she's laying right now, you're as guilty as you can be..."

"Don't you think I know that?"

Jimmy was slowly breaking her, slowly getting under her skin. Jimmy needed to keep her mind going a mile a minute so Britney wouldn't be able to settle on one train of thought, to prevent her from coming up with a fabricated tale. She was going to break soon; he could sense it.

"You're as high as you can go now on the guilty scale, you have nothing to lose. This is already the most serious thing that you're being charged with, it doesn't get any worse than this.

"I'm telling you the truth."

Britney was waiting for another quick-fire response from the detective, only to be greeted with stone cold silence that lasted several minutes. The soundproof walls made it so that any noise generated in the room was quickly snuffed out, and as the minutes ticked by, Britney began to grow more restless, tapping her fingers off the table top and coughing loudly, to make any sound at all, than face the silence of justice before her. Eventually, after what seemed like an eternity, Jimmy let out a soft sigh.

"What way was Stephanie lying on the ground? Was she lying on her back or lying on her tummy?"

"I want to say that she was lying on her tummy, but like I said, I only kept glancing over so, I don't know, especially when she got wrapped up, it was hard to see what way she was lying. I know at one point he had her curled up on her side."

"Was she still alive?"

"Yeah, she was still moving, struggling, then Sebastian started belting her with the hammer."

"Did she say anything?"

"She was moaning, that was it." The floodgates opened once more, and Jimmy reached behind to grab the box of tissues off the ground, there were a few tissues left in the box. He handed them over to Britney, who eagerly swiped one from the box, and held it close to her face, almost like she was about to regress and suck her thumb. She treated the tissue like a security blanket, another defense mechanism in order to prepare herself psychologically for the rest of the interrogation.

"How many times did he hit her with the hammer?"

"I only saw, like, a couple of times, I don't know if it was three or four, it could have been three, I just heard the groans and the thuds, and I don't even know which side of the hammer he used..."

Britney's ramble was so quick and sudden that Jimmy lost interest in her reply. A crime of that magnitude, you remembered everything in vivid detail, your senses were enhanced, sharpened, that noise of the hammer hitting the skull would be so precise, an innocent victim or bystander would be able to recall exactly how many times the weapon was used. Jimmy had to amp up the pressure now, Britney wasn't as innocent as she was claiming to be. She was hiding something.

"When Sebastian was hitting her with the hammer, was there just a bin bag wrapped around her head, or was it..."

Jimmy was cut off by Britney blowing her nose. He never heard anything like it. It was like a foghorn going off, for a girl her size and stature, you would think it was an old man blowing his nose the way she was able to destroy the tissue.

"...was her whole body covered in binbags?"

"Just her head, he covered the rest of her a few minutes later."

"Did he make you help him?"

No reply, Britney looked at the floor, her face looked pained, as she relived horrific, gory details that flashed through her mind.

"He made you help him, didn't he?" Whispered Jimmy, leaning into her space, ever closer. "He made you cover her body in those bags. There's no way, even with a little girl that size, he could put her in those bags on her own, is there?"

Britney had stopped sniffling and fidgeting, she then covered her face with her hands and began to mumble, Jimmy could just about make out what she was mumbling.

"I opened the bags for him, I opened the bags so he could pick Stephanie up and lift her into the bag. I looked away when he was doing it. When he finished putting her in he put another bin bag over the top half of her and tied them together with rope."

"Did you see any blood on her body?"

"Around her...crotch."

"Okay." Jimmy leaned back in his chair and

crossed his legs, placing his arms behind his head. “Britney, what you’ve told me today, not a lot of people have the strength to do that. I appreciate everything you have told me, it’s very brave of you to do so. What I need for you to do now, is to help me piece in together the final bit of the puzzle.

Her parents are absolutely fuckin devastated, they’re at the point of no return when it comes to their grief. They’ll never feel whole again. What I need for you to do now Britney, is tell me where Stephanie is. I need you to help me bring her home, so the parents can at least mourn their child properly, and put her in her final resting place… We need to bring her home, Britney.”

“I told you before, we left her in that field… We, like, covered her in rocks, or something.”

“How many rocks was there?”

“I don’t know, three or four…” Britney was mumbling, ‘three of four’ seemed to be her answer when she didn’t have one or didn’t want to share what really happened.

“Three or four rocks? They must be extremely heavy rocks, to cover her with rocks of that magnitude, would they not crush her?”

“There was, like, this rock pile.”

“Okay?”

“There’s a tree beside the rock pile.”

“So you’re saying, in this field, this lush green field, with sheep, there’s a tree and a large rock-pile.”

“Yeah, the rockpile is at the edge.”

“The edge of what?”

“The field.”

“Along with the tree?”

“No, I mean…yes…and there were big green things.”

“Big green things?”

“Yeah, like, bushes.”

“Mmhh?”

“And he like threw her next to the rock pile…”

“That’s next to a tree, at the edge of a field, surrounded by bushes?”

“Yeah, and just, like dumped her in the rock pile, and like, pushed some rocks down on top of it, and treated her like trash and…”

Britney stopped abruptly and placed a red tear-stained cheek on the cooling surface of the metal table. Her lie was so bad that she had stopped believing it herself.

“Did you get any of her blood on you, on your

face or on your clothes, when you were helping Sebastian?"

"No."

"Are you sure?"

"Positive."

"Did you help lift rocks and place them on her body?"

"Yeah, I like, lifted one rock."

"Did you help Sebastian lift a rock?"

"No."

"So, there were three or four of these rocks."

"Yes."

"So, these were really big heavy rocks?"

"Yes."

"And you managed to lift one, all by your teeny tiny self?"

"I...don't know."

Britney kept her cheek pressed against the table, she let out the odd sniffle, she was there in body, but her mind seemed to be a million miles away.

"How did he make you help him; did he blackmail you, or, what did he say?"

"He said, 'You're in this just as much as I am.'"

"When those rocks were on top of her, can you still see her? Say for instance, if I went to that field, and in the corner of the field, at the tree, next to the rock pile, surrounded by the bushes, would I be able to see her?"

"You could probably see the garbage bag poking out from under the bits of rocks, but that's it."

Jimmy had developed a solid understanding of this suspect, in terms of her grace, mannerisms and her tone and tempo when answering questions. What he was able to gather now, was the body was covered in rocks, wrapped in garbage bags, most likely under a tree. What Britney was hiding was where the location of the body actually was, and her involvement in the murder, this was evident in how she lied, she mumbled and spoke far too quickly.

When she was telling the truth, her eyes filled with clarity, she spoke softly, almost robotically. Jimmy had to make sure that his form of questioning was baited with understanding, to play along with her lies until she was so emotionally exhausted, she had no choice but to tell the truth.

Jimmy began to collect the plastic cups that were scattered along the table, along with his casefiles and the box of tissues, He removed his hanky from his shirt pocket and placed it on the table.

"So, say this Kleenex box is the car..."

He placed the box in front of Britney and noticed her body language begin to wilt. Jimmy was setting the fictional scene, using anything he could find in the room as props.

"And, say, my hanky, here, is the rockpile..." He moved the hanky next to the Kleenex box.

"And these papers, are the bushes..." Jimmy neatly stacked together all of the papers into a neat pile and placed them on the opposite side of the Kleenex box."

"And...let me think..." Jimmy began to root around in his trouser pockets before taking out his vaping pen, with its large, blue design, placing it on to the table next to the hanky.

"This here...my vaping pen. Let's say that's the tree."

Jimmy moved his chair back, so he was sitting perpendicular with the table.

"Where I'm sitting now is the main road, and where you are, that's the dirt road that you guys drove down?"

"Yeah."

"So as you headed down the main road, you

saw the tree and rock pile on your left, and you turned left down a dirt road, that led down to the field and you parked next to the tree, that was surrounded by bushes, with the rock pile here, you parked next to the rock pile?"

"Yeah."

"And where was Stephanie lying?"

"Here." Britney pointed at the space on the table between the hanky and the Kleenex box.

"So she was in between the car and the rock pile?"

"Yeah."

There was a sudden, loud rapping on the door that caused Britney to flinch. Jimmy turned around in his seat, as the heavy door squeaked open, to find Linda, case file under her arm. She nodded politely to Britney.

"Jimmy, can I see you for a second?"

"Sure thing, Britney, if you can give me a few minutes, do you mind?"

Britney shook her head, wiping at her eyes with her sleeve. Jimmy left the room and walked with Linda down the hallway to the main offices.

"What is it?" Jimmy asked, as they both sat on the edge of Kiki's desk and began to observe Britney on the LED monitor, through the cctv camera pointing at her from the top right-hand corner of the room.

"You told me to get you out of there after thirty minutes, to let her stew."

"Oh sorry, I forgot."

"It's okay."

"How's Abed getting on?"

"Abed has been grilling Sebastian now for two hours, but the guy hasn't flinched. Just keeps demanding a solicitor. He's tried to deny the murders a couple of times, but Abed has shot down the denials quickly. No matter how long he spends in there with him, I don't think the guy is going to crack."

"No, the guy knows the system too well, I do think Britney knows more than she's letting on."

"I noticed the mumbling act all right."

"She can't see the gravity of it. She's treating this like it's just a trip to the principal's office.

"Do you think the emotion is real?"

"Oh yeah, but she's stating that Sebastian did everything. The rape, the murder, everything."

"And you don't believe her?"

"She had countless opportunities to run for help, every time they stopped for supplies, she could have easily asked a clerk, or a passerby, anyone, to call 999. But she didn't. Not to mention the fact she's lying about where the child is buried, whatever they did, they brought the body with them, it makes no sense to bury her where they killed her, there'd be evidence, plus I've never heard of fuckin rockpile next to a tree, in the very cor...."

Jimmy stopped mid-sentence. Something caught his attention on the CCTV footage.

"What?" Linda asked, frowning.

"Do you not see?"

"What? I don't see anything."

Jimmy walked over next to the monitor and tapped the screen, pointing at Britney's face.

"She's not crying, she's not even upset."

Linda moved in for a closer look, squinting, she put on her reading glasses. Britney looked pale, her eyes wide, staring into space. There wasn't an iota of emotion etched on her face.

"She hasn't wiped at her eyes once since I left the room."

"So what are you thinking?"

"What if she did it?"

"What, raped her?"

“No, Sebastian raped her, what if it was Britney that killed her?”

“Why?”

“Love, devotion, who’s to say they weren’t planning to do something like this for a while?”

“I can’t see it, what is she, eighteen?”

“Yeah.”

“I don’t know, Jimmy.”

“Think about it, your first boyfriend, bit of a bad boy reputation. Manipulates her into his way of life. Convinces her that whatever he decides is above the law. That they can do anything they want. Why else is she lying about the burial? Best case scenario, she’s accessory after the fact...”

“Worst case is, she beat the shit out of that girl with a hammer.”

“If she was in fear of her life, or Stephanie’s life, she would have done everything in her power not to let that happen. Now...that we’ve caught up to them, the best thing she can do is look as cute and innocent as she can and blame everything on him.”

The two detectives fell into a silence. On the screen next to Britney, Abed was looking relaxed, sipping his coffee, speaking non-stop, giving Sebastian no chance whatsoever to open his mouth and form any kind of false alibi. Sebastian looked very effeminate in the manner in which he sat, he was covered with a blanket, and seemed like he was shivering. A packet of Tayto crisps and a coffee lay untouched on the table, next to him.

"...Listen man, I know that you've been through a lot and it's been tough on you, especially going through the withdrawals that you're having, so I'm going to break this down and make this simple okay?

I like honesty, I was raised to be honest, and I respect people who are being honest with me, anything that you want to get off your chest today, I'm here for you dude. I've been doing this a long time, so whatever you say, it's not going to shock me...people make mistakes, I make them all the time, and people who say they never have dark thoughts, they're lying dude.

Everybody has dark thoughts, and whatever happens today, whatever you tell me, we'll do it, okay? We'll sit and deal with this. I look at you and I don't see a cold-hearted killer, I see someone who's made a grave mistake, and I think the best way with dealing with this is to sit here and talk about it, Sebastian? Hey..."

Jimmy watched as Abed reached in and grabbed Sebastian by the shoulder. He was trying everything in the book, and doing it very well, as well as any detective would. He was coming across as understanding, caring, being the good cop in the situation, before Jimmy would burst in later on and hail down a rain of abuse upon the suspected murderous pedophile.

"You can do it, I know you have the capability to explain what happened. There's two people you can be right now, one is a guy, who's made mistakes, and wants to atone for his mistakes, or else I'm dealing with a psycho kiddy fiddler, which one is it Sebastian?"

No reply, Sebastian remained hunched over in his chair, his arms covered by his blanket.

"We can do this, and I'll sit here with you and listen, and we'll get through this together, no matter how long it takes, I'll sit with you dude. If someone manipulated you, or framed you, or made you do something that you didn't want to do, I'll be here man, every step of the way. But you need to be completely honest with me, as I have been here with you. If there's anything I said about what happened that isn't right, or something that I've deducted that's completely way off course, you need to correct me on it, help me do my job, or else I can't help you."

"No one gives a shit about what I have to say."

"What makes you say that?"

"Whatever I say, you're going to presume me guilty anyway, so what's the point?"

"Oh, there are plenty of points, my friend."

"It doesn't matter."

"Of course, it does, how can you helping me today not matter, eh? You can be the guy who after I leave here today, I can go up to my superiors and say, "Sebastian is alright, you know? He's willing to talk and help us find the little girl." What's the downside to that? I don't see one, everything you say matters, no matter how minute the information, everything that you say, whatever you heard, whatever you saw, will be for the greater good, and I'm all for the greater good, look my friend, look here."

Abed slid the CCTV photographs of the Silver Audi in front of Sebastian.

"That's you driving away from the cathedral, and here, that's you coming back into the city that very same night, that's you there, see? And see here, in the back, where it's circled? That's Britney, hiding. You see? We know all this already, we've gotten past the point of figuring out what happened? What we want to know now is why? Whatever else happened, Sebastian, you saw the little girl, you spoke to her..."

"No, I didn't..."

"Yes, you did, you see? It's all right here in front of you, you drove her and Britney out of the city that day, and here's Britney at the fast-food place, and here she is at the DIY place, and look, see there, that's your car outside both of these premises. So, anything you tell me today, is going to help everybody involved. Why not do the right thing? And help everybody involved, this is..."

"How long did you say Abed has been speaking?" Jimmy asked, admiring Abed's approach to the interrogation.

"He hasn't stopped since the interrogation started." Linda replied.

Abed was deploying a mentally draining form of interrogation. It was simple, speak until the suspect was completely sick and tired of hearing your voice. The timestamp on the screen showed two hours and eighteen minutes.

"We should call the Guinness World Records."

"I think the holder of that record, did he not speak for a week straight? Or something?"

"It was about 100 hours."

"No problem to Abed."

"Keep an eye on it, I'm going back in."

"Good luck." Linda watched Jimmy exit the bullpen and stride down the hallway towards the interrogation room at the end of the corridor.

#

As Jimmy re-entered the room, he glanced down to his right where Britney was seated and saw that she quickly picked up her tissue and began wiping her face with it. Jimmy sat down in his chair and rolled up to Britney, blocking his tall frame from the door, from any hope of Britney leaving this room as the victim.

"Before you covered Stephanie with these... rocks...was there any conversation between yourself and Sebastian, anything about what you were going to do next? Were you going to take her with you? Anything like that?"

"I don't know."

"Here's the problem I'm having, Britney, why in the world would you cover a body in bags, just to leave her at the same spot where she was assaulted and murdered?"

"Because, that's what happened."

"No, that's not what happened, you hid her somewhere else, you hid her deeper in the countryside, somewhere hard to find. You didn't want the body to be found."

"Why would I do that? I mean, I've been honest with you..."

"You're not going to get into any more trouble telling me where the body is."

"I know that."

"I have no doubt that she was molested and murdered at the spot where you said it happened, but I'm having awful trouble believing that you didn't take her with you. You know why? And I'm making no secret about this, okay? My colleague believes the same thing because she just told me so..."

"No, I'd never..."

"Because if you wanted to help that little girl, you would have."

"I tried, and I couldn't."

"You didn't try hard enough, you had ample opportunity to help her, and you just turned your back on her."

Britney broke down crying again, she really went for it this time, summoning up as many tears and as much sadness as she could muster.

"What kind of person would do that Britney? Unless you were involved in it."

"She's buried in a pile of rocks; I'm trying to help you where she is."

"What about the hammer, is that buried with her?"

Britney grew quiet all of a sudden, her tears stopped almost automatically.

"Britney, you have to help me out with this,

please? Is the hammer buried with her, or did you get rid of it?"

No answer. Britney tried to bring her face down to her chin as much as she was physically able to.

"I believe you when you say she's buried under a pile of rocks, believe me I do, I have no doubt in my mind that's where she is, and I'm thinking the hammer and the bags are buried with her, do you know why I'm thinking that?

Because it makes sense, because it's something I would do, bury the body in the middle of nowhere, a place so discreet it's difficult to get to, and throw the hammer in on top of it. No point risking taking it back to the city with you, or throwing it somewhere where a farmer or hiker could find it, because of all the blood, and throwing it in a bin, well, what bins are out in the countryside? Hmm? I mean it makes sense to bury the murder weapon with the body."

Jimmy was merely fishing, but it seemed to be working. The truth of the matter was that if they had pulled over next to a trash bin and disposed of the hammer, chances are it would never be found, especially if it got hauled off to a landfill. It would be like finding a needle in a haystack.

"So, here's what I'm going to do, because you

have been brilliant so far, you really have, but what I need you to do right now, is draw for me where she's buried, so that we can find her and bring her home…"

"I don't know where she's buried…"

"Oh Britney, I think you do know."

"No I mean, like I couldn't see where we were."

Britney clammed up again, Jimmy knew she would have put her foot in her mouth if she had followed the sentence by saying, "because I was hidden in the back." Jimmy had to be delicate now in his approach, Britney was the only shot at getting Stephanie.

"So, you did take her with you."

Britney contemplated the question for a long time, before nodding her head up and down, very slowly. When she spoke again, she spoke quietly, slowly, her voice strained.

"But I don't know where she is…"

Britney was crying for real now, the remorse was getting the better of her.

"You couldn't see where Sebastian was going?" Jimmy asked, softly, trying the coax her into the information he needed.

Britney shook her head from side to side.

"Can you remember any details of the place. If you close your eyes can you see the area? Was there a river, or trees, or a barn, or cattle? Something that might help us in narrowing the search.

"Yeah, I remember we were up high…"

"Like on a hill?"

"Yeah and there was this fence, that had like, a strange pattern to it. Like, it was fine, and then it seemed to sink into the ground, and then there were bits of wood missing, and then fine again.

"What else was there?"

"There was a house."

"A big house? Small?"

"A really small house, like what you see from the olden days, in like, old pictures and stuff."

"Like a cottage?"

Britney nodded her head.

"Was there anybody living there?"

"No, it was really rundown."

"Derelict?"

Britney nodded her head.

"What else?"

"There was a dirt road that led up to the

house, and it was surrounded by trees. Behind the house was this big oak tree, and next to it was a rock pile."

"Are there any other houses around the area? Any other people?"

Britney shook her head.

"No, it was like in the middle of nowhere."

"Could you hear anything?"

"I could hear running water, like there was a stream nearby, and it was really green. And the view was pretty special, it was full of hills and the sky was purple, going dark."

"Any idea where this house could be?"

"No, I know there's a small wooden bridge that you have to go over to get onto the dirt road, but I didn't have a clue where we were.

"Somewhere special?"

Britney nodded again. Her eyes were becoming droopy, her face becoming pale.

"I feel sick." She said.

"Are you going to throw up?"

"No, I don't know, I feel like shit, I need methadone."

"I can't authorize that Britney, I'm going to have to get a doctor in here to check up on you."

"Well I need something; can't you get me smokes or something?"

"I can do that."

"And a coke, something with sugar."

"Okay, but Britney, you're going to have to do something for me."

"What?"

"I need you to draw a picture, a map of where she's buried, can you do that?"

"Yeah, yeah, but I need something before I start cramping up."

"Okay, just give me a minute."

Jimmy leapt up from his chair and exited into the main hallway, closing the door gently behind him, before jogging down to the main offices. Kiki was back from her search, looking glum.

"No sign of her, nothing, we've been looking for hours."

"Where's Linda?"

"She's gone to get you the cigarettes and the coke."

Jimmy began rummaging around in his desk drawers for some pens and some blank A4 paper. Kiki sat on the edge of her desk, studying the monitors in front of her. Britney was now depleted, her head in her arms, which were crossed on the table.

“She’s a funny duck, that one.”

“Do you think there’s more than what she’s letting on?”

“I think, and I know from growing up, hearing stories, abused people abuse people. They think it’s normal. She may play the innocent girl, but she knew what she was doing, I don’t think she could keep her eyes away.”

“Do you think she killed the girl?”

“If she did, I’d say it was out of mercy.”

Jimmy was still rummaging, Kiki turned to watch him flap around at his desk.

“You call yourself an intellectual, and you never have a pen. Here take mine.”

She took a pen out of the breast pocket of her neat business blazer and tossed it to Jimmy.

“Thanks.”

“The man in charge wants to get helicopters in and around the Connemara area, he said there’s a rockpile next to a tree down at some vantage point past Spiddal. I told him you’re wasting your time man. I told him he was searching in the wrong direction, that we had footage of the car in Mayo, he said that it would be stupid to bury a body close to where they killed it, I called him stupid. Things got heated. So, I said, 'fuck this, she's not here, I'm leaving. I had to change my clothes; I was covered head to toe in muck."

"Who's leading the search party again?"

"Lieutenant Gray. Pure and utter gobshite. She's in Mayo, I feel it in my bones. You look tired boss."

"I'm okay, I'll sleep when I'm ready to sleep."

It was Jimmy's go to catchphrase, something he always said when he looked like he was about to pass out from exhaustion.

"I'm thinking of bringing Britney in to see Sebastian, see how he reacts when he finds out that we got info from her."

"I've been watching Abed, motormouth, he hasn't stopped talking. This is the guy who needs to go for a piss every ten minutes. Bladder on him like a woman. Must be ready to pee his pants."

Jimmy had to sit down, that sway of exhaustion was back, his vertigo was completely messed up.

"When was the last time you ate?"

"I don't know, yesterday. I think?"

"Go for a break, I'll get her to draw the map,

and sit with er. Go and get something to eat."

"I'm fine."

"Man, ya know who you're talking to? There's no option, Mama Kiki insists."

"You're talking to your commanding officer."

"Who's going to drop dead cuz he's stupid. You're starting to piss me off. You don't think I can watch her draw a map. Boi, ya think I'm stupid?"

Kiki was deftly guilt tripping Jimmy, it always worked, her method never failed her, not once.

"Go for a nap, get something to eat and go for a drive, it's not like they're going anywhere."

"Are you sure?"

"I say fuck off man, now go!"

***

CHAPTER 19 --- LICENCE TO KILL

The Sun hung low in Jimmy's visor as he sped through the Mayo countryside. He had eaten a salad, more to get Kiki off his back, and had a refreshing nap in his office. Kiki was right, it wasn't like the suspects were going anywhere, and Kiki knew Jimmy long enough that driving cleared his head. He was enjoying the drive so much he would be happy if he died in a car smash right now and never have to look at the city again.

He felt more organic driving through the countryside, more at peace with the universe. The streets would be too busy at this time of the evening, the buildings all lit up with 3D advertisements and promotional videos. Out here, in the glowing dusk, it felt more like the real world, he felt warm and content listening to Lateralus by Tool on Spotify.

He replayed the interrogation with Britney

over and over again in his head. The bridge, near a stream, the cottage in front of the tree. The rockpile, up on a hill. It was like he could picture it vividly, and was racking his brain as to where he had seen it before. Did he drive by it? Did he see it in a photograph? It was forming in his head more like a memory than an image. No, Jimmy was never really down in this neck of the woods, he was associating it other cottages he had seen throughout his life.

He had driven around Ballinrobe, down towards Castlebar, and on towards Westport. He had to think like Sebastian, if he didn't find where this girl was he'd be walking straight out into the public again. He was evolving. Shaking his stepson to death was an 'experiment' so to speak, the power in taking a human life, just to see what it was like. It was difficult to know at this point whether his autism gave him such a disregard for the law, or was he faking it?

Jimmy got as far as Newport and pulled over at the bridge. He took out his tablet and began flicking through the notes from the Ryan Adams case. Going through all the testimonies with all of Sebastian's family and relatives. Because of his total recall, he could speedily pinpoint any old documents relating to Sebastian's background. Anything that could give him a clue as to why Sebastian chose a specific burial site. Something, anything to do with Mayo. There was nothing.

Jimmy's mind was going a mind a minute now. He tried to picture all routes from where he was, there wasn't that many he could take. Newport didn't seem like the right place. Could Sebastian have driven to Achill? No, Jimmy had been there a few times and knew it was a bit too far away, considering the team knew what time Sebastian had arrived back in Galway.

There was a turn at Mulranny towards Ballycastle and Belmullet, again…too far, it had to be somewhere around Mulranny. Had to be.

The logistics of the journey made sense. They had pulled over somewhere remote, where they had abused and murdered Stephanie. By the time they would have gotten her wrapped and placed back into the car, dusk would have been forming in the sky. It would have to be a place Sebastian had been to before, or at least known about. And if they had murdered Stephanie outside of Castlebar, God knows there was enough countryside to hide in, they would have had to bury Stephanie at a location pre-planned by Sebastian, in order for them to transport the victim, bury her under a pile of rocks, and get back to Galway by the specified time.

What was special about Mulranny? Jimmy went onto the google search engine and searched Mulranny. He pulled up the Wikipedia page. He didn't find anything of interest, until he searched under notable people. Desmond Llewelyn, Q from the James Bond movies, used to own a house in the area.

Jimmy frowned, Sebastian really thought he was that clever. Maybe his low IQ did cloud his judgement. Sebastian was a huge James Bond fan, Jimmy remembered that from the interrogation. Bond this and Bond that. And what was it Ryan Adams grandparents said? He spent all of his time playing 'Goldeneye.' Jimmy knew the game from his youth. And what was it Britney said? "Somewhere special." They were going to take Stephanie somewhere special.

Jimmy's gut instinct was in overdrive. The derelict cottage was here, in Mulranny, and Jimmy had to keep north of the village, there was nothing to the south but Clew Bay. Where John and Yoko bought an island and screamed their heads off. He was now on the lookout for a derelict house, which was out of the way, near a stream, up high in the hills.

Jimmy googled Desmond Llewelyn and found an article covering his life and work, how the property now belongs to his grandchildren. Meaning that property was not derelict. Interesting. It didn't deter Jimmy. Whether or not the derelict house belonged to Q, it didn't matter. Sebastian thought it did.

He cursed himself for not thinking of the

destination sooner. As he drove down a tiny back road near the village, the tarmac sinking under the weight of his Ford, he noticed a small wooden bridge form in his headlamps. Jimmy thought back to the time he found the farmer hanging from the big oak tree, feeling nausea grow in the pit of his stomach.

He rumbled over the small wooden bridge, hearing the noisy bustle of the busy stream gushing below him. Out of the darkness his headlamps shone on a rundown, derelict, cottage. The bushes and long grass growing out from its foundations only highlighted the banality that stood before him, the lost memories of a time forgotten. A tree stood proudly behind the house.

Jimmy sat in his car for the longest time, thinking of nothing. He lowered his window the let in the cool fresh country air, smelling the sweet scent of bog that lingered in his nostrils.

The moon was forming, about to shine down a light on the small path ahead, as if lighting the way. This was fucked, this whole situation was fucked. Sebastian's mindset and motive was becoming ever so clearer, killing filled him with an evil primal power, making him realise that he wasn't like the rest of the world. Killing made him feel different...special. Killing can provide you with such a huge thrill very few can imagine, because very few can deal so well with the moral consequences.

As long as society would remain politically correct, the blame would always be shifted away from Sebastian. It would always be somebody else's fault, somebody who didn't sympathise with Sebastian's autism, somebody who never killed anybody in their life. This realisation pissed Jimmy off to no end.

He couldn't procrastinate any longer. He could feel death linger around him and hoped it was just his paranoia. He grabbed his flashlight and stepped out into the evening, pleading with the gods, hoping that this was a dead end, that he was merely wasting his time. He took his time preparing himself, making a mental checklist of all the items he needed, praying that he didn't need any of them.

He walked to the back cottage as night fell quickly. Visibility was limited, and Jimmy had to use his flashlight to find his way, carefully picking his steps along the jagged path. As he clambered over fallen branches around the back of the run-down cottage, there, sitting in front of the tree, was a large rockpile. He could hear the stream faintly nearby.

"Fuck." Jimmy whispered.

He edged closer to the rock pile and saw

a small piece of black plastic, poking out from the rubble, whipping in the wind that whistled around him.

"Fuck" Jimmy whispered again.

He placed his torch on the rocky grass, making sure to aim the beam at the rockpile. He proceeded to lift heavy rocks off the pile and throw them to one side. The more he cleared rocks from the top of the pile, the blacker the plastic began to appear, until he could see the shape of a small body outlined through the plastic. This was her all right unless some kind of freak occurrence was going to happen.

"Fuck it anyway."

Jimmy grabbed his pen knife and tore away at the plastic, revealing the face of Stephanie Madden. Her angelic blue eyes stared motionlessly towards the sky. Even in the darkness he could see how vivid and beautiful here eyes...were. Her dried blood caked along her little face. Her skin was gray, she was beginning to decompose. Jimmy felt tears spring into his eyes.

She looked so peaceful. Jimmy was overwhelmed with sadness. He cried for her, praying that wherever she was now in the cosmos, she was smiling and happy. This face was going to haunt him more than any other, this one hurt the most. Protector of the dead. He absent mindedly reached for his phone and rang headquarters.

Linda answered.

Jimmy couldn't speak for a second. "Linda… I…"

"Jimmy, is that you?"

"I…eh…I found her."

Silence, Jimmy had to turn away from Stephanie, she was resembling one of those paintings where their eyes followed you around the room.

"I can't hear you Jimmy, you're breaking up."

"Get an ambulance down here, and a coroner, I found her."

"Where? Where was she?"

"Just outside Mulranny…"

Linda could hear heavy breathing, followed by whining.

"She's here, where Britney told me she would be."

"How?"

"James Bond…" Jimmy was trying to speak but his vocal chords weren't responding.

"James who?"

"I'm sending you the location. She's…eh… she's out here in the sticks."

"Are you okay?"

"No...I'm going to sit with her and look after her. Has Joe Perry made it down from Dublin yet?"

"He can't make it until the morning."

"Good...would it be a bad thing, if I killed him?"

"Don't talk like that."

"The world would be a better place, wouldn't it?"

The line went dead. Jimmy sat next to Stephanie, meditating, letting the night air sooth his anger, his frustration. He mentally tried to send a message to her, wherever she was, letting her know that everything was going to be all right, to watch down over him and to guide him. How he was taking her body home, back to her family.

He tried not to let the horridness of the reality destroy him, as he sat on the ground in silence next to Stephanie, waiting for his colleagues to arrive.

***

CHAPTER 20 --- THE TROUBLE WITH SEBASTIAN

Abed had spent almost 3 hours talking nonstop, assessing three factors to the case. He was able to build a criminal profile just from reading the suspects body language, his reaction to comments, his history, to be able to build an understanding of the suspects character.

Abed was then able to perform a psychiatric analysis to use this knowledge in the hopes of gaining a confession by influencing his thinking, his emotions and his decision making.

Abed's rouse of a threat level assessment didn't matter, he just pretended it did. Threat level assessments are used to see if a suspect will commit a crime again, whether it be assault, robbery, or rape, the fact that Sebastian was the prime suspect, and having already receiving Britney's full confession claiming he raped the girl, and partook in her murder, meant that a child killer pedophile didn't need threat level assessment

As Abed put it once to Jimmy, cases like this, the suspect is already at 'Threat Level Midnight.' This was a reference to another classic TV show that Abed enjoyed watching on his time off.

In the past three hours, Abed had tried several different interrogation approaches to get a confession from Sebastian. It was his own unique approach, a mixture of The REID Technique cleverly cloaked in to the PEACE Technique, to avoid a possible Garda inquiry later down the line.

Abed began with the approach that he already knew everything that happened and needed to perform a threat assessment to see if Sebastian would do it again, this caused the suspect to break down crying, but nothing more.

Abed then tried the 'Cleanse Your Soul' approach, stating that now was the time to come clean, before more DNA evidence would be found on young Stephanie's corpse. Better to tell your side of the story now before no one would believe you. Sebastian merely stated that his solicitor told him not to say anything that might incriminate him.

What followed was the 'Alternative Question', When Abed said to him, "there's two people you can be right now, one is a guy, who's made mistakes, and wants to atone for his mistakes, or else I'm dealing with a pyscho kiddy fiddler, which one is it Sebastian?" Sebastian heard the alternate question before. He saw it being thrown out of court. He was like granite, he just stared at the bare bricked wall six feet in front of him, refusing to speak.

Finally, Abed tried to evoke emotion from Sebastian, a chink in his defensive armor, bringing up his sick mother, who was suffering from cancer, to appeal to his better sense of nature.

"Think of your mother, my friend, think of her and what she must be going through right now, what would your mother want you to do in this situation?"

"Get a solicitor," came the cold hearted, cynical reply.

Sebastian wasn't going to crack. It was like chipping away at cement with a butter knife, his prior meeting with Jimmy had hardened him. Abed left the room, promising to get him a hot meal, he then rushed to the restroom to empty his bladder, before sitting down at his desk, exhausted. Kiki was smirking at him.

"So what ya going to get him? They have fish

and chips in the canteen today."

"Shite and sawdust."

"Are you not going to get him anything?"

"Fuck no."

Abed saw Linda hunched over at her desk in her corner office. She was preparing her notes for the next part of the interrogation, making sure she knew the approach she was going to perform, inside and out. Abed leaned on the opened office door and gave it a quick rap to get her attention.

"You're up." Abed said, his voice had a strain to it, like it was beginning to crack. "Are you ready?"

"As ready as I'll ever be."

Linda stood and looked at her reflection in the wall mirror, she fixed her hair and straightened out her business suit. Abed began to rub her shoulders, like a boxing trainer, motivating her.

"Watch his counters. Be patient. And when you're ready, try and go in for the kill. You're an animal, a beautiful animal, he's not going to know what hit him."

Linda laughed, she turned and faced Abed with her fists up and started shadow boxing in front of him, Abed put his hands up and encouraged Linda to throw combinations into his palms. She performed a few triple combos before shaking out her arms and picking up her copy of the casefile.

“Not bad,” Abed smirked, flashing his pearly white teeth, “you could have been a contender.”

Linda laughed again and briskly began walking to the interrogation room.

“Remind Jimmy to bring Britney in he comes back!” Linda shouted over her shoulder, as she exited the main offices.

“Sure thing!” Abed’s voice trailed off as Linda’s high heeled stilettos echoed down the empty corridor. She stopped in front of Interrogation Room 2, took a long deep breath, and gave a gentle knock on the door, before entering.

“Hi Sebastian,” She said warmly, smiling. Sebastian broke from his trance and looked up at the brunette professional looking figure with the pretty face.

“I’m not sure if you remember me, my name is Dr. Linda Ní Gorman.”

“Sure, I remember you.” His tone had changed, from his sly cold-hearted replies, to a more gentle, shy tone, trying to sound as innocent as possible. He grabbed his blanket and tucked it up under his chin, covering his entire body.

"I'm just here to check up on you and see how everything is going." Linda said as she placed the case file neatly on the table and sat on the office chair across from Sebastian.

"I'm hungry, the fella said he was going to get me some food, but he hasn't come back."

"Oh, well I'm sure that I can find something for you in a while, I just want to check in with you first, if that's all right?" Linda kept her tone friendly, trying her best not to be overly friendly.

"It's not like I have a choice in the matter."

"I promise, the quicker I get through this and the quicker you help me, the quicker I'll be able to get you some food, I just need to go through this process with you, you know? For the big wig upstairs." Linda whispered, one hand cupped around her mouth as she pointed towards the ceiling, Sebastian broke a smile from the corner of his mouth.

"So what do you liked to be called, is it Seb or Sebby? I don't know about calling you 'Sebastian,' I'm not sure I'm that with it you know, on the streets." Linda threw a hilariously bad attempt at a gangster hand signal, this time Sebastian chuckled.

"Sebastian is fine." He said smiling, shaking his head.

"Cool, Sebastian it is." She opened the case file and took out an A4 writing pad and a pen, opening the pad onto a clean, empty sheet of paper.

"I know the last time we spoke, we talked about your family a bit and I'm here to check on your mental wellbeing after being processed." Again, Linda kept her tone and composure warm and friendly. "You mentioned that your mum is sick. Which I'm very sorry to hear. I know what it's like to watch a family member suffer with cancer, it's not nice. Unfortunately, my father died of cancer, and I hope the same thing doesn't happen to your mum, and I want to assure you that she'll get all the help and assistance and care she needs while you're in here and that you shouldn't worry too much because I know she relies on you to look after her..."

"What kind of cancer did he have?" Sebastian asked, his interest peaked.

"Colon cancer. Stage four."

"Did he get chemo?"

"He did, he fought bravely, but unfortunately cancer doesn't care about who you are."

"How long...was the cancer?"

"Six months...he was very sick."

"I'm sorry to hear that."

"Well thank you Sebastian, that means a lot."

Linda leaned over and gently patted his arm, she then clicked her pen and rested it between her fingers.

"The last time we spoke I felt a bit of a connection, I'm not sure you felt that. But I certainly did."

Sebastian shrugged, going back into his trance like stare.

"I know you're in a rough spot in your life, with your mam and your granny...would you be able to look at me Sebastian? Would that be possible, do you mind?"

Sebastian slowly turned his head, his blazing empty black eyes looking right into Linda's soft green eyes. Linda felt a chill run down her spine, Sebastian's eyes were so clear, yet so menacing, it was like he was able to see directly into her soul and knew all of her fears and doubts and mistakes she had made in her journey through life.

It was like he was possessed by some unknown evil entity and could smell fear, like a horse sensing trouble in the distance on a lonesome highway. Linda couldn't break eye contact with him now, even if she wanted to.

"Thank you, Sebastian, I appreciate that. I know when we talked before, we made good eye contact, and I think it'll help moving forward."

Linda watched tears flood into those evil black eyes, she pondered whether he was crying for his sick mother or feeling sorry for himself, she quickly concluded that it was probably the latter.

"I've spoken with your mum, she's such a lovely, gentle person and she's terribly upset about what has happened. I promised her that I'd do all I can to help. She really is a warrior, especially with everything that's going on with your step-daddy, what's his name?"

"Geoff."

"That's it. I know I've been heartbroken like that in the past, it's hard to understand when someone you love just ups and leaves like that suddenly."

Sebastian looked down at the floor and merely shrugged again.

"I know after being processed and having to hear my colleague talk for so long, I know that you might be influenced. What I mean is, I don't want your opinion swayed or feel coercion on any level when it comes to this...matter, what they said to you or vice versa, that's between you and them.

I've been helping out on this case since the beginning. I've spoken to your girlfriend, your mam, your nanny, your friends, I've also spoken to the victim's family, I've spoken to all sorts of people in relation to this case. I can deeply empathise with your situation. I know you've been on the benefits, I was on it myself for a few years there, after college, and I know it's rough, with food and bills and clothes, and the rent, Jesus wept, I mean, it's not so bad now but when I was in college about fifteen years ago, it was really bad then…can you look at me again Sebastian? if that's possible."

Sebastian averted his gaze once more, directly into the window of Linda's soul, another long, spinetingling chill shuddered through her solar plexus, she felt her anus and crotch tighten up as goose bumps began dancing up her arms.

"I know about the amount of stress you've been under since your mammy got sick. I know you've been trying to get any work possible, legal or illegal, to help pay for her treatment and her pills. Britney has gone into great detail explaining how much you're underappreciated in your home, and now there's the oxy addiction…"

"I'm not addicted, I can stop anytime I want."

"I'm sure you can, what I'm saying is that all these factors can play a major role that can lead to much more personal, darker issues, later down the line. Do you understand what I'm saying?"

Sebastian slowly nodded, keeping his gaze firmly on Linda.

"I know that you've been trying your level best, juggling your relationships and responsibilities... your social life, it's a lot for one person. It really is. I think what's most admirable is your girlfriend's resilience, especially coming from a broken home. The violence, the abuse, the drugs, to get hooked onto drugs by your own mother at thirteen, and then being passed around from pillar to post...her own mother...it's monstrous. I know you feel a special connection with her, and that you feel you can tell each other anything, that you're remarkably similar in a lot of ways..."

"Is she okay?"

"Oh yeah, she's a strong-willed person."

"Can I see her?"

"She's been interviewed at the moment, but I instructed my colleagues that once they're finished, that they will bring her in here to see you..."

"When will that be?"

"Oh, quite soon, possibly within the next hour."

"Are you sure? you're not going to run off like that fuckin Paki, are you?"

Linda ignored the racist slur.

"Cross my heart, hope to die, stick a needle in my eye." Said Linda, drawing a circle around her upper chest with her index finger.

"All right then."

"So...the circumstances have led you to undertake some bad, possibly illegal decisions. You got caught up in a frenzy of sex and drugs and guilt and responsibility..."

"That's not true."

"What's not true?"

"What you said."

"About the frenzy?"

"No...about whatever you said there, about making illegal decisions, it's not true."

Linda repositioned herself in her chair and took out Sebastian's criminal record sheet, including a list of all charges and information, along with his mugshot.

"I have your criminal record here."

"Oh sorry, I didn't know that's what you meant."

"What did you think I meant?"

Sebastian became gravely quiet, breaking eye contact, resuming his trance like state as he stared once more at the carpeted floor. Linda let the guilt linger for a few minutes, it was so thick she could almost smell it.

“Anyway, as I was saying, you’ve been caught up in a whole bunch of stuff. I was talking to Britney, and she told me that you’ve kept in touch with her, since all of her troubles started. You’ve brought her clothes and food and you’ve helped take care of her when her mum kicked her out, and she told me everything...your...desires... how you wanted to do it, the plan afterwards, where you were going to emigrate to, the death of Ryan Adams, and the whole media circus surrounding that...what happened with Stephanie...there’s no doubt in my mind she’s telling the truth.

We saw everything on video. Britney and Stephanie walking down to the cathedral, and the car, I mean, thirty years ago, there’d be a load of Silver Audi’s, now...they’re a unique sight. With the rims, and the special exhaust, and them big speaker thingies...”

“Woofers.”

“That’s what they’re called, I don’t like driving myself. I don’t like the thought of a car driving me around.”

“It’s a bullshit law.”

“I can’t argue with you on that. The thing is, and this is where it gets beyond my control, the car was seen at 3:22pm, driving away from the cathedral, just at the same time when Britney is seen walking towards the cathedral with the little girl."

"What a coincidence." There was a real smarmy tone to Sebastian's reply, Linda ignored it.

"The Audi, pulling away at around that same time, the backseat taken out, the car is unique, there's no question about that. When you arrive back in Galway, Stephanie isn't in the car with you, and cameras pick up Britney, hiding in the back, hunched over on the floor. Why would she hide, Sebastian?"

Sebastian was about to answer, before Linda jumped in again.

"Don't answer that, it was a rhetorical question." Linda's tone became more authoritative. "What I have here are facts...I have everything. I have video evidence; I have a full confession."

"Coerced."

"Is that what you think? The poor thing has been in there crying for the past six hours."

"She's not as innocent as she lets on."

"Yet, you say her confession is coerced."

Sebastian was about to retort, Linda cut him off once more.

"You see this is where it gets tangled for me. All I'm looking to do is to help and to make things right, for your family, for Britney's family, for Stephanie's family, and your silence is stopping the whole process, there's nothing I can do, it really is getting out of my hands. What are you going to think when the forensic team finish searching the car? I assume you know about how DNA works?"

"It'll show Britney was in her car. The car she bought for herself, with her tax, insurance, and registration"

"Naturally, don't you also think it'll show Stephanie's DNA also?" Linda was beginning to flow now, letting her voice ring out with a mixture of authoritative friendliness.

Sebastian shook his head.

"I think when you get two people together, who can influence each other the way that you and Britney do, it mixes some kind of reaction that leads you both to do very bad things. You heard of the term 'bad influence.' This isn't about trying to lie your way out of it, this is about redeeming yourself, for your own sake."

"I have nothing to redeem."

"That's a shame to hear, better to redeem yourself now before all of the DNA evidence is found..."

A loud knock on the door caused both Sebastian and Linda to jump an inch out of their seats. The door was sharply opened and in walked Jimmy, escorting Britney, who was handcuffed, wearing a blanket over her shoulders.

Britney sat in the plastic chair next to Linda, as Jimmy sat on the edge of the table. Linda noticed a look on Jimmy's face she had never seen before. His eyes were red, it was getting to him, he was barely holding it together.

"Seb, I'm not going to beat around the bush anymore, quite frankly I'm getting sick of all the bullshit."

"Call me Sebas…"

"Fuck what you want to be called. It's time to listen to me. You wanted to see Britney, here she is…"

Sebastian kept staring at the wall.

"You've been calling her a liar, you're claiming this and that, crying like a little bitch, well here's your opportunity now. Are you going to sit there and say that your girlfriend is a liar?"

"Britney is a liar."

"Why don't you man the fuck up and look at her when you say it."

Sebastian looked directly at his girlfriend across from him. And said in the most terrifying mundane tone that Linda had ever heard...

“Britney is a liar.”

Britney began to cry; Linda gently patted her knee.

“Linda, can you get Britney out of here, bring her to the canteen or something, get her a cup of tea, if that’s okay? I need to have a word with my buddy boy here.”

Linda stood up and opened the door, escorting Britney out of the room, who was bawling.

“Big man Sebastian. I tell ya something though, as fucked up as this may sound, I admire that girl. To go through all the shit she’s gone through, and then on top of all that, unwittingly falling for a paedophile...”

“I’m not a...”

“Shut the fuck up!”

“You can’t talk to me like that.”

“Maybe, how about this Sebastian, maybe if you don’t go around raping and killing little girls and shaking babies to death...”

“I didn’t...”

“Shut the fuck up!”

“My solicitor advised me on the phone, I didn’t have to say anything.”

"Who advises who, Sebastian?"

"What do you mean?"

"Exactly what I just said. Who advises who? You said your solicitor advised you, the thing is, you advise your solicitor. It's how it works. And hiding behind Perry doesn't make you look innocent..."

"I am..."

"Shut the fuck up! I'm fucking done with you. Have you even stopped for one second to think of the avalanche of forensic evidence that we're going to find?"

"You're going to have to ask my solicitor that question."

"How does your lawyer deal with the evidence of your semen on a 13 year old's dead body? Do you know what prisoners hate more than anything? We have some scum locked away, some of them I have had to deal with, people who'd have no problem slicing my head off with a machete if given the chance. But, do you know what they hate, more than anything else? Paedophile child killers. If they get a sniff that you're in a cell nearby they're going to go baying for blood, probably even something worse, do unto others as they have done unto you."

"That may be true if I was, but I didn't do

anything."

Jimmy moved from the table and sat down on the desk chair, cutting off the entrance, making himself as big and as lanky as he possibly could by stretching out his legs and placing his hands behind his head.

"I'm not here to kiss your arse, I couldn't give a fuck about your mother. I don't like your mother, you know why? Because she had you. I hope she suffers because you don't seem to give a fuck. My colleagues they want to know why, get inside your head, build a profile..."

"You all work together, I'm not stupid."

"Yeah we do. I like to think we live in a society where people can walk around and not have to worry about their children being abducted, raped and murdered. I like to think that we live in a city where people think a little bit more about what they're going to do with their lives rather than do something as horrendous as that. What do you think you're coming off as right now? Do you think you're coming off as an innocent guy, seriously? Do you think you're coming off as somebody who's wrongfully accused in all of this?

"Nothing I'm gonna say is gonna change your opinion, so what's the fuckin point?"

"You're right there, nothing you're going to

say is going to help you walk out of this station tonight. Nothing you say will prevent you going on trial for the abduction, rape and murder of Stephanie Madden. The thing is that every single part of Britney's confession, every single part of her story so far checks out, and we've only started delving into the details, we haven't even scratched the surface yet… The system just wants to chew you up and spit you out, doesn't it Sebastian? Because no-body gives a fiddlers about you. We picked up Britney's trail when she was identified on 'CrimeCall.' You weren't even in the reckoning. But low and behold, there you are driving away from the cathedral moments after she's spotted walking there with Stephanie…"

"Big coincidence."

"But it's not…is it, Sebastian? It really isn't, if it was, you wouldn't be sitting here in front of me right now. You need to get ahead of this thing. This is the evidence leading me to this point. How can I say to myself, after hearing what Britney had to say…and say to myself, 'this is bullshit,' I wouldn't be a good cop?"

"You're not anyway…"

"Oh, I can't be that bad, I have you."

Jimmy got to witness the ice-cold stare of Sebastian, who stared him right in his pupils. Jimmy didn't flinch, he was at this racket a lot longer than Linda, so he stared right back, to the point Sebastian had to look away.

"You know, we're going to have so much DNA evidence to tie you into this case, it's going to make your head spin."

"So what's your point?"

"Just tell me what happened, and that way then fifty people won't have to be pulling these all nighters to get the evidence that's going to nail you anyway. And you can give peace of mind to Stephanie's family."

"Sucks to be them."

"No…Sebastian, sucks to be you, they'll work until the end of time to make sure your arse sits in a cell, similar to this room, for the rest of your natural born life. Now, will you just help me out with this? So we can move past this, and save the long and arduous process you're subjecting yourself to, putting your mother through hell, for what? You know how much the media has been given on this case already, and you know what they're going to do when they catch up to your family tomorrow.

You're going to be labelled all the worst things a person can be labelled. You think we've been harsh? That's nothing compared to what the newspapers and the media are going to be doing. This is a huge scoop for them. This is going to make all those corpse excavations uncovered from those IRA assassinations a few years ago look like a teddy bears picnic. It's fair game with you buddy boy. It's going to be a frenzy. A clusterfuck of the highest proportions. Did you know your mother is a suspect?"

"No."

"We're interviewing her right now. I know, it looks bad, but we have to be arseholes when it comes to something as severe as this, if we don't interview all of your family and friends, and rule them out as suspects, my superintendent, the senator, the government would order us to be arseholes. Now this is going to sound like a deal to you, but believe you and me, it's not, but if you want me to lay off your friends and family you need to tell me the truth, right now, or else it's open season."

"I've got nothing to say."

"Well, you better, because if you don't say anything, I can guarantee you the media will go for the more drastic option."

"Drastic? What?"

"They're going to either report on the fact that two teenagers, under the duress of drugs and bogged down with stress, made a horrendous, horrible mistake, or they're going to say that two cold blooded psychopaths raped and murdered a teenaged girl. I've experienced it first hand, unfairly, no thanks to you. It's up to me to decide whether they'll take the drastic option with you or not. You can control that to a certain extent."

"No, I can't."

"Yeah, you can, because when they ask us, what you had to say about it, we can just say..."

"He wanted to speak to a solicitor."

"And then, once that's done, they can say whatever the fuck they want."

"I really couldn't give two fucks."

Sebastian yawned. Jimmy leaned his elbows on the table.

"Oh I'm sorry, am I boring you?"

"No, I'm just tired is all. I've been in this room for God knows how long, I haven't had anything to eat since breakfast, all I got was a shitty packet of Tayto that I didn't want and you're throwing all this bullshit at me."

"Well just think about things for a minute, just think it over. Bar all of the camera evidence that we have, think for a minute about how Stephanie's blood has seeped into the interior of your car."

"Britney's car..."

"Just think about it. I'm sure you've seen all of them crime shows. Think about how the blood seeps into the fabric, even after you think you've wiped it down and gotten rid of it, think of how all of her blood seeped into the carpet of the car, into the driver's seat, into your clothes. It's all there, it may be invisible to the naked eye, but it's all there. Not just blood, but all of the skin cells, the hairs…the semen. Just think about that for a minute."

"I can't believe you're grilling me over some made up story an eighteen-year-old girl told you…"

"What does her being nineteen have to do with anything? She saw what she saw. You told her if we came knocking on her door asking questions, not to say anything. And if somehow, we found proof that she abducted the girl, you told her to tell us that you drove Stephanie to another car to be taken away, and you don't know where they went after that. Wasn't that going to be your story?"

"It's not my story."

"That's what you told her to say?"

"I didn't tell her to say anything."

"Do you know what a psychopath is?"

"Never met one."

“Well I have, quite a few actually, I’m looking at one right now.”

“I just can’t believe that you’re so gullible that you investigate a story some junkie made up.”

“When somebody tells me, that a fully grown man killed teenaged girls, when that happens, we don’t say, ‘feck this, lets go to Croke Park this Sunday and watch Galway play in the league,’ instead of arresting our main suspect in a rape/murder case, that’s not the way it works.”

“Well, it should be, isn’t she libel?”

“Not the way she was crying, the sick shit she told me. Stuff that you did to that girl. Now I have to go and tell her parents that we have you both in custody. The first question they’re going to ask me is, why? “

“I’m sure they’ll have the answers.”

“What are you getting at? Are you insinuating that they did this, to their own daughter? Now that, I know for a fact, to be bullshit. You see what I did there? I know when someone’s bullshitting me and when someone is telling me the truth. If you’re going to go and throw out hints like that, it’s not going to work because I’m not in the mood for any of your mind games, there’s nobody involved in this except for you and Britney.”

“We’re done.”

"Is that what you said to Stephanie before you killed her?"

"Funny man."

"You think this is funny?"

"I think you're a funny man."

"I think you're a cold-blooded killer."

"You're getting nothing out of me, whatever else you want to say to me you can say to my solicitor."

"I don't want anything from you. Why would I want anything from the likes of you? I just wanted to see what it felt like to sit across from somebody who abducts, rapes and kills defenceless girls. You are one sick fuckin puppy Sebastian; I make no bones in saying that. You think a judge is going to free a monster like you? Because that's what you are, no remorse, no empathy… nothing. Burn in hell you rotten piece of shit."

Jimmy didn't give Sebastian a chance to reply, as he swiftly stood and exited the room, leaving behind the cold, cold existence of Sebastian Rivers.

***

CHAPTER 21--- THE BIRTH OF JACOB KRISP

Wesley first claimed divinity at The House of Novalis, six months after arriving at the commune. Up until that point, he merely surveyed his Novalis brothers and sisters, their habits, personalities and day to day routines.

The screaming sessions became so intense that Wesley became the centre of attention at each therapy session. While he could not confess or admit to himself that he had taken a human life, the rest of the small dedicated community could sense he was battling some serious demons.

Every morning and evening he would convulse, vomit, cry, pull chunks of hair directly from his skull, and would feel actual physical pain ricochet through his entire body as he purged all of his hateful, sinful desires from his system.

Because there was no pornography readily available to him, and technology being scarce in the house, his purging was a key technique and vital to Wesley overcoming his pornographic addiction. The purging side effects, which included, cramp, sweating, dizziness, vomiting and headaches, were 'cold turkey' symptoms similar to somebody overcoming an opioid addiction.

The more he divulged into his therapy, the more he changed...physically. It was as if some kind of strange metamorphosis washed over Wesley. He gained weight after he found pairs of dumbbells and old gym equipment in the old storage shed out of the back of the house. His eyes changed colour from blue to violet.

His voice became deeper and more purposeful, he became taller in height, gaining about two inches. He shaved his head, and his features, which were once withering and thin, became fuller. He smiled more and wasn't crippled by the black dog of depression.

Wesley became a supremely confident person, and through his confidence and rapid change of appearance he realised he had a kind of magnetic charm, almost unrecognizable from the creepy, strange child man who was interrogated only six months previously.

His intelligence now became vital, especially for Polly, who was trying to make The House of Novalis a charitable organization. Wesley's knowledge of the law became invaluable to business matters involving the house as an organization.

Wesley quit eating meat and was put off from eating any kind of junk food, he preferred brown bread, vegetables and fruit. He became an avid fan of marijuana and found that using it helped his state of mind, it relaxed him.

This transformation didn't go unnoticed by the female members of the group, especially Bonnie and Lulu, and when Wesley announced that he would abstain from sex until he was married, that only made the women lust for him even more.

There was one major important change in his metamorphosis, he began to respect and admire women. He didn't hate them anymore. He found that he preferred the company of women rather than the men in the group.

Wesley spent his life watching people, studying people, a man who was always on the outside looking in, now that he lived in close proximity with a group who were strangers to him merely months beforehand, he studied them very closely and realised that the group were sensitive and advocates of free speech.

Polly preached her belief that passive aggressiveness was the root of all evil, people with issues needed to voice them right away, in order to advance their treatment, this led to torrid arguments, arguments so vicious it left the house in duress for days on end before they were able to become stoned in harmony once more.

Wesley learned two things when he observed these arguments, that the men were gutless in the face of confrontation, preferring to cower in the shadows of an evening fire rather than attempting to resolve the situation, and that the women had no control over their emotions, unapologetically so, they were gullible, extremely vulnerable and were eager to love.

If Wesley was extremely careful in his actions, and placed his thoughts, ideas and beliefs correctly, he could make the arguments stop, and fill their heads with such grand ideas, visions and philosophies they would forget why they were so vulnerable in the first place.

The argument that really drove home this conviction was the one between Bonnie and Lulu which almost ended in a violent, physical altercation. The group had just finished a primal session, and had gathered in the common room, smoking weed and listening to blues records.

Wesley was sitting next to Bonnie at the large fireplace, while Lulu sat on the floor near Bonnie's feet. The rest of the commune sat on beanbags and sprawled out on sofas, feeling lazy from the warm heat which generated from the turf fire. Almost out of the stoned silence, when everybody was afraid to speak, probably because she was so stoned, Bonnie began to ramble about her thought process.

"Being where I'm at, experiencing life every day and feeling what comes up, you can't grow older feeling what another person needs and being yourself, you can't become yourself if you're trying to live up to other people's expectations. You can never attempt what you want to be when other people want you to be like them. You shouldn't be doing what they want when it preoccupies what you want to do. I have to express myself, in my own way, take Lulu for instance..."

"Wait...what?" Lulu seemed legitimately surprised that Bonnie suddenly made her the topic of conversation.

"It doesn't seem to matter to her about how she can talk about relationships and about sex. It doesn't seem to matter at all that she can blurt out whatever is on her mind. I couldn't sit here and feel 100% comfortable talking about sex. It's far too delicate and private for me. I can't talk about sex the way she can."

Lulu looked completely shocked by the honesty and the meaning behind the words, making it seem to her that Bonnie was trying to assassinate her character. She shook her head from side to side, frowning, as she knotted her soft, pale hands into tight fists, her eyes blazing with anger.

Polly encouraged everybody to express their true feelings, heightening emotions rather than downplaying comments and Lulu found herself in the unlikely position of defending herself in the face of the firing line.

"Do you know something Bonnie? That made me utterly and violently angry."

"Why do you feel angry? I'm only speaking the truth."

"I hate the way you're talking about me. The way you're characterizing me. Like I have no opinion."

"Why?"

"Because I just fucking do? I don't have to explain myself; I didn't ask for my character and honesty to come into question. I hate the fact that you think I'm nothing, as if you're on top of me..."

"What's so terrible about it?"

"You're dismissing me like I'm nothing! Like I'm just some kind of statistic in your life! The whole wild world doesn't revolve around you

Bonnie! It's as if you hate me!"

"I do hate you!"

The accusation was sneering, full of hate, Bonnie didn't like to be challenged, and it was at that moment Wesley realised that Bonnie liked to stir the pot.

"Well I don't like it! There's no reason for you to talk about me. Why don't you sit there silently so I can say things about you and make accusations about your behaviour? I think you're a five star cunt for saying such horrible things about me and I think you're shit and I think it's fucking horrible that you treat me like I'm nothing! I hate the way you treat me, sitting there all prettier than me. I hate you for getting boyfriends more than I do, I hate the way you treat them and trash them when you get bored of them."

"Why does that upset you? I don't know why that upsets you. I can't change that. I don't think that I've been acting horribly, I've just been acting the way I feel."

"I don't like you for it, and I don't like the way I'll be perceived after. Everyone is just going to think, "oh look! Bonnie's all right now, Lulu was a bitch to react the way that she did. Bonnie needs to get all the support from Polly and Tara, let Lulu sulk in the corner!"

"So it's a rivalry now, is it?"

"Fuck you."

Thus, began an hour-long argument, where everybody except for Polly and Tara, made their way into the kitchen and sat next to the stove as the argument raged on.

Wesley admired Lulu's defiance in the face of passive aggressive accusation, and Bonnie for speaking her mind, although he didn't see why she would stir up emotions. The group didn't speak, and Wesley watched as it was Ruby who made her way to Lulu upstairs to console her while all the men grouped around Bonnie, supporting her.

Wesley could see the group tangents and the politics and made a mental note to use this to his advantage when the time was right.

It was around this time that Wesley first smoked DMT, and the experience was so profound it caused him to claim divinity to the rest of Novalis. He experimented under the supervision of Gideon and Polly and was shocked to discover the trip only lasted roughly ten minutes, to Wesley it felt like he was hallucinating for days.

He understood what Gideon meant when he said that "he felt like god." They had talked about it for hours, sitting in the front garden, smoking joints. Gideon was happy that he was able to smoke again without any paranoid delusions, the therapy was working wonders for everybody. Wesley felt that Gideon had done a good job of explaining his trips, but it was now, only now, only when Oscar grew the plants in the greenhouse, and extracted the DMT, only after Wesley experienced it for himself, that he knew what Gideon truly meant.

Wesley's hallucination was one of clairvoyance and spirituality. He was kneeling, high up on a mountain, donned in a white robe. He could see a town in the distance. His alter was all set up. An old stone settlement, it was built for the most important day of his life.

He set down his belongings on the alter, taking each of them out of his brown leather bag. They included a black Isis band, frankincense, earthen censer, ashes of the heliotrope plant, rose oil and an oblong stone.

Now came the most painful part. He screamed aloud as he tore a fingernail from each of his index fingers, and then went about chopping at his hair with his trusted knife. Once he had botched all of his hair off, he placed the fingernails and hair in a bowl of honey and milk.

He was ready, he felt weak, yet he felt prepared. He sensed his stomach was empty, but he was not entirely sure. He knew he needed to abstain from any kind of animal meat, for a whole night and day, yet he couldn't think of the previous night or day. He couldn't remember anything about it. That was odd. Maybe it was the hunger, yet he didn't feel hungry. All he knew was that he was ready, he knew what he needed to do, and he was ready to do it.

"Come to me good husbandman. Good daemon. Come to me oh holy Orion, you that lies in the north! Who causes the currents of the Shannon to roll down and mingle with the ocean, transforming them with life as it does, man's seed with sexual intercourse, a god that has established the world in an indestructible foundation. A god who is young in the morning and old in the evening. A god who journeyed through the great subterranean sphere and who breathes fire. A god who has parted the seas in his first month, and who ejaculates his seed into the baby trees. This will be your authoritative name! Arbath, Abaóth Bakchabré. When I dismiss you, go without your shoes, and walk backwards."

He gripped his falcon staff tightly in his left hand and knelt before his alter. He admired the view as he watched the sunset in behind the town in the distance. As the last remnants of light disappeared from the sky, he began to chant, he had to chant the same phrase, over and over again. The language was new to him, yet he knew exactly the words he had to utter.

"ÓRI PITETMYAMOUNTE AINTHYPH

PICHAROUR RAIAL KARPHIOUTH YMOU ROTHIRBAN OCHANAU MOUNAICHAPTA ZÓ ZÓN TAZÓTAZÓ PTZAZÓ MAUIAS SOUÓRI SOUÓ ÓOUS SARAPTOUMI SARACHTHI AYÓI RICHAMCHÓ BIRATHAU ÓPHAU PHAUÓ DAUA ÓUANT ZOUZÓ ARROUZÓ ZÓTOUAR THÓMNAÓRI AYÓI PTAUCHARÉBI ÁOUSÓBIAU PTBAIN AAAAAAA AFÉIOYÓYÓOIÉEA CHACHACH HACHACH CHARCHARACHACH AMOUN B EI IAEÓBAHREN EMOUNOTHILARIKRIPHIAEYEAIPHIRLIRAHTHON OMENERHABÓEAI CHATHACH PHNESSHÉR PHICHRÓ PHYNRÓ PHÓCHÓCHOCH IARBAIHA GRAMMÉ PHIBAÓCHNEMEÓ

Where are my bay-leaves? Come, Thestylis; where are my love-charms? Come crown me the bowl with the crimson flower o' wool; I would fain have the fire-spell to my cruel dear that for twelve days hath not so much as come anigh me, the wretch, nor knows not whether I be alive or dead, nay nor even hath knocked upon my door, implacable man. I warrant ye Love and the Lady be gone away with his feat fancy. In the morning I'll go to Timagetus' school and see him, and ask what he means to use me so; but, for tonight, I'll put the spell o' fire upon him.

So shine me fair, sweet Moon; for to thee, still Goddess, is my song, to thee and that Hecat infernal who makes e'en the whelps to shiver on her goings to and fro where these tombs be and the red blood lies. All hail to thee, dread and awful

Hecat! I prithee so bear me company that this medicine of my making prove potent as any of Circe's or Medea's or Perimed's of the golden hair.

Wryneck, wryneck, draw him hither.

First barley-meal to the burning. Come, Thestylis; throw it on. Alack, poor fool! whither are thy wits gone wandering? Lord! am I become a thing a filthy drab like thee may crow over? On, on with the meal, and say "These be Delphi's bones I throw. Wryneck, wryneck, draw him hither."

He chanted the phrase seven times over, he could remember it forwards and backwards, he felt happiness for being able to remember such complex words so easily. He was asking for a god to anoint him. He was asking one of the gods to appear before him, to be the son of that god. It was a long process getting a god to appear before you, much longer than summoning demons. This path was the better path, this path was his initiation into becoming a druid.

Once his adjuration was complete, he grabbed hold of the black Isis band and tied it around his head making sure to cover his eyes until he was blind. He made sure not one shade of moonlight deflected in, he also made sure he couldn't see anything when looking down, he had seen that trick being used by other druids, when performing rituals. He knew the ones who had failed in performing their rituals because they didn't allow themselves to be blindfolded properly, who knows? Maybe they were afraid of the dark? Now he had to sit there, holding his staff in his right hand. He had to sit there all night long, and try not to fall asleep. Thankfully it was the height of summertime. So, he really only had seven hours. Still, it was going to be a long seven hours. Best to meditate, and think of nothing, let nature envelope you.

Sunrise came after an eternity. He could feel the warm rays of the sun bounce against his tired eyes.

He was only beginning the second phase of the ritual. The Pnouthis operation was draining, a lot of people couldn't endure it, a lot of fellow druids had failed this ritual at several attempts. Completing it brought ultimate rewards and power. Your very own God who could send dreams, summon anybody you wanted, he could acquire gold or silver, stir up winds from the earth and free you from bonds if you are chained and shackled in prison. He could open any door, and provide food of any kind.

The recipient of the rite is exhorted not to share his secret to another living soul. He needs to be worthy, as worthy as the lord God.

He shook his falcon staff at the rising sun and recited the passage one more time. He then burnt some frankincense on the brazier. He then placed his censer on the ashes of the heliotrope and poured rose oil into the censer.

As he spoke the passage, he began to visualize a blazing white falcon swooping down from the sun, and after being sleep deprived and blindfolded for seven hours straight, the visual was quite easy to conjure up. He had never seen a falcon, only sketches that the druid priest had shown him as a youngster. The great white falcon let out a deafening scream and dropped an oblong stone at his feet before swooping back up into the heavens above.

He picked up the stone. He carved in an inscription. ACHA ACHACHA CHACH CHARCHARA CHACH, the magical words to summon the sun God Helios. He descended down the mountain, back to a temporary hut which he had built from branches and began to sculpt the figure of Helios out of the stone. It took him most of the day, but he was pleased with the result. He was pleased that 18 years of training prepared him so well to adapt and survive, to heal, to cook, to hunt, to sew, to read, to gain knowledge in law, medicine, astrology, music, mathamatics and ancient languages. He was also very pleased that he took the time out to learn how to create art. Whether that was writing poetry, or painting portraits or...sculpting. The fruits of his labour were on display.

After hours of carving and sculpting and polishing, a detailed, miniature figurine of Helios stood before him on his makeshift work table. In his left hand Helios held a globe aloft, while in his right hand his whip ran around his body, which metamorphosed into a serpent biting his own tail. He then bore a hole through the stone and laced a string of leather through the hole, enabling him to wear the amulet around his neck. He spent the rest of the day, cleaning and prepping the hut, laying out plates of fruit and vegetables he had picked from his own self grown garden and preparing a makeshift shrine of candles and sketches next to his sleeping quarters, so his God had a place to rest.

Just as the sun began to set, he ascended his way back up the mountain, amulet around his neck, back towards his stone alter. It was a full moon tonight, a super moon, the most powerful of all the moons, and he smiled as he could see the outline of the moon appear in the evening sky. As dusk turned to twilight, he faced the moon, speaking to the goddess Selene. He sacrificed myrrh troglitis in the censer, and as he lit the fire, he held a branch of myrtle up toward the moon, and began to shake it, reciting a poem to salute the goddess Selene.

INOUTHÓ PTOUAUMI ANCHARICH CHARATOUMI ANOCHA AIBITHROU ACHARABAUBAU BARATHIAN ATEN DOUANANOU APTYR

PANOR PAURACH SOUMI PHORBA PHORIPHORBARAUÓÉTH AZA PHOR RIM MIRPHAR ZAURA PTAUZOU CHÓTHARPARACHTHIZOU ZAITH ATIAU IBAU KANTANYOUMI BATHARA A CHTHIBH ANOCH!

He saw a blazing star above him, blazing so bright it blinded him. He had to avert his eyes, squinting them shut as he shielded them with his free hand. Whatever doubts he had about the ritual before, the truth behind the summoning, was it real or imaginary? Well, those thoughts were laid to rest now. There was no way he was envisioning or imagining this. He had recited an old ancient spell and now a bright blazing gold star had ascended from the heavens, it was the capsule, holding the God he had summoned. The star came down to barely a few feet over his head, and as the light began to dissipate, he was able to blink once more. With his eyes becoming accustomed to the darkness, the outline of a human figure hovered in front of his eyes as the star vanished. He had summoned his God. He actually did it. He kept his composure as he beheld his God.

As his God stood before him, he approached his God and grabbed his right hand, kissing his God on both cheeks.

ÓPTAUMI NAPHTHAUBI MAIOUTHMOU MÉTROBAL RACHÉPTOUMI AMMÓCHARÍ AU-

THEÍ APHANTO TAMARA CHIÓBITAMTRIBÓMIS ARACHO ISARI RACHI IAKOUBI TAURABERÓMYANTAI TAUBI.

"What is your divine name? Reveal it to me freely, so that I may call upon it."

"SOUESOLYR PHTHÉ MÓTH"

"Hither to me King, I call you God of Gods, mighty, boundless, unemployed, indescribable, firmly established Áion. Be inseparable from me from this day forth through all the times of my life. My name is Jacob Krisp, I beseech you to guide me on my path of enlightenment. Protect my body and the entire soul of me.

He showed his makeshift hut to his god, and allowed his god to rest next to his sleeping quarters, once three hours had past, and he could see the sun rise once more, he turned to his god and said, "Go Lord, blessed God, where thou lives eternally, as is thy will."

As the god vanished, he sat at his makeshift table and ate the food and drank the wine as a sacrifice to his god. After fasting for so long the meal was the best he ever had, a plate of fruit, vegetables and meat, along with a bowl of porridge and a cup of gooseberry wine.

Before he went to sleep, he stood outside and watched the dawn spread over the countryside, as he admired the view, he noticed a shooting star. This was at the break of dawn...seeing shooting stars at the break of dawn was a bad omen.

His initiation had arrived just in time. He would be able to show his amulet to the high priest, to notify him that his initiation was successful. There was a war brewing between the Druids and the Romans.

He went to his knapsack and grabbed a dead pigeon he had found on his travels, he gently placed the carcass on his alter and offered a prayer to Matrona, the mother goddess and Lugus, chief of the gods. He cut open the carcass and examined the entrails for divine messages. The Romans were trying their best to spark feuds between chieftain tribes, to cause unrest so they would turn against their Druid authority.

The Romans had no time for Druid authority, and any Druid throughout Europe captured by the Romans were crucified without trial. They were denied citizenship by the Roman's, who considered them masters of the black arts rather than philosophers, doctors and judges. The Vinetti Tribe in Gall, France were stealing cattle from the Reydonay tribe, more than likely under the supervision of the Roman's. He would have to return to France to settle the argument, the shooting star was an omen that if he did not return to France soon and resolve the matter, the war would arrive sooner than expected...

#

Wesley awoke, incoherent, muttering about Chieftain tribes in France and dead pigeons. Once he got his bearings he was questioned by Polly and Gideon about his experience. He explained the vision to them in great detail, explaining how he was a druid from the middle east called Jacob Krisp and how he had journeyed from Israel to Ireland over a period of 18 years as a druid apostle. The entire vision seemed like a clear memory, not only that, but events from Jacob's life, everything that happened to him, all came flooding into Wesley's mind as memories.

When he told Polly that he was fasting and praying for three days as part of an initiation into becoming a druid, and had succeeded, he was able to recount in great detail the items in his possession and the God that appeared before him. To have all of this happen in 10 minutes was a mind altering, life changing experience for Wesley.

Polly came to the conclusion that Jacob was real, and that it was another life Wesley led, somewhere in another dimension. She described how DMT could not only cause visions, but evaporate the meaning of space, time and matter. That there were countless dimensions, and we all existed in each and every one of them. Wesley said he felt like he travelled back in time, Polly went onto explain that all timelines, from all points in history, can exist at the same time in different dimensions.

She had seen it happen before with DMT experimentations, and it always led to a major development in their primal therapy. Wesley requested that if he was living the life of a druid in that dimension, that he should continue doing so in his existing dimension. He asked Novalis to call him Jacob and declared that his DMT trip had claimed him with divinity, the commune gladly obliged. Henceforth, Wesley Harding was now known as Jacob Krisp.

#

Once Jacob claimed divinity, He began to study and read through the large collection of books, that were stacked high on shelfs in the Novalis library. It was quite the eclectic collection, ranging in everything from philosophy, to chemistry, to art, science, astrology, music, poetry and classic literature.

Jacob began to open his mind to new ideologies and the more he learnt, the more he became inspired, the more enthusiastic he became. He would burst out from the library and race to the common room to eagerly share his newfound knowledge with the rest of the commune. The more they listened to Jacob's findings, the more enlightened they became.

They began to see Jacob as their unofficial spiritual leader, they saw that his experience with DMT had opened a portal to a dimension where he was a prophet, who could summon the Gods, now that he had given himself the title of the prophet, there was no doubt in anybody's mind, that he could become an even greater prophet over many dimensions.

Once Jacob had completed studying everything that was to be found in the library, a process that took many months, his thirst for knowledge grew ever greater. What he needed to further his studies was to gain broadband access, and after a large discussion with the entire commune, it was decided that Jacob could access the web via an old computer that Gideon was able to rig up in the basement.

Nobody else was interested in re-connecting with technology, they felt happier and freer without it, it was for Jacob's work, and he spent hours at a time, writing and researching in the basement, while the rest of the commune went about with their daily business.

Jacob would embark on major spiritual rabbit holes, he wrote about his findings, and every time he would emerge from a rabbit hole, the community could sense a warm serenity radiating from Jacob. Jacob's teachings and prophecies became as important as their daily primal sessions. Jacob still participated in the sessions, but he was more of a guidance rather than a participant, his calming presence assuring the commune that they were in safe hands if they were to embark on a physically and emotionally dangerous primal.

It got to be that after every evening session, the commune would gather in the chapel at the east end of the building, and Jacob would share whatever newfound knowledge he had acquired that day.

He would teach them everything he learnt about DMT, otherwise known as dimethyltryptamine, he would preach about experiences of DMT visions from people on message boards and social networks, that were just as inspiring and life changing as his own.

He read out passages from the bible and proclaimed that the heavenly visions and miracles that occurred throughout the bible stories, were brought on by the effects of DMT.

One prime example is the fable of Moses and the burning bush. 'There the angel of the lord appeared to him in flames of fire, from within a bush.' Jacob explained how the story was real, it was because the bush was of acacia origin, and when it burst into flames, a vision of God appeared before Moses.

Jacob's teachings were eclectic, enlightening and fascinating to the House of Novalis. He would read passages from lectures given by the legendary spiritual guru, Terrence McKenna, stating that, "for the past 500 years, Western culture has suppressed the idea of disembodied intelligences, of the presence and reality of spirit. Thirty seconds into a DMT flash, that's a dead issue."

He taught Novalis about the origins of Hermetic Philosophy, and about its founder, Hermes Trismegistus, a prophet around during the time of Moses, and how all religions in the past 2000 years are relative, as they all link back to his accurate spiritual philosophy. He spoke about how art, philosophy, music, astrology, poetry and mathematics, all derive from Hermetic philosophy.

He spoke about how your conscious is a living entity, and because our brains possess certain levels of DMT, our muse is actually a cosmic broadcast used by higher beings that send us ideas via electromagnetic wavelengths.

He would play Bob Dylan Records that lay dusty in the collection amassed by the commune and would go into grave detail on each of his records, pointing out where the lyrics were interpreted with Hermetic meaning. How Dylan was able to describe the meaning of life through his poetry and how he is probably our greatest living man since William Shakespeare.

He played the commune Dylan's recording of 'All Along The Watchtower' and explained how when you take the last four lines of the song, and put them at the beginning, the story and the interpretation of the song become completely different.

He explained how the song was the greatest poem ever written, how society should rebel against the idea of the bourgeois and rise up against it. He described the main characters in the song, the Joker and the Thief, as two outcasts, spiritual prophets who are riding into Babylon to begin an uprising and break the city from their bureaucratic mindset, how the path of the mind is greater than the path of the flesh, a path that includes creature comforts and items that numb you from your true self.

He read passages from 'Finnegan's Wake,' claiming it to be the quintessential work of literature of the 20th century. He quoted how Terrence McKenna once claimed, "if the whole universe were to be destroyed, and 'Finnegan's Wake' survived, you could rebuild the universe with it." Jacob went on to say, "It's a work of magical complexity, there is no time in the reality of life, an age can happen in thirty seconds, hence the stream of consciousness. It's as if Joyce has taken 1000 years of history and melted away the boundaries."

What the commune got a kick out of the most, was when Jacob described the reason why Joyce wrote 'Finnegan's Wake,' it was because Joyce loathed the work of Carl Jung and psychoanalysis in general, that psychology never tapped into the true meaning of the universe, not in the way 'Finnegan's Wake,' was able to do.

Jacob went onto read a hermetic text he had found and printed off the web, written by Basilides of Alexandria, the text was titled 'VII SERMONES AD MORTUS', and Jacob read passages from the text in one of his classes. If Jacob had researched the origins of the text and its author, rather than accepting it at face value and believing it to be the work of an ancient Egyptian, he would have discovered its author to be Carl Jung, who had become Gnostic in the latter years of his life.

He had prayed to Basilides and had transcribed what Basilides had prophesied to him in his prayers. Few copies of the book were printed, Jung had used the pseudonym of Basilides, claiming him to be the true author as so not to lose his audience of readers. 'VII SERMONES AD MORTUS' became the foundation for the 'Novalis Manifesto,' a gnostic philosophy that incorporated their roots of primal therapy. Although the commune despised Carl Jung and his teachings, he had accidently become their spiritual inspiration.

Over the months, The House of Novalis became so enlightened by Jacobs's lectures, the urge to spread his teachings far and wide became overwhelming. They began to wonder with glee if Jacob Krisp was something more than a mere mortal. Gideon asked Jacob, on a whim, if he could video record Jacob giving one of his lectures to the commune?

Jacob agreed on the condition that it was recorded in such a manner that his identity would remain hidden. His argument being that he wished for his teachings to be merited by what was said, not by who said them. Jacob requested that he wear a white druid robe, his face covered by a large hood, and that he stood on the alter, in front of his fellow Novalis members.

The speech was recorded by Gideon and distributed online via social networks, where it garnered attention, both good and bad. The speech was pivotal in The House of Novalis developing from a primal commune into a gnostic, theosophic…cult.

#

"The eternal parent, wrapped in her ever visible robes, had slumbered again for seven entities. Time was not, for it lay asleep in the infinite bosom, universal mind was not, the great causes of misery were not, for there was no-one to produce and get ensnared by them.

Darkness alone filled the boundless all. Father, mother and son were one in all. The son had not awakened yet for the new wheel, and his pilgrimage Theron. The seven sublime lords and the seven truths had ceased to be. The universe, the son of necessity, was immersed in Paranishpanua, to be outbreathed by which is and yet is not.

The causes for existence had been done away with. The visible that was, and the invisible that is, rested in eternal non-being. The one being. Alone, the form of existence stretched boundless, infinite, causeless, in dreamless sleep, and life pulsated unconsciousness in universal space.

Throughout that, all presence, which is sensed by the open eye of the dangma. Such is cosmic evolution. The universe is expanding. It is getting increasingly organized and energetic. It will gradually develop into supernova wonder world, a dimension on the eight level, our final destination.

Western civilization has been trying to brainwash us for centuries. This prophecy of free will is nothing but an illusion. Our cosmic journeys have already been mapped out for us by a higher being. While our destinies are set in stone, the West try to bog us down with bureaucracy and laws. Let it be known henceforth, from this day onwards, **we are all above the law.** We will rise together, as one, and our draconian, Babylonian, bourgeois state will crumble and fall.

Our modern industrious world fills our water with chlorine, they warp our minds with advanced technology to a point that we spend more time in a virtual world than our own. They tax us for being alive, and they govern so many rules and pile them upon us until we reach breaking point, and if we don't comply, they will destroy you.

Here at Novalis, we are free from the shackles of our, draconian, Babylonic state. We are free from the bourgeoisie, and we can once again nurture a pure civilization and proud culture that was once lost to us.

When the soul, failing to discriminate, extends itself beyond the cosmos, it becomes submerged in the plemora and becomes nothing. The West have tried to convince us since the Roman era that the word, 'nothing' is used in a negative sense. All is all, all is nothing...nothing is everything. We are living in a hivemind, where you are told how to think, how to feel, and we take everything at face value.

Question everything. Question the true

meaning of words. Question my words. Question our existence. The western civilization has never envisioned a permanent dissolution of human individuality in humanity. Desire for self-knowledge is just as much a desire as food or sex. When desire is dampened by conscious efforts, what remains is a psychic force from which the libidinal cosmic force of the vital surge has been artificially removed.

It is important not to confuse freedom with mere permissiveness. Strive after your true nature, force natural energy and channel its power. Provoke the bureaucracy and let the authoritarians know you will not be diverted from your cosmic destiny.

When we all rise together, rise above the draconian law to the point it will cease to exist, use your libido as a principal of pleasure, as its motivating force, even as it has the individual principle as its driving force. We deserve gratitude for the wisdom we seek, not guilt and shame.

An anxious individualist can be in as much psychological trouble as the yogi seeking the endless void. Had the bourgeoisie managed to stay in touch with us, we who follow the cosmic journey, they would have never been given a chance to force their agenda. Wisdom's final say is that freedom and life belong to that solely who must reconquer them everyday."

#

Over the course of a period of twelve months, The House of Novalis became one of the leading spiritual centres in Europe. This was mainly down to the popularity of Jacob's lectures that were posted online, which unbeknownst to his followers was a philosophy which was copy and pasted from a variety of philosophers and visionaries throughout time.

Jacob's lectures hit a nerve with people, not just around the country, but from Europe and further abroad. The house became so popular it was decided that they should hold a public spiritual retreat. 30 people attended the first event, paying €300 each. The other factor that intrigued the hive mind of the public was Wesley's belief that all nations should rise above bureaucracy. To do whatever felt right in their hearts, in their minds and in their souls.

Some people took this statement for granted, and large protests turned ugly and violent any time they marched on the houses of the Oireachtas. There was an uprising occurring, and The House of Novalis were the root cause.

The spread of religious freedom in Jacob's manifesto was sanctimonious to those who were starved of spirituality, living in a politically correct, censored culture, a civilization where publicly displaying your thoughts had you put on trial.

What the followers of Novalis could not apprehend, was how they unwittingly fought free of one fascist regime to inadvertently join another. Jacob was in his element, he felt untouched, nothing could knock him off his high perch, no criticism could penetrate his large defensive shell. He was right and everybody else was wrong. He could now manipulate people into emotionally doing his bidding, without any remorse, faking concern and understanding.

After Jacob's lectures became a viral hit, the house noticed that the air of mystery Jacob brought by concealing his identity only made him more intriguing to listen to. They bought him a rooster mask, made in the style of the venetian masks that were popular during the Renaissance Era. His masked face became synonymous with quotes from his lectures, which were plastered all over the internet. Jacob Krisp became as quotable as Martin Luther King.

The House of Novalis was the new "in" thing, something to distract people from their mundane lives. When Gideon suggested to Jacob that he do a live stream, to gauge the public reaction as it happened, nobody expected the popularity the stream would bring.

Jacob "The Rooster God" Krisp, sat in the Magik Theatre Church, wearing his white robes, his hood shadowing the golden rooster mask which covered his face, and as he spouted his philosophy, Gideon purposefully used an editing trick to make the broadcast look scratchy and distorted as it was beamed live, making it seem otherworldly.

Roughly 20,000 people tuned in at various times throughout the two-hour broadcast to hear what this new age prophet and mystic had to say. After completing his sermon, he spent the next hour repeating the phrase "I love you" over and over again, causing something quite profound to occur.

The more Jacob repeated the phrase, the more people replied in the live messenger claiming they loved him back. Over the space of three hours, The House of Novalis raised close to €9,000 in charitable donations to help maintain the house, website, publicity and living costs for all active members.

Polly and Tara in particular, were overcome with joy, flabbergasted by the amount of people who were starved of love in the world. They saw this as a unique opportunity to promote primal scream therapy.

Thus, the weekend spiritual retreat came to pass. A three-day seminar over the Easter Bank Holiday weekend which was entitled, "Finding your inner self," promising peace, happiness, fortune, and tranquility. Jacob, Polly, and Tara, with massive help and input from the rest of the members, went about setting up a plan that would keep the customers entertained and enlighted for the entire bank holiday weekend.

Patrons partook in primal scream therapy each morning, before Jacob would lead them in prayer and silent meditation, meals would be provided by the house, followed by a spiritual seminar each evening.

The guided mediation and prayer involved sitting cross legged for hours on end without any food or water. At the end of the session, plastic cups filled with cordial were passed out to the patrons, who drank it gleefully. They then formed a line waiting for Jacob to embrace them in a warm hug. Because they spent so long in an isolated mantric stance, once they were touched by the hands of Jacob, a divine ecstasy flooded their bodies.

They felt at one with the universe, like the hand of God had touched them.

The weekend retreats were held every month at first, normally on a bank holiday weekend, but grew in stature and popularity that after six months, they decided to begin doing the retreats on a weekly basis, and raised the attendance fee to €1,000 to cover the costs of having extra people staying with them.

Their gardens turned into a large camp site. And with the extra money, they were able to hire people to teach extra activities, whether it be choir singing, yoga, or art. They held discos in the common room, where there were three rules if you wished to partake. No alcohol, no speaking and you had to dance for the entire two hours. The evening time was filled with people drinking cans and smoking joints, and free love was allowed and encouraged.

The House of Novalis set up a Facebook account, which had close to 400,000 members. They had an Instagram account, which had 200,000 followers, on Twitter they had close to 100,000 followers and the website was free to anybody who wished to browse the philosophy of Jacob, or read up on the profiles on the founding members of Novalis, or even just browse the hundreds of photographs of people attending the spiritual retreats. All relaxed, smiling, and happy, all looking like they were enjoying themselves.

Their official YouTube channel was full of videos of Jacob's sermons and sessions of Primal Scream Therapy, and after 8 months, had notched up more than 2 million views combined. While Jacob, Polly, Tara, Lulu, Bertie and Bonnie helped Gideon with promoting and distribution, Oscar kept himself busy in the old greenhouse, growing magic mushrooms and Phalaris arundinacea plants that produced copious amounts of DMT.

The plants and mushrooms were easy to grow, and the temperature settings in the greenhouse meant that he was able to widen his network of plants and began to grow cannabis.

Before long Oscar had so many crates of drugs for distributing, he didn't know what to do with them. The solution came via a contact Polly knew in Belfast, she had kept in touch with an IRA sergeant by the name of Bernard Brennan, who was running a splinter group of paramilitary soldiers out of West Belfast.

Along with being a political paramilitary group, they also had a large drugs network and were in the business of smuggling weapons to and from the Middle East and Russia. They even offered training to those in war torn countries in the art of guerrilla warfare.

Bernard agreed to smuggle and sell the mushrooms, cannabis and DMT into the north and the U.K. for 40% of the profits on the promise that Novalis agreed to shelter any IRA soldiers on the run from the law and hide any crates of weapons that were deemed too hot to handle until they were able to find a buyer.

This led to Jacob requesting that Bernard and any of his soldiers they shelter, provide them training in handling and shooting weapons, which led to Brennan agreeing to providing soldiers as security to Novalis, in the event of authorities landing on their doorstep with search warrants, or despondent anti-commune groups protesting at the main gates.

As Bernard set up his drugs operation, Novalis began to strum up new innovative ideas to expand their growth and popularity. Jacob and Polly had to come up with new ideas to promise eternal bliss, peace and happiness. They began to think of ways to expand their weekend retreats to entice members into spending more money on weeklong retreats using buzz words in their advertising such as, "find nirvana in three easy steps," or, "realise the absolute truth in seven days!"

Jacob knew this would take extra time and effort to prepare, so he began to write a doctrine that would be given to new members at the beginning of a retreat, his main aim, to create an enlighted, ecstatic, global society. To buy a large plot of land to expand their commune, and create an enlightened city by the year 2035.

When he told his plan to the rest of the founding members, they fell around the common room, hugging each other and crying with glee. Here was their chance to build their emphatic eutopia, to help civilization find their true path to glory. "We'll be the forerunners in achieving goals only others would ever dream of achieving, where we can all live in harmony with one another, away from prying eyes. To follow the path of the mind while the damned in society venture down their hedonistic path of the flesh.

Co-operation will be our main vocal point, where everyone will blend together in peace and tranquility. We need to guide one another. This all needs to happen by using clarity, where technology is dismissed and anything you require will be at your immediate disposal. There is something so simply beautiful in finding a new way of living. Something so gratifying and satisfying in building your own community, freeing yourself from the chains that have weighed you down throughout not only this life, but through all of your past lives."

Jacob was in the groove, in the moment, Gideon began recording him.

"I am the music maker, I am the dreamer of dreams, I wander by lone sea-breakers, and sit by desolate streams. World losers and world forsakers, upon whom the pale moon gleams, I am the prime mover and shaker of the world forever, it seems."

***

CHAPTER 22---
WE NEED TO TALK ABOUT WESLEY

The second murder trial was another absolute media circus, however the heat wasn't as heavy on Jimmy. There was a lot of interrogation footage to get through, and another Voir Doire was announced. Joe Perry was going for another dismissal, using the same tactic as before, the controversial technique of one Detective Sergeant James Daniels.

The heat wasn't as heavy on Jimmy because the public were beginning to see through the media façade of defending a suspect with learning difficulties. This was down to the fact that Sebastian had overwhelming evidence against him. While no semen was found at the crime scene or murder scene, (Jimmy found this odd,) Sebastian's hair and DNA were found on Stephanie's cadaver.

Joe Perry's defence was that Sebastian was coerced into committing sexual acts by Britney. The biggest revelation in the case came when Britney confessed to murdering Stephanie with the hammer. Which meant, Sebastian Rivers was not going to be charged with murder.

This was a theory that Linda and Jimmy went through during the interrogation, Britney's ghostly face on the monitor not showing any hint of remorse nodded to this, but Jimmy never thought she'd confess to it. No chance in hell. Sebastian was playing her like a fiddle. It seemed like love held no bounds. She was willing to spend life in prison to protect the man she loved, no way was she going to sell him up the swanny.

She killed Britney, but Jimmy knew that this was Sebastian's plan. Much like Charlie Manson ordering his family to kill all the 'piggies,' Sebastian sat in the courtroom smirking, as charges of violence against a minor, sexual abuse against a minor, kidnapping, assault, manslaughter and other nit-picky charges were read out to him.

Joe Perry immediately requested an inquiry be held into the interrogation of Sebastian Rivers. The one thing on Jimmy's side was he didn't have to be sat in court looking at the shrivelled chestnut face of Her Honourable Judge Elizabeth Lyndon. She was on a sabbatical, her son had gone missing, and she was dealing with personal issues in relation to this trauma. Jimmy knew she was dealing with these personal issues by sunbathing in France.

His Honourable Judge Eddie Francis was now holding proceedings, and he wasn't as patient to Joe Perry's antics.

The cross examination went much like before. Only this time when Perry went for the kill, Jimmy was ready for him, stating that the evidence against the suspect was overwhelming. The two men held a verbal back and forth, as Perry once again accused Jimmy of attempting to coerce a confession out of his client. The booming voice of Eddie Francis cut him off.

"There is nothing in the footage to suggest that a confession is being coerced. The Gardaí already had a confession, they had found the body of the missing girl, and were waiting on the DNA evidence they were sure would collaborate the confession! They showed a degree of professionalism, excellence, and thoroughness seldom seen in any police work, and although he was brazen and rude in his approach, he had every right to be, given the behaviour of your client throughout the entire interrogation. Am I right, or am I right, Mr. Perry?"

"Your honour if it may please the court..."

"No, it may not. I'm dismissing your claim

and the video will be submitted to evidence. Which means we'll converge back here with the Jury on Monday morning at 9am. I must also advice any journalist who enters my courtroom, if you so much as utter one lie in covering this trial, if you accuse the Major Crimes Unit of not doing their job properly, after me stating right here they did an excellent job, I will banish all of you from the courtroom. And I mean all of you. I will not have you convince or sway the public with false information, are we agreed?"

All of the young new age journalists nodded with enthusiasm, as the mainstream, traditional journalists solemnly nodded in unison.

After a month of opening statements, witness testimony, prosecution, defence, and closing statements, the jury reached a verdict. Sebastian Rivers was found guilty of kidnapping, assault on a minor, sexual abuse of a minor, and **not** guilty of manslaughter. They couldn't prove beyond a reasonable doubt, that Sebastian partook in the actual murder, especially not after Stephanie confessing to it.

Jimmy put his head in his hands when he heard the not guilty verdict. He'd done it again. The bastard had gotten away with it again. Sebastian was sentenced to nine years in St Francis's mental institution for treatment and analysis, with the last four being suspended, and could be out sooner than five years depending on co-operation and good behaviour.

He would have access to doctors, phones, television, video games. St Francis was a cushy place. He'd get all the medical and psychological assistance his heart required. The mainstream press called it justice, claiming that people like Sebastian needed help and treatment to help further Irish society and banish the stigma of people with mental illness. To Jimmy, karma was playing a cruel joke on him. He was going to have to keep a close eye on Sebastian. Something which would be difficult to due to the ever-changing landscape of the Major Crimes Unit.

Over the period of ten months, the team dealt with their share of kidnappings, rapes, assaults and the odd murder, Galwegians weren't prone to murdering each other easily, it was mainly gangland violence in the city, and the ever-growing threat of another IRA presence in the north. While they had a high turnover of solved cases, one unsolved case grew colder and colder, the disappearance of Myia Dawkins. Hobbs and Rodge had covered every angle, every blade of grass, interviewed everybody, followed every lead diligently, only to find themselves running straight into brick walls.

It got to the point Hobbs knocked on Jimmy's office door, causing Jimmy to startle away after falling asleep at his desk. The faces of the dead were growing stronger, and larger, causing Jimmy to lose more and more sleep.

"Come in." Jimmy shouted.

Hobbs entered, dishevelled, pale, as he sported a week-old beard, he looked as good as Jimmy was feeling.

"We need to talk about Wesley."

"Who?"

"Wesley Harding, our former prime suspect. Nobody's seen him in almost a year. The profile fits Jimmy. Fits him to a tee. We've looked at every possible angle, he did it Jimmy, I know he did, I can feel it in my bones. I still feel bad about what happened, I know I fucked up, but you got to help us Jimmy. Rodge is on the verge of quitting, and I can't blame him, I don't know how to close this case, it's baffling. But one thing I do know, one thing I'm sure about, as much as I'm sure how much my ex hates me, he did it. I just don't know how he did it."

Jimmy nodded in agreement and pulled up the interrogation footage of Wesley on his computer.

The two men sat in Jimmy's office, late into the night. Watching and re-watching the two hour long footage. They took notes on every mannerism, every tick the suspect had. Jimmy knew Hobbs was right. The profile helped, and Hobbs and Rodge had eliminated every other possibility, Hobbs couldn't help wince every time he watched back on his mistakes, this was encouraging to Jimmy, it meant Hobbs was learning from his mistakes.

Jimmy had written the word BLEACH into his notepad and had circled it every time he heard it.

"So, there was no blood in his apartment, or any trace evidence of any kind?"

"Nothing." Hobbs replied.

"Did he smell like bleach?"

"It was faint, but it was there, my guess is it was on his clothes, he seemed like the type of kid who didn't change his clothes much, I reckon personal hygiene wasn't a high priority on his list."

"And he told you he couldn't remember the last time he cleaned?"

"Correct."

Jimmy kept staring at the word BLEACH, the connection was on the tip of his brain, he couldn't quite reach it.

"You didn't find any evidence in Myia's place, nothing at all?"

"No."

"What about her bedroom?"

"Sure. We checked, just to rule it out more than anything. We used lumisol lighting, but all of the evidence found led back to her. It lit up the way a normal young ladies' bedroom would light up. Nothing out of the ordinary."

"No trace of discharge, or semen, or anything to say there was somebody there the night she disappeared?"

"No. Her boyfriend, or whatever you want to call him. He's clean. We did find hairs, but that was after her friends used a spare key to let themselves in and search the place."

Jimmy frowned. "Was Wesley with them when this happened."

"Yeah, he said he wanted to help."

"Did you find his hair at the scene?"

"Yeah, in every room, but we found the hair of all the people who trampled around the place that night."

"No sign of forced entry…"

"For the millionth time, no, I swear to the angels and the saints up in heaven, the door or windows were not violated in any way, shape or form whatsoever."

"Did you find any bleach?"

"No, he didn't have any."

"What if Wesley had a key?"

"To Myia's place? Doubtful. No way would she give him one. By all accounts they were friendly, but witnesses say he creeped her out a little."

"He did some work for the landlord…"

"Some property sitting, anytime he was out of town. Nothing strenuous."

"Very cheap and easy to copy keys."

Hobbs looked at him, he too was now frowning.

"He stole a key, copied it, and replaced it?"

"He could have done it on his lunch break."

"Sure, that's a great theory and all, but that's all it is, a theory."

"Let's take a drive over there."

Hobbs didn't protest, they were both exhausted and wanted to get home. Jimmy grabbed his evidence kit, just in case, another gut feeling was growing in his stomach.

They had reached Hollywood barely ten minutes later, pulling up outside Myia's empty apartment, with Wesley's empty apartment ominously watching them from across the road.

The landlord was there to greet them and didn't look so happy about it. As he unlocked the door to let the detectives in, he grumbled how he was unable to shift the property, or the one across the road, he couldn't even rent them, nobody wanted anything to do with them.

Jimmy tried to envision the killers' movements as he slowly made his way through the apartment, Hobbs tried not to laugh as Jimmy walked across the room like a mixture of Jesus and the Bee gees, arms out before him clutching his evidence kit tightly in his right hand, his eyes half closed, as if he was about to bless the space around him.

Jimmy tried to envision the empty apartment with Myia's belongings. He tried to image how it smelt, he read in the report that Myia was an avid vapour, so the room would smell very sweet, like lemon and strawberry, a very pleasant, welcoming smell.

He floated his way into the bedroom and envisioned Myia sleeping in front of him. The room was empty but he could quickly formulate an image of Myia, looking like an angel with her blonde locks tussled over her pillows.

"He killed her, right here."

"What makes you say that?" Hobbs said as he watched his old colleague at work with an old envy that burned as strongly as ever.

"It's where she would least expect it, the element of surprise. He had the power, he was a God standing over her, watching her, deciding her destiny."

Jimmy unzipped his evidence kit and took out his lumisol flash light.

"He'd be too neat to leave her body, he would have had to follow through with what he started."

He looked at the entrance to the bathroom, the door swung in the emptiness, revealing the mirror, sink, and toilet. Jimmy noticed his reflection in the bathroom mirror. His eyes looked large and lifeless.

"There." Jimmy said as he readied the flash light and killed the lights, leaving a blue orb as their only light source.

Hobbs and McDonacha watched in horror as Jimmy passed the lumisol light over the tiles of the bathroom, revealing blood spatter, the vicious blue made the entire scene look like something out of a psychedelic horror film.

"He smelt like bleach because he used her bleach. He cut her up in here. We need to get a CSI team down here, and cadaver dogs, there may be a trace of something left…he cut her up, and put her body parts into bin bags and threw her in the dumpsters outside like everyday rubbish. We need people scouring the landfill, especially around the incinerator, for any trace of bone..."

Jimmy's voice was so low and menacing that he was cut short by the landlord vomiting into the toilet.

#

The team were hard at it the following days, wading through mountains of shit to find any trace of Myia's body. CSI found remnants of DNA, skin cells, belonging to Wesley Harding, and the blood matched that of the victim. The team's problem now was finding Wesley, he too, had vanished without a trace.

There was silence as the team sat around with their arms folded, staring into space, wondering what to do next, hoping that Wesley didn't kill himself, just so they could catch the bastard. They had units scouring the river along the cathedral and any river and stream around the West of Ireland that they could think of, but they found nothing, if there was a body, it would have appeared by now.

Their silence was shattered by the office phone ringing, Jimmy answered.

"Yeah?"

"Turn on channel two." It was Deeley.

"What's going on?"

"Harrison has gotten word from the Deputy Minister for Justice that there's a drug smuggling ring operating from Achill Island, the IRA are involved, and they're armed to the teeth."

Jimmy walked over to the television and switched it on, as the picture flickered, he went rooting for pen and paper at Kiki's desk.

"What's that have to do with us?"

"They've done a documentary, about this... commune...or cult...or whatever you want to call it."

"Who's they?"

"Some production company, they spent a week down in Achill, they're a bunch of hippies walking around with AK-47's, smoking pot, or whatever, talking about creating a free society. Commissioner James wants heads to roll. He wants you on the case, Jimmy."

"Is there any proof, or is this a witch-hunt?"

"See for yourself, Harrision has got his knickers in a right fuckin twist over this."

"What about vice, can they not handle this? Or the terrorism unit, or both?"

"He wants all hands on deck for this, top priority he says."

Jimmy once again, couldn't find a pen, and Kiki once again, took a pen from her blazer pocket and threw it at him.

"We're kind of busy here with a case..."

"Just watch the fuckin telly Jimmy!"

With that, Deeley abruptly hung up. Abed turned up the volume as the screen portrayed spectacular, jaw dropping views of Achill Island.

"Is this about drugs?" Abed asked. "My mind reading skills are a bit rusty at the moment."

"Some fuckin IRA operation, I don't know in the fuck, the terrorism unit couldn't find their arse from their elbow even if they tried."

"What kinda drugs?" Kiki asked.

"I don't know! Fuckin drugs, the kind that get you high. Deeley mentioned something about drug smuggling..."

"SHUSHHHH"

It was Rodge who shushed Jimmy, which made him angry. There was nothing Jimmy Daniels despised more than passive aggressive behaviour, especially shushing. Before he could say anything, the narrator's voice boomed across the bullpen with his confident, smooth sounding, D4 tones.

"The picturesque Achill Island is home to many things, poets, painters, basking sharks, you may even see the odd dolphin pop up its head up from time to time, they have had everybody live here from the likes of artist Robert Henry, to Nobel Prize Winning author Heinrick Boll, but never in Achill's long and illustrious history have they ever played host to a spiritual centre, not just any spiritual centre, but one of the leading spiritual centres in Europe, The House of Novalis. Which incorporates Primal Scream Therapy with hermetic teachings, lead by their spiritual guru, Jacob 'The Rooster God' Krisp."

"I'm gonna get popcorn ready, does anyone else want popcorn?" Abed declared, as he made his way into the small kitchen, everybody shook their heads, engrossed to the screen, except for Linda, who waved her arms around excitedly.

"Make me a hot chocolate, and get me a doughnut from the fridge!"

"Yes Ma'am.' A minute later the team could hear the microwave whirring softly.

The documentary was now showing the members of the house, sitting on cushions in the large common room, screaming their heads off.

"The therapy, which first came to the attention of the public when it was created by American Psychologist, Doctor Art Janov, back in the 1970's, has found a resurgence in the House of Novalis,

where they take in all people of race, colour and creed, anybody who is need of spiritual healing. The process involves screaming for two hours per session, every morning and evening, to help cure any psychological ailments that they may have. At the former convent in the parish of Keel, which can house up to 25 people, we caught up with its founder and owner, Polly Applegate, to find out just exactly what primal scream therapy entails."

The footage cut to Polly Applegate, sitting on the floor against the wall of the common room. The first thought that struck Jimmy was how much she looked like punk singer, Patti Smith. Polly began to speak in the footage.

"Our society puts a premium on mediocrity, on politeness whereas we put an emphasis on aggression, like an animal looking to hunt, not in an evil way, just in the way nature was intended for humans. If you hurt someone deliberately, because of your truth, it's up to them how they want to take it.

"So you feel the aggression is helpful?"

"Oh, absolutely. You need to get out every horrible thought that poisons your mind."

"Won't that just cause more harm than good?"

"No, because it's there anyway. If it's not out in the open, if you don't control these feelings, they formulate as vibrations and tensions. Better to get it out there than let it fester inside of you. We want

everyone to express their aggression to one another because it can be dealt with and we can move on from it. If you can't honestly say to someone what's on your mind it all just boils up inside of you.

"Is that the fundamental reason why you scream?"

"When you're hurt really bad as a child, when you're prevented from crying, when you're slapped, that affects you as a person. I just feel in every part of the world, children are not allowed be themselves, and Jacob, he testifies to this when he preaches. There's nothing special about the people who come here. People who think outside of the box are having a tough time in society, they're being harassed and bullied for not following the norm. everybody these days have been brainwashed by social media. There's barely any gardens or parks for children to play in. Mothers are frustrated and take it out on their children. The world today is selfish, it's not built for children."

"Have you a message today to anybody out there who can't visit this place? Who are craving spiritual comfort? Is there any advice you have for those who need it?"

"Yeah...turn off social media."

Jimmy looked over to Linda, who was frantically taking notes, a doughnut half shoved into her gob. Abed sat beside her, engrossed in the documentary, shovelling handfuls of popcorn into his mouth.

"Is anything she says true or is this all-psychobabble nonsense?"

"I did a paper on Janov in Uni." Linda said, taking the doughnut out of her mouth. "Not everything he said was bullshit. The repressed pain of a traumatic childhood generally leads to an emotionally stunted adult, even when it comes to small matters such as being unable to comfort a crying child. There's 70 years of papers and studies by different psychologists claiming it works, my lecturer didn't see it that way, but my lecturer was an asshat."

The narrators voice boomed from the television once more.

"Of course, not everybody is happy with their new neighbours. They've being condemned from the pulpit, and some are apprehensive. There is a reason for this apprehension."

The documentary showed footage of armed IRA soldiers patrolling the grounds.

"This is what makes the centre so controversial, along the pathways, corridors and gardens of the old convent, armed men patrol the premises. The guru of Novalis, Jacob Krisp, claims it is merely protection from the outside world, however critics see this as a call to arms, it is no secret that Krisp des-

pises bureaucracy, when asked if they had permits to carry weapons, the armed guards refused to comment, what was more alarming…

The footage cut to the greenhouse around the back of the house, where the camera panned along rows and rows of magic mushrooms and marijuana plants.

"Is this…the unlicensed practice of growing and distributing marijuana and the illegal manufacturing and distribution of 'magic mushrooms.' There are rumours a plenty that the house uses the fishing harbour to smuggle said drugs and crates of automatic weapons to and from the island. We caught up with one local, who wanted his identity hidden, to hear about what way the locals feel about 'The House of Novalis.'"

The silhouette of a man sat next to a kitchen window, his voice is altered to protect his identity, The Minaun Cliffs could be seen through his kitchen window.

"They're a nuisance, I would prefer to see them out of Keel, and away from Achill. I don't think there's any room for them around here. It's affected not just our tourist trade but the mental wellbeing of the locals. You can't sleep at night when you hear the screaming, it travels for miles, they sound like banshees haunting the roads. It really is horrible when you hear it."

Jimmy looked at the phone, waiting for it to ring. It lay there dormant. But Jimmy knew it wouldn't take long before a member of parliament called demanding an investigation. A judge was probably writing a warrant, but Jimmy guessed they were as well to wipe their arse with it, there was no way this hired 'security' was just going to comply, The Armed

Garda Unit would have to be on standby, the military would have to be called in.. These thoughts flashed through Jimmy's mind in seconds as the narrator spoke once more.

"The technological age and the stress and strain of everyday living has brought with it a lot of new and complex mental issues. The people who live here are typical products of society. For most of them, their problems began in childhood, their inability to cope stayed with them as they grew up. Oscar Boyle, from Galway worked at Dublin's Botanical Gardens."

The footage portrayed Oscar, who sat in the common room next to Polly, looking so excited he looked like he was about to burst ftom the scenes.

"I couldn't control my feelings. I couldn't control when I was scared. I couldn't tell people when I was scared. That was the first thing I needed to do. I was dreaming of someplace like here, where I could enjoy being with plants. I felt I wanted someplace different than Babylon and the pollution of the city. I was trained in university. I couldn't teach I was so afraid of everything. The child within me had been so suppressed and so scared. I could not display my feelings, especially by the Christian Brothers..."

Oscar's interview was cut off mid sentence as the footage cut to a church alter. A red leather chair sits empty on the alter.

"We caught up with Jacob 'The Rooster God' Krisp, to find it what the long term future entails for The House of Novalis, and whether what he feels the commune is doing is illegal. Viewer discretion is advised.

Jimmy's eyes widened as he saw a well built man

in white robes sit in the chair. He wore a golden rooster mask which covers his features, his head covered by a white hood. Jimmy smelt something sweet and turned to find Linda standing next to him. He pushed down the small flutter of butterflies growing in his stomach. It was unprofessional to develop feelings for a work colleague, especially one that he saw all day, every day. He hadn't even been physical with a woman since his last relationship finished seven years ago.

"This is...new." Linda said, her eyes were just as wide as Jimmy's as they watched the interview begin on screen. The narrator was off screen as he addressed Jacob.

"What I'm trying to get out of this philosophy, Jacob, is what is it about your lectures you want to teach people?"

"What can you teach people?"

"What I mean is, what is the fundamental message in your teachings."

"To be reborn, to start all over."

"Like a born-again Christian?"

"Yeah, or whatever, I don't know."

"What do you mean, you don't know?"

"What the fuck!" Hobbs shouted as he nearly bucked out of his seat. "Kiki..."

"I'm on it, I'm on it." Kiki was frantically typing on her keyboard, bringing up files related to

Wesley Harding. Abed did his usual routine of leaning over Kiki, watching her work. Jimmy was shaking his head in dismay.

"He wouldn't be that brazen, would he?"

"It fits the profile." Linda retorted, as she bit down on another chunk of doughnut before scribbling on her notepad.

"I'm here to help people, not give them an underlying way on how you should live your life, that's not up to me. The whole point is for the people to free themselves. I'm here to help them free themselves."

"Is there anything you can pass on, to tell society, what it is that they are missing, what it is that can help them?"

"Society knows what it wants to know, I'm here to tell them not to follow the herd, not to be a sheep, or a cog in the machine, you have your own mind, yet you still go and use technology and listen to everything that is spoon fed to you through the media, you take the truth from what is given to you rather than what it actually is. Society knows everything, they would just rather choose to follow the herd rather than carve out their own path in life. Everybody knows that everybody is lying, do you know anyone who tells the absolute truth? Who can you trust?"

"How would you teach parents how to raise

their children?"

"I would teach children how to raise their parents, the parents are the children, the children see more truth around them than their parents do."

"Is there anything you would like to say right now, to the country, to everybody that's going to listen to this interview, is there a certain message you would like to give them, in terms of where they are going right now."

"You can go wherever you want to go. I'm a divine messenger, here to spread the word of God, I can't stop you going where you want to go, it's up to you, I can't force you to do anything. You're going to your destruction, not mine, I've already went through mine, I used to hate myself, now I love myself, and everybody can love themselves if they really want to."

"Is that not disrespectful to the masses of people in Ireland who suffer from depression, who suffer from anxiety, who are suicidal?"

"They suffer from those ailments because they are chained to lies and corruption that is fed to them by disgusting people who only want to profit from the misery of others. I feel for them, but I can't force them to do anything, all I can do is try to help them, and if they need me, I am here."

"What about the accusations about your...society...that supports the right to ignore the law,

the use of illegal drugs, there are even rumours of this commune having amassed a massive arsenal of weapons to arm yourselves with..."

"We have nothing to hide, we're here to build our very own society, nothing can stop us. People can say what they want to say, if there is proof, show it, and we'll deal with those individuals accordingly."

"Why not give that information over to the Gardaí?"

"We're above the law."

"Isn't that not a wild statement to make, doesn't that make a mockery of the law system we have pride ourselves upon in this country?"

"It's the truth, the law is governed by bureaucracy, they make up laws according to how they feel they could profit from people personally. Why, there was a time in this country you were fined for coughing. If you say the wrong thing, to the wrong person, you are fined..."

"I take it you're an advocate of free speech?"

"You say it like it's a bad thing."

"What you are describing, has been fully welcomed by the public..."

"I have a man who joined Novalis, who had to pay a 5,000 Euro fine for calling a member of the travelling community a 'fuckin tinker' after he caught this member of the travelling community,

breaking into his shed, red handed. He was fined and the traveller walked free, where is the justice in that?"

"What about the people in the world who have threatened to rape, murder and bomb cars and homes?"

"You're not making any sense..."

"How do you mean?"

"I'm surprised a renowned journalist such as yourself can't tell the difference between freedom of speech and a verbal threat."

"Yet you claim that your right to criticize the law out trumps a person's right not to be offended?"

"You use that right to ask me questions and put me on the spot, isn't that why freedom of speech is used? I refuse to go to prison over opinions I have expressed. The Gardaí are not dissimilar to the thought police. It shouldn't be illegal to express your thoughts or to criticize someone..."

"Well I disagree, I think the hate speech law shows we're a tolerant, loveable nation..."

"Fuck you..."

"I beg your pardon?"

"Fuck you..."

"I see what you're trying to do there..."

"Fuck you, fuck you, fuck you, fuck you, fuck you, fuck you, fuck you, fuck you..."

"Please stop..."

"FUCK YOU!!"

"You're not being civil about this..."

"I'm trying to show you that words can't hurt you, once you become immune to them, they can't hurt you, and you shouldn't be jailed for saying the word cunt, slut, arsehole, tranny, bitch..."

"All right..."

"Wanker, pussy, dickhead, knob, tinker, knacker, he, she, ..."

"Please refrain from that kind of language..."

"You get fined for calling someone the wrong gender, yet I hear they still use the phrase 'Paddy-wagon,' in America and in other countries. Where's the justice in that? I think the phrase 'Paddy,' is just as offensive as other certain words used to describe indigenous people and people of colour. Who else was on the signs?"

"What?"

"Who else was on the signs, 'no blacks, no dogs, no what?"

"We're getting off track here."

"No blacks, no dogs, no what?"

"Irish."

"Exactly, I want to put it on the record that Ireland is a proud land full of history and rich with culture and art, and these social justice warriors try to tear away our history, culture and art by describing us as 'Western Europeans', and 'White privileged,' never mind the 800 years of tyranny we faced at the hands of the British. There is nothing they haven't done to us in that time, you talk about rape and murder, go and ask the British. They burned us out of our homes, raped and murdered and starved us…"

"We're not indigenous…don't be ridiculous."

"I'm not being ridiculous, I'm being very rational, and I refuse to sit here and watch my people get washed up in this tide of bureaucracy and law that is governed by a continent, not by our country, where is the justice in that? These bureaucratic soldiers who want to come down here and evict us from our home, they want to arrest us and lock us up, all because we're trying to help people find their true cosmic path. That's all we're trying to do."

"I see your point, but might I remind you that you're fined for using those expressions, not jailed."

"What if I don't pay the fine?"

"You have to pay the fine."

"No I don't, and if I do, they put me in prison.

I'm not paying any fine."

"And what if you are convicted, of a hate speech crime, and put in prison, what then?"

"I'll starve myself to death. I'll go on hunger strike"

"In terms of your philosophy, the videos you have put out on social media, the sermons you give are quite detailed, and cover a wide range of topics, that seem to be utilized by quoting everybody from widened philosophers to hardened criminals, one common criticism against your sermons, is that it tends to go over a lot of people's heads, is there a way of expressing your philosophy by describing it in layman's terms?"

"It's sad all over. It's hard to describe how much pain and loneliness and sadness I went through in my life to reach this point of understanding where I am now able to express myself with such liberty and hope. How are you meant to help somebody who clearly doesn't want your help? You can't hit them over the head and make them do it, although, I believe that is what my critics are trying to do. They disregard my message because to them, like you put it so keenly, it goes over their heads. They don't understand it because they don't want to understand it, it's as simple as that."

"Tell me about your life."

"Why?"

"I just want to know a bit about your background, that's all."

"There isn't that much to say on it, really."

"Do you have any family?"

"No."

"Do you have a girlfriend."

"No."

"Did you study."

"I don't know."

"What do you mean you don't know?"

"I study now, do you mean did I go to school?"

"Yes."

"No."

"You didn't go to university?"

"No."

"So you did go to university?"

"I don't know. It was another lifetime ago."

"I can see this isn't getting me anywhere. Going back to your philosophy. Will you try?"

"Will I try?"

"In the future, surely it's your goal to spread your philosophy far and wide?"

"To people who want to listen, I can't help those who choose not to listen. You can hear something and choose not to listen. People choose not to listen because they don't like what I have to say, they're made of rubber and lead, and will get an absolute shock when their rubber fingers fly off their hand and into the universe."

"That's a prime example right there, what does that mean?"

"And there's a prime example of choosing to hear rather than listen."

"Why do you say that?"

"Because the people who you let run your lives, aren't very nice. The people that govern you, that make the rules and the laws, that tell you what to do, they're not good people."

"So, you're saying we shouldn't let other people run our lives?"

"Now you're starting to listen."

"What is the primary purpose, of your philosophy, what is the primary message running through all of your teachings."

"The harvest."

"Can you explain to everyone what that is?"

"It is what it is, it's a harvest, we harvest people and spread happiness and joy."

"Why use the expression, harvest? It sounds so very ominous."

"No, it's not, I'll tell you what is ominous. Time is ominous. The harvest shows that we can transcend above space and time."

"But why that particular phrase?"

"There's a tradition down here, that the locals still use, they call it 'The Keelman's Fortnight.' Straight away I was intrigued by what this meant. I found out that every year, during the summer, while the rest of the island went about harvesting their hay, the people of Keel opted to wait until September to harvest, when it was quiet and there was less traffic on the roads. The reason they opted to wait until September, was because, every year, without fail, Achill gets two weeks of glorious sunshine. A lot of people call it "The Indian Summer", but down here, they call it "The Keelman's Fortnight." They are able to harvest their hay in two weeks rather than toil in the fields all summer. They do it at an alarming pace, and the entire community chips in and helps each other. I thought there was something so very special and unique about that. It sounded very similar to something I am trying to achieve here. Anybody who wants to come here and study and live with us, can realise what the absolute truth is in two weeks."

"What does the harvest entail?"

"We are disciples of the universe, we are trying to prepare ourselves into the entry of evolutionary level which is above mankind, which is synonymous with the kingdom of heaven. Planet earth is about to be recycled, we want to put an end to the tyranny and corruption that technology brings to us in this patriarchal, capitalist society. We want to go back to our roots. To live off the land, to harvest the knowledge and way of living of our ancestors who settled here over 10,000 years ago. Everything has a cycle, it has a beginning, a season, and an end. We want to break the cycle of capitalism that rots us to the very core of our souls. We want to be ready when planet earth decides to start over and become a garden to a fresh, new civilization..."

"Any final message you want to put out there, before we wrap things up?"

"But John forbade him, saying, I have a need to be baptized of thee, and comest thou to me? And Jesus answering said unto him, suffer it to be so now: for thus it becometh us to fulfil all righteousness", and he finished with "Hear now—permit it. Do not restrain me."

Out of Kiki's computer speakers, she began playing a loop of Wesley saying the phrase, " I don't know," over and over again. Jimmy held in a breath for the longest time, exhaling it slowly. The suspect they wanted for first degree murder was a guru for one of the largest cults in Western

Europe and the only evidence they had to prove that it was him, was a matched recording of Wesley using the phrase, "I don't know," from his interrogation footage.

Linda tore off the notes she had written from her notepad and handed the page to Jimmy, who read the note.

- Glib and superficial charm

- Cunning

- Manipulative

- Lack of remorse.

- Grandiose estimation of one's self.

- Wesley Harding has developed traits of malignant narcissism, a psychological syndrome comprising of a volatile mix of narcissism, aggression, and anti-social behaviour.

Underneath these notes, Linda had written in brackets:

(The mentally disturbed aren't cut out to be good solicitors, but they can easily build an army.)

Jimmy let out another long, slow breath. There was a lot of work that had to be done. there'd probably be a sting operation, maybe infiltrate the commune by going undercover? Jimmy wasn't sure yet, the only thing he was certain about was they would need to act quick, before he killed again.

As the team converged around Jimmy, every phone in the bullpen began ringing. Things were about to get crazy, and Jimmy and his team needed to board the crazy train before it screamed off into the night.

***

EPILOGUE

Isabella Di Maria admired herself in the reflection of her Victorian style, full length mirror. She had just finished applying the final touches to her make up and was now in the process of making sure her appearance met her overly critical standards.

She poked and prodded at the padding that lifted her breasts, trying to ensure she showed off a nice amount of cleavage. She smoothed out her elegant, summer dress, making sure there were no lumps of fat bulging out from any part of her full, curvaceous body.

Her friend, a male friend, had asked her to attend him to the opening of a William Blake exhibition that was on display at the Galway City Museum for the next six weeks. Her male friend was an artist by the name of Terry Isaac, who she had met through an art class that he taught once a week down at the old Arás Na Gael building. Isabella had admired his teaching ability, his technique, his inspiration and his warm, comforting personality, and after being friends for six months, began to wonder whether Terry was romantically interested in her or if he just saw her as a friend.

She was unsure if she wanted to be actively involved in a romantic relationship, but after reflecting on the fact that he had asked her to be her date for this evening, decided that there was some interest on his side, so she decided to make the effort.

She began to throw on shawls that matched her summer dress, twirling in front of her reflection, seeing how the different colours and patterns clashed with the mellow purple fabric of her dress, before deciding on a shawl that had a deep mix of purple and red. She willed herself to have a wonderful time, and to go with the flow and to not force the issue, if they were destined to be in a relationship, than it was meant to be.

Even though she was blessed with eye catching beauty, and a personality to match, Isabella had never been in any kind of long-term relationship, yet it was never from the want of trying. She was married to her profession, and her profession in turn, had rewarded her heavily when it came to financial stability. She was an extraordinarily successful, highly sought-after graphics designer, and was a successful entrepreneur, having not only designed for major business chains across the country, but for film and television as well.

Like many foreign nationals, she had visited Galway on a whim, when she was travelling Europe as an eager, bright eyed, young artist. After slumming in hostels for a couple of weeks, she fell in love with the city so much she decided to live there and ended up renting a room in a huge Edwardian house with about seven other art students in Upper Salthill. It was a mellow house, all of the tenants were co-habitual and likeminded, and had become close friends. She found a job waitressing at a high class, modern coffee shop in the city where she met many bohemians, poets, and raconteurs, and began taking night classes, working her way towards a degree in graphic design.

Because of hard work, study and diligence, everything came easy to her, except for men. She remembered hearing about the famous quip the Galwegians liked to use, where they would proudly say that 'Galway is the graveyard of ambition.'

After hearing the phrase countless times, and thinking of it as a negative, she finally mustered up the courage to ask a work colleague what it meant. She was surprised to find out that it meant that anybody who visited Galway, who only wanted to stay a short period of time, fell in love with the city so much that they would throw away their original ambitions to begin a new life in the city.

After hearing the explanation, Isabella proudly used the quote in conversation on many occasions. It was men, more than anything else, that became her graveyard of ambition. Being a workaholic and not a major advocate of the drinking culture in the city, limited her chances in meeting a partner. She did try online dating, but she found the men that she dated to be self-centred and loutish, interested in looking good rather than pleasing her.

Now that Isabella was reaching her mid-thirties, she was getting lonely, and had given up on finding a man completely until she decided to do an art class as a hobby, to keep her skills sharp, and had struck up a close friendship with Terry. Terry was a potential partner, but if he didn't sweep her off her feet soon, Isabella would lose interest and remain content on being friends. She was an old fashioned romantic, and she hoped the Terry was the same. He was extremely sweet, very funny and somewhat handsome in a fat, goofy kind of way.

As she finished admiring her reflection, she heard the doorbell clang loudly, and fluffed at her hair quickly before running down in her bare feet to answer the door. Had Isabella not been so wrapped up in her gleeful thoughts, she might have noticed a pair of cool grey eyes staring at her from the shadows of her wardrobe.

Robie Dechamp let out a long shuddering breath once Isabella ran excitably out of the room. He had been hiding in her wardrobe for the past hour, thinking she had already left for the evening. He knew that she was on a date this evening because Isabella was hired to design all of their marketing propaganda for his upcoming election campaign, and had overheard her telling one of his aids about her date.

He had broken into her home the usual way, she was absent minded when it came to locking her back door, and had been skulking around her kitchen when he overheard her humming to herself as she worked in her office, a large, creative space that sat adjoined to her kitchen. He slowly tiptoed his way upstairs and went to hide in the walk-in closet in Isabella's bedroom. He shut the doors over to a point where he was able to peek out around the entire bedroom and en-suite.

Robie was used to hiding in closets, he did it all the time in college, he'd always spy on the girls in the house down the road from his digs. It was the thrill of watching, the thrill of being caught that turned him on the most, he was good at hiding, and he was never caught, generally because he would hide in obvious places, he was good at remaining unseen.

Robie wasn't planning on hiding, he was planning on stealing more of Isabella's underwear, it was his third time in her house, and the two previous break ins had gone by without any incident. He cursed his own luck that she was still at home and wondered had he gotten the wrong day. There was nothing left to do now but wait, he had a gala event for the G.A.A to attend at nine o' clock, and he'd have to pick his moment to escape, he just hoped he hadn't gotten the date wrong or else he would be stuck in this closet all night...

Isabella had finished work in her office and Robie could hear her climb the stairs, before she entered the bedroom and slowly began to undress. To Robie this was a bonus, he had never expected to see her naked, he had tried searching her computer for nude photos, but to no avail, he had to settle on some bikini photos he had come across. Now she had stripped down to her underwear and the excitement was almost too much for Robie, who had to bite into his hand as she stripped out of her underwear. Her breasts were large, her nipples dark brown, she had a mole on one of her ample bum cheeks that only made her more desirable. She checked her reflection in her floor to ceiling mirror and prodded at the hairs around her vagina before she strolled into her en suite and turned on her power shower.

To Robie's surprise, if he craned his head out of the wardrobe at a certain angle, he was able to watch Isabella shower through the reflection of the en-suite mirror. And had to refrain from orgasming right there and then as she lathered her curvaceous, sallow body with soap. Robie was in a perverted dreamland. It had been years since he had spied on a woman showering and the dopamine rush that soaked his brain was totally worth the risk.

Watching her slip into sexy lingerie and her summer dress was just as erotic. Robie hoped that Isabelle didn't need anything from the closet, if she opened it he would have to overwhelm her, knock her out, he was twice her size so to Robie that wouldn't be much of a problem, the problem was that she could recognize him before he was able to knock her out. He should have brought a mask. He'd remember the next time. Right now, he had to control the urge not to jump out of the wardrobe and attack her.

The sound of the doorbell came as sweet relief to Robie's ears. As he watched Isabella run excitedly out of the room, he braced himself for escape. He craned his ear, listening to the front door opening followed by the muffled sound of greetings and pleasantries. Was she leaving or was he coming in? Robie willed for the voices to disappear and the door to slam shut as he snuck out of the wardrobe and across the bedroom into the hallway.

To Robie's dismay, the voices only began to grow louder. His heart jumped as he heard footsteps on the stairs, he ran back into the wardrobe and closed the door before Isabella re-entered the room, along with her friend Terry.

Terry was a big man, 6 foot 5 inches tall, weighing roughly 300 pounds, a different kind of animal to take down. He was very shy, his cheeks a ruddy red, his eyes wide with innocence as he took a glance around Isabelle's bedroom, as she sat down on a wooden chair that sat next to the window, putting on her high heels.

"Are you looking forward to the exhibition tonight?" Terry asked her curiously.

"I am and thank you for asking me. I don't often get a chance to go out and let my hair down. You look very handsome!"

"Oh…thanks…you look…beautiful." Terry replied, attempting to sound suave and debonair but failing miserably.

"Thank you, you're so sweet."

"I hope you don't mind, and I can always cancel the booking, but I booked us a little table in that Spanish tapa restaurant on Dominick Street.

"Smart." Robie thought to himself. "This guy knows how to plan a good date."

"Oh, I've never been there, I heard it's wonderful!"

"So, you don't mind."

"Oh no, there's only so much time you can dedicate to standing around, looking at paintings and drinking wine, before you get sick of the bullshit."

Terry laughed heartily. "Yeah, some of them do take the piss alright."

"Okay, let's see if I have everything."

Isabella began to rummage to her handbag before picking up her keys from the bedside dresser.

"Do you want to know the weirdest thing?"

"What?"

"I can't find my dildo?"

"...right?"

"I had it in this bottom drawer, here... but look..."

She opened the drawer to show Terry the contents.

"It's not there anymore, plus I'm pretty sure some of my underwear is gone."

She was right. Robie was wearing a pair of Isabella's black panties under his tracksuit.

"Do you think someone broke in?"

"If they did, I would have been here. Anyway, let's not worry about that now."

"Why don't you report it to the police?"

"No way, they'd laugh me out of the building! I'm sure it's fine. I'll probably come across it at some point. Maybe I'm just over-reacting, maybe I left it down somewhere...anyway, come on, I've been looking forward to this all week."

Robie closed his eyes tight shut and waited for the front door to close. He listened as the footsteps faded away. Finally, when he heard the front door close, he slowly stepped out of the wardrobe and wiped the sweat away from his forehead with his sleeve. He could never remember a time when he sweated so profusely. What a rush, what a high! He placed his hands on his knees and began to breath slowly, as the sweat dripped from his shaved head, and dripped off the end of his nose. He had to get out of there, and fast. But there was something he had to do first, he needed to leave his mark, to show her and prove to her that he was right there, watching her. His calling card, so to speak. He wanted her to know he watched her get naked, spied on her during an intimate moment.

Robie made his way downstairs into the kitchen and opened the fridge, looking for something to drink. He found cold beer stacked into the vegetable box, he took one out and opened it, drinking it down in one go, as he finished the bottle, he noticed the door to Isabella's office was left open. He slowly walked over to the PC and place the empty beer bottle next to the keyboard. He brought up the 3d typing interface and typed a message in bold white capital letters on a blue background, he then opened the PC options and made sure the message was saved as a screensaver, preventing the PC from switching itself off, before slipping out through the front door and disappearing off down the street into the darkness.

It was past midnight when Isabella and Terry got back to her house. She unlocked the front before pinning the large frame of Terry against the wall and kissing him passionately. The night had gone splendidly. They had enjoyed the exhibition and Isabella could not get over how knowledgeable and talented Terry was to not only his art, but to art in general. They had stayed long enough that they had talked to anybody they deemed entertaining without getting roped into the bullshit arty farty fancy talk of certain artists over selling their own work rather than appreciating the work of one of the greats.

They had a fine meal in the Tapa's restaurant and had stayed there drinking bottles of Spanish beer until closing time. It took Terry some Dutch courage, but he managed to muster up enough of it to confess to Isabella that he thought of this evening as their first date, that he understood if she didn't, and that he'd be over the moon if she agreed with him, Isabella responded by holding his hand, and nodding yes.

She felt giddy on beer and lust. She asked Terry to sit down in the living room as she ran into the kitchen to grab some beers from the fridge. As she did so, she noticed a blue glare emanating from her office.

Terry jumped from his seat when he heard the ear shrilling scream let out from Isabella, he ran to her side, finding her sobbing uncontrollably in front of her computer monitor. When he placed a hand on her shoulder, she spun around into his arms, sobbing hard into his chest, shaking like a leaf. A message was blinking on the monitor, no doubt to catch Isabella's attention, it read:

GO AHEAD, CALL THE POLICE. I DARE YOU!!! THEY WOULD NEVER BELIEVE YOU ANYWAY.

P.S. THANKS FOR THE DILDO XX

***

ABOUT THE AUTHOR

Adrian Lavelle

Adrian Lavelle is a writer/playwright who hails from the West Coast of Ireland. He is the proud author of three stage plays, 'A Fig For A Kiss', 'Memento Morte,' and 'Godhead'. which have been staged on numerous occasions in Galway City and throughout the West of Ire-land. 'The Keelman's Fortnight - (Volume One)' is his first novel. He currently lives on Achill Island.

Printed in Great Britain
by Amazon